Ghost Stories and Supernatural Tales

by

I0461132

P G Sharp

Acutus Press

Published by Acutus Press 2013

http://www.acutuspress.com

ISBN 978-0-9575893-1-5

CONTENTS

ACKNOWLEDGEMENTS

No book worthy of the name should be published without a merciless editor. Alison Brunger trod fearlessly on my toes whilst providing more than enough encouragement and support to prevent excessive screams of hurt pride.

My thanks also to my excellent cover designer, Andrew Brown, at www.designforwriters.com, who amazingly managed to distil the essence of twelve very different stories into a single image.

I am deeply indebted to both.

DON'T GO BACK

Sipping Jack Daniels and water, Charles Gregory and Michael Hobbs gazed appreciatively through the panoramic windows of the lounge bar in Oremouth's Westcliff Hotel. To the east, over the resort's rooftops, a dangerous red sandstone cliff, subject to frequent rockfalls, reflected the dying rays of the setting sun with a warming glow and sharp-edged shadows marked the irregularities of the soft rock as the light glanced across it.

Beyond the peaked red wall was another cliff-face, yellow this time and flat-topped, equally magnificent and equally friable, reflecting sunlight with its own dazzling quality. Far off beyond that, a chalk cliff stood out in brilliant and slightly pinkish white against the calm aquamarine sea. This splendid scene accounted for much of the hotel's success, attracting photographers and artists from far and wide. Adding to it was the westward view from the hotel's well-named Vista Bar, encompassing the beautiful Ore estuary and the ships sailing in and out of Hadwell, seven miles upriver.

But there were other more dynamic attractions than cliff and estuary views for the holidaymaker to enjoy. Oremouth boasted several popular tourist sites. A large fairground was the most obvious and included the coast's largest Ferris wheel, a rollercoaster of national fame and a range of spine-wrenching and, for some people, emetic rides. There were also the usual seaside arcades, bars, ice-cream kiosks and crowds. Fortunately for the hotel, none of these features were either audible or particularly visible from its elevated position. Residents could enjoy their drinks, admiring the cliffs or the estuary, looking down like eagles upon the beach below and the tiny figures that played happily upon it.

After scanning the marine horizon, his attention wandering, Michael gazed round the bar, not at anything or anyone in particular, until his eye came to rest on a picture he had noticed the night before.

"Let's go over there," he suggested to his friend. "I want to show you something."

He walked across the room to one of its few lengths of wall, with Charles trailing in his wake. Hanging there was a framed black-and-white photograph of Oremouth, taken from the sea. It was a professional job, in pin-sharp focus and high definition.

"Take a look at that," said Michael, pointing to the picture. Charles did as he was bidden.

"It says 'Oremouth,'" remarked Charles. "Probably some time ago, I'd say."

"Correct," replied Michael. "1939, to be precise."

Charles studied the framed photograph again, then commented,

"Thirty years ago. But how do you know? There's no date. Have you examined the back or something?"

"No," said Michael. "I didn't need to. You see that tall chimney?" he asked, referring to a large factory chimney in the middle of the picture.

"Yes."

"Well, that was built in 1939 and demolished five years ago. And over here," he added, directing his friend to an empty piece of land to the left of the photograph, "you can see there's nothing there."

"Yes. So what?"

"Because of its proximity to Hadwell, Oremouth was militarily useful during the Second World War. Hadwell was quite a base. Alongside its civilian docks, a small naval depot evolved, and the large flat area just inland provided the perfect place for an airstrip. B17 Flying Fortresses were based there and eventually the place became home to thousands of GIs preparing for D-Day. There were all kinds of guns and defences. Ack-ack. Guns pointing out to sea. Guns pointing across the estuary. Tank traps. And pillboxes. They put one on that patch of ground, in September 1939. It's still there. So, as the chimney is there, but the pillbox is not, this picture must have been taken in the middle of 1939."

"Gosh!" mocked Charles. "OK, the picture was taken in 1939. But how do you know about the chimney and the pillbox?"

"Elementary, my dear chap. I asked the barman last night. He's been here since God was young and filled me in. Anyway, I thought it might be fun to take a picture from the same place myself. We could do it tomorrow if the weather is fine."

The pair had been friends since being in the same

class at school ten years earlier. Now in their early twenties, they had driven to Oremouth the day before, towing a Wayfarer sailing dinghy, for a week's holiday shortly before Charles's scheduled wedding day. "Your last fling before the manacles snap shut," Michael had quipped.

Charles, still studying the photograph, said "yes, good idea. We could combine it with taking a closer look at the lightship."

"Yes. I saw that. Don't know much about it though."

It was Charles's turn to show off. He pointed to the estuary.

"You see the river," he started, "well, at the mouth of the estuary, there's a sandbar called the Staggers. It used to claim lots of ships until they moored a lightship there to warn vessels away."

"Never heard of it."

"You should have," said Charles airily. "I've known of it for years. Almost as famous, or should I say notorious, as the Goodwin Sands."

"Right," said Michael, wondering at his own ignorance on the subject.

"But the sandbar is fine for boats like ours at high tide," continued Charles. "They don't draw enough water. It's the bigger vessels that cop it. We could easily sail over the Staggers and do your picture as well. The lightship's about two miles off the beach. You can see it from here, flashing in the twilight. Piece of cake."

The weather next day was perfect for a boat like the Wayfarer. The sun was bright, the sky cloudless and a warm wind was blowing at about Force 3, with a forecast for more of the same.

The two young men were experienced dinghy sailors, and their boat was a good choice for light duty inshore sailing on the kind of budget they could afford. Glass fibre, with a white hull and bright blue deck, there were built-in buoyancy tanks to stop the vessel sinking in case the crew capsized it, which they often did. The boat was also equipped with a paddle, a small anchor which could be heaved overboard in shallow water if required, and a marine compass, recently acquired with sea-sailing in mind.

Clad in black wetsuits and armed with flasks containing hot drinks, a light lunch packed for them by the hotel and Michael's camera in a waterproof bag, Charles and Michael rigged and checked the boat, launched it off its trolley from the beach and set off.

They had to rely on memory to judge where best to position themselves to take a photograph approximating the one in the bar. After a good deal of sailing across, away from and then back towards the beach, they eventually settled on a position about half a mile offshore, with the Ferris wheel in the middle of the view.

"We'd better anchor for a while," Michael said. "There's no point doing this if I don't take steady shots. Anchored, I'm sure to get some good ones."

So they lowered the sails and Charles dropped the anchor, which grounded on the sea bed with plenty of rope left aboard. Michael started his photography.

Charles knew Michael took his camera-work very seriously, and that his perfectionist friend would take time finishing to his own high standards. Charles looked around. The sunlight was coming from the south and shining straight onto the beach and the town's frontage. It danced and glinted like transient diamonds on the green wave tops, and Charles wondered whether those reflections might upset his friend's pictures. He mused that, if they did, there was nothing he could do about it, and his mind wandered lazily off in other directions.

He thought about Neil Armstrong and Buzz Aldrin and watching their feat of being the first men to walk on the Moon. Had it been only a few weeks ago that he had sat glued to a TV screen, like millions of other people around the world, watching Armstrong take 'one small step for a man, a giant leap for mankind?' He looked up at the sky and felt very small. In another few weeks he would be married, and his thoughts returned to the present.

The new compass was doing what it should, indicating that northwards lay Oremouth and southwards lay the sun. Everything in the boat seemed in order, and Charles began to study the cliffs they had admired the night before. Compared to their evening appearance, the reds and yellows were bleached in the midday sun, but the view was still spectacular.

Charles reflected how owning a boat, even one as small as the Wayfarer, yielded an enormous degree of freedom unknown to landlubbers. He did not really want to lose that feeling, and wondered what effect marriage would have on his waterborne activities. Paula had never expressed much enthusiasm when he had mentioned boats before, but he decided he would try to bring her here and take her sailing after they were married. If she could only experience the sheer pleasure of a day like this, she would be an instant convert, he thought.

Through his binoculars, Charles watched the mail boat rounding the jetty at Oremouth. The Staggers lightship was manned, and every day the mail boat, which must have weighed about twenty tons, brought out mail and other supplies to the crew. During the summer, the mail boat also carried trippers to defray costs, and Charles could see that the deck was packed. For a small fare, trippers were able to enjoy the sights of Oremouth from the sea, a pleasant boat ride and a close-up view of the lightship, plus the additional fun of wondering whether packages transferred to and from the lightship might fall accidentally into the sea. There must have been boats doing this for decades, if not for centuries, thought Charles. He tried, and failed, to recall when lightships first appeared around the English coast.

Thinking of the lightship, Charles decided it was time to embrace the other reason why he and Michael were afloat that beautiful day.

"Done enough yet?" he asked his companion. "You must have taken hundreds. If we leave now, we might make it to the lightship whilst the mail boat is there. That should give you a few more good shots."

"Just one more … hold on. Yes, that's … it," said Michael, the shutter clicking for the last time as he finished the sentence. "I think I have taken enough in case the movement of the boat blurs some of them. But that's the lot."

Michael carefully stowed his camera back into its waterproof bag whilst Charles weighed anchor. They hoisted the sails and started towards the lightship, Michael at the helm.

About five minutes after restarting their journey, Charles glanced towards the south-east. "Looks like there's a mist coming in," he said. Michael looked over his left shoulder. Sure enough, the horizon was becoming less and less visible.

"What do you think?" asked Charles. "Time to go back?"

They both knew coastal weather could be very changeable and unpredictable. They also realized they were approaching a shipping lane. Not being able to see would be highly dangerous to a small boat.

"We've no choice," answered Michael. "It's too risky to go on in mist. Now where's that mail boat?"

The pair looked dead astern. To their horror, they found the mist was rising more rapidly than they had thought. Neither mail boat nor beach were visible. They looked ahead again. Nothing. They were suddenly and completely surrounded by a thick sea mist.

How quickly the familiar and safe can change into the strange and dangerous. Within moments, the sunny day completely disappeared. There was no brightness where the sun had been, just a uniform cold, damp greyness in which sea and sky merged into one, with no horizon, no town and no lightship.

"The mail boat was coming at us from the east and, from what I recall, was on a course a little to the south of us" said Michael. "So if we turn north, we'll miss it. If he turns back there's no danger anyway. We're also bound to hit the beach if we go north. It's all sand along there, no rocks. OK?"

Manning the jib sheet, Charles agreed, waiting for his friend to shout "Ready about!" to warn him of an impending turn. But the warning did not come. Instead, Michael exclaimed,

"Holy cow! Look at that!"

He was staring at the compass, fitted as a precaution against just the type of conditions they now faced, in which no points of reference were visible.

Charles looked. The compass was spinning slowly round and round, never stopping, completely useless.

"Oh," said Charles, equally uselessly. He tapped the compass, but it continued its pirouettes. "What's causing that?" he wondered. "It was fine a few minutes ago; I was watching it."

"I don't know," answered Michael. "Maybe there's something magnetic nearby; a buoy or wreck or something."

"I didn't see any buoys," said Charles, "but in this fog I don't like the idea of being near anything large and magnetic enough to mess up the compass." He paused. "That's not right, though, is it? A wreck or something similar would just make the compass point a different way. It wouldn't spin continuously. It needs energy to do that. Where's that coming from?"

"We've no time to wonder now," responded Michael. "We'll have to work without it."

There was a pause whilst two minds grappled with the situation.

Charles spoke first.

"The wind was from the south. If we turn and run before it, we'll get back to the beach. Or we could drop anchor again and ride this out. But it could take hours and I don't fancy sitting here blind wondering what's out there heading our way."

Michael agreed, but before they had a chance to turn, the wind died away to a complete calm.

The two looked at each other. Then they studied the pennant atop the mast, still vaguely visible through the clammy murk. It drooped lifelessly, and the sails slumped. The sea, too, became rapidly calmer. For all the wind and wave it was now experiencing, the tiny boat might have been floating on an indoor swimming pool.

"We've got to drop anchor," said Michael. "If we don't, we could drift hopelessly on the tide or with a current. We can't risk getting into the shipping channel. Or getting caught in the outflow from the estuary and being swept far out. At least we know where we are at the moment, even if we can't see anything."

Charles threw the anchor overboard immediately. It again grounded, but more of its rope was paid out than before. The boat drifted a little and the rope tautened slightly.

"I reckon we're on the edge of the channel," said Charles. Michael said something he would not have wanted his mother to hear. He looked over the stern, down at the water.

"There is a current, or a tide," he said. Charles joined him aft. Sure enough, in the now uncannily calm sea directly behind their boat, there were some slight and feeble eddies.

"Let's hope that means the anchor is holding and not dragging a little," said Charles. "The trouble is, there's no way to test it."

"No," said Michael. The pair fell silent for about ten minutes, each privately wondering what was going to happen next.

"What would Robin Knox-Johnston do?" thought Charles, trying very hard to keep calm. "He must have suffered far worse than this." He momentarily considered the bravery of the man who, back in April, had become the first person to sail solo around the world non-stop, and how terrifying that must have been.

"What about the foghorn?" suggested Michael.

"Of course!" replied Charles, highly relieved by this sensible suggestion. "I'd forgotten about that. Where is it?"

Michael rooted around his waterproof bag and produced an aerosol-powered miniature red foghorn. He waved it triumphantly at his friend.

"Got it!" he exclaimed. "How about SOS?"

Without waiting for a reply, Michael dashed off a couple of SOS sequences. Then the pair listened for any response.

There was none. There was, in fact, no sound at all. It was as though the world no longer existed, and they were cocooned in a cosy soundproof box lined with cotton wool. But they knew their environment was the complete opposite of cosy. Michael tried again. Still no answer. He tried a third time, with the same result. Charles stopped him trying a fourth time.

"We'd better use the horn carefully," he said. "It won't last long. Why not give it a blast every five minutes or so, to give anyone out there the chance to come within range? Don't forget, sound doesn't travel far in fog, and if anyone is out there and moving, they will probably be going slowly."

"I wonder where the mail boat is," said Michael. "I didn't hear it pass, did you?"

"No," answered his friend. "It probably went back to base."

Charles fished a couple of chocolate bars out of his kitbag. "Might as well have one of these," he said, offering one to his friend. "We could be here for a while."

Michael took the bar, unwrapped it and began to eat. Charles unwrapped his, and then observed, "funny about the lightship."

"What's funny?" enquired Michael.

"Well, lightships don't just have big lamps, do they? The Staggers vessel has foghorns as well, so ships know there's danger even when they can't see it. For fog like this."

"Well, I haven't heard any foghorn, except ours," said Michael.

"I know," answered Charles. "Why haven't we heard one? I'd have thought they would have sounded away for all they were worth in weather like this. But there hasn't been a peep."

"You said sound doesn't go far in fog," his friend helpfully reminded him. "We might not be able to hear them."

"Maybe," mused Charles, "but still, lightship foghorns are of industrial strength, designed to penetrate a long way. I'd have thought we would have heard something, only a mile or so off."

"And what do you make of that?" asked Michael, giving Charles no chance to reply before launching into his own thoughts on the subject. "Maybe they're bust. Or maybe this fog is very local and they don't have any. Maybe there are some peculiar local atmospherics. Maybe something very logical."

"I suppose so," said Charles, doubtfully. "But it's odd, anyway." He took a bite from his chocolate bar, and swallowed.

"I don't like it," he said. "This isn't right. I've got a funny feeling about it."

"Apart from the obvious fact that being becalmed

in a small boat in thick fog close to a shipping lane in the English Channel near a port isn't most people's idea of fun, what do you mean, 'funny'?" retorted Michael, sardonically.

"I don't know. The way the fog came up so quickly on a warm day. The compass behaving strangely. The wind falling away to nothing just as we'd worked out how to get back home. The absence of the lightship's foghorn. It doesn't add up." Charles paused.

"I get the impression that … oh, nothing." He stopped.

"Impression of what?" pressed Michael.

"Nothing. It's just my imagination, I suppose."

"What?" persisted Michael. But Charles would only say, "forget it."

Michael gave up, and the pair lapsed into an uncomfortable silence. There was no change in the fog, not a breath of wind, and not a sound. The water was flat calm. The feeble eddies at the stern continued silently as before.

"What was that?" Michael shot out the question as a splash sounded, apparently close by.

They both stared into the fog, but in different directions, as it was impossible to decide from which quarter the sound had come.

"Could have been anything," said Charles, uncertainly. "A fish jumping, perhaps?" He did not sound convinced.

"Try the foghorn again," he said. Michael did so, twice. The sound died without echo against the dampening cushion of fog. There was no response. Michael put the foghorn down again, and the two fell back into nervous silence.

A few more minutes passed. Then Michael stammered, "what was that?" They both listened, ears straining to detect any sound that might indicate their ordeal was coming to an end.

They could hear nothing.

"What do you think you heard?" whispered Charles.

"I don't know. Something, something …" Michael's voice tailed off inconclusively. They passed more minutes in silence, their ears alert for any noise, however slight.

A sudden loud scream above them made both men almost jump out of the boat in terror. They looked up involuntarily. A large white bird wheeled round the top of the mast, barely visible in the fog, and then disappeared.

"A gull!" exclaimed Michael.

"Was it?" asked Charles. "I couldn't tell. Do gulls fly low in fog? How can they navigate?"

As neither knew the answer, silence returned again. Then Michael said, in a low voice,

"I feel it, too. What I think you were almost going to tell me a little while ago."

"You mean something's about to happen and we shouldn't be here?" Charles shivered.

"Yes. Or, rather, the other way round. We are here and something's about to happen that shouldn't." Michael looked at his friend. Both felt a sudden sensation of terror. Almost automatically, without speaking, each put an arm about the other, and they hugged tightly.

"We're going to die here," said Michael, into Charles's ear.

Charles, looking over Michael's shoulder, said,

"no, we're not. Look!"

He wrested himself out of Michael's grip.

"Look!" he repeated. "The fog's going!" He pointed through the lightening gloom.

Michael spun round to observe the view. Sure enough, Oremouth was rapidly taking shape before them. Over to the east were faint outlines of the familiar red and yellow cliffs, with what could be white as well, far off to the right. To the west he could see the Westcliff Hotel, perched overlooking the town on its own low cliff. In between, mist still lingered, though dispersing rapidly.

"Thank God for that!" he shouted. "Thank God! Let's get going!" He returned to his position near the stern.

But his friend did not move. Charles stayed staring at the clearing view to the north.

"Wait a bit, "said Charles. "There's still no wind, and, and … something's not right."

"Not right?" parroted Michael.

Charles did not answer immediately. Then he said, hesitantly,

"It's Oremouth sure enough, but it's not the same. There's something missing."

Across the flat calm sea, they silently studied the resort, now bathed in full sunlight and still about three-quarters of a mile away. It was Michael who saw it first. Or, rather, did not see it.

"The Ferris Wheel!" he gasped. "It's gone! And the fairground. I can't see the rollercoaster!"

With a flash of insight, his friend said, "you're wrong. They aren't there, but they've not gone: they've just not come yet! I can't believe it … it's not possible! Can't be!"

"What do you mean?" stammered Michael, wildly.

"Look again. You were right. Something that shouldn't has happened, and there may be more."

Michael examined the coast. At first he could only notice what was not there. Then, suddenly, he saw what was.

"The chimney! The chimney I was telling you about last night. It's there!" He stared at the view, and paused. "Pass me those binoculars of yours."

Charles did as he was abruptly bidden. Michael scanned the shore through the lenses.

"And the pillbox isn't there. This is the picture we were looking at last night, the mid-1939 view. But it can't be." He paused. "We can't have gone back in time," he muttered, half to himself. "Dr. Who isn't real."

Neither of them could quite believe their eyes. "Maybe we're in some kind of weird dream," said Charles, also muttering out loud. He leant forward and picked up the crinkled wrapper of his now consumed chocolate and scrutinized it. He smoothed out the wrapper and found the small print stating the maker's details and what was in the bar. There was a tiny copyright symbol, which reassuringly declared 'Copyright 1969.' He focussed on the resort again. There was Oremouth, as real as the chocolate wrapper, but now with its tall chimney and no pillbox. He held the wrapper up against the view, and was able to read '1969' and see 1939 at the same time.

Charles put the wrapper down again. His fear, which had fled on seeing the shoreline re-emerge through the fog, returned. He fought it back, and said to his friend with forced evenness, "we can't do anything. There's no wind and, even if there was, I wouldn't know what to do if we landed in Oremouth thirty years earlier than we left." He took the binoculars from Michael and began to study the landward horizon in more detail.

"Incredible. It's like déjà vu, but in reverse," he said. "I can see that blasted mail boat leaving port, just as I did earlier today." Then he added, "or whenever it was."

He scrutinized the boat again.

"It's the same colour, and it's full of people, just like, just like before. Different boat, though. A much older style."

Michael said, "but it's going to the same lightship. See." He pointed towards the mouth of the estuary. Charles looked round. Sure enough, there was the lightship, bright red in the sunshine across the flat water, with the single word 'Staggers' painted in large square white lettering along the side. He examined it through the binoculars.

"It is the same one: you're right. The same we saw last night, or this morning." Again he added, "or whenever it was."

"No reason why it shouldn't be the same," replied Michael. "Even if we are in 1939, that ship could easily have been here then. It wasn't new."

He began retrieving his camera bag, saying, "I think I'll take some more pictures."

Once again Michael selected the view of Oremouth, clicking his shutter several times before letting the camera dangle round his neck whilst he watched the mail boat journey towards the lightship. It passed close enough for the two friends to distinguish the late 1930s fashions worn by the happy day trippers. Michael photographed the boat as it approached. They heard its diesel engine and the constant splash of the bow-wave. Michael stood up and waved violently, but there was no response from anyone on board.

"You'd better sit down," said Charles. "The wake might rock you over." Michael sat down.

Unable to avoid it, they watched the mail boat's wake approaching as it spread out in an ever-widening 'V' across the flat calm sea. They watched as the waves advanced. One wave was higher than the freeboard of their own boat, and should have flooded them. Yet the Wayfarer did not move in the slightest, and no water came aboard.

"What the … ?" said Michael.

"Oh my God," said Charles.

Temporarily, they were utterly aghast, as they wrestled with the implications of what they had just experienced.

"Over there!"

Charles looked up at his friend's shout. Michael was staring towards the west. Steaming very fast out of the Ore estuary was a sea-going ship. Charles instantly thought of John Masefield's 'dirty British coaster with a salt-caked smokestack,' for the ship belched thick black smoke, which swirled momentarily and then lingered where it had been emitted in the windless air. Then he grabbed the binoculars and studied the ship. A jack fluttered from a staff on the stern, bearing red, white and blue bars. Otherwise, the entire vessel was black.

"Not British," said Charles, but before he could comment further on the vessel's nationality, he noticed a man standing on its prow. The figure was leaning forward on the rail, looking ahead of the ship, his lower half hidden behind the upper plating of the bow. Charles's binoculars were powerful enough to see that he wore a black overcoat, with a high collar covering the lower half of his face. Charles tried to pick out more details. There was something unusual about the man, he thought.

"They're going to collide!" screamed Michael. With his view restricted by the binoculars, Charles had been unaware of anything other than the black ship itself. But Michael could see the lightship and the mail boat as well.

Charles dropped the binoculars onto their restraining strap round his neck.

"How can you tell from here?" he began, refocusing on the wider picture. But as he began explaining to Michael the difficulty of judging from a small boat whether two other vessels were going to collide, he stopped in mid-sentence. Suddenly, screams from the crowded mail boat cut across the water. Terrible screams. No-one could ever have forgotten them: the hopeless, mortal screams of those who could see death only seconds away.

The black coaster rammed the mail boat amidships at full speed. A violent explosion tore the air, with an orange fireball and an immense cloud of oily black smoke. As debris, driven by the force of the blast, rocketed out of the smoke, the black ship disappeared into it. And never came out.

Whilst bits of debris fell splashing all around them, Charles and Michael stared horrified at the disastrous and incomprehensible scene. Where moments before there had been two vessels, one laden with happy, laughing holidaymakers and the other a complete mystery, nothing now remained but an almost stationary cloud of evil black smoke, dispersing only very slowly in the still air. Beyond lay the Staggers lightship, now with two tiny figures against its port rail, and two more trying to lower a small lifeboat.

"We must help!" exclaimed Michael. "We can paddle over and see if there are any survivors." He started to raise the anchor.

Charles said nothing. He looked round at the nearby, dreadful sea. The current which had produced the eddies behind their anchored boat was now yielding a sombre harvest. There were some broken timbers, patches of oil and everyday items of clothing and personal effects any group of trippers might have. There were also several blackened lumps which had recently been living human beings. Except that some of them were much smaller than the people of whom they had once been part.

Nauseous, Charles turned away. But something else caught his eye. On the surface of the water directly below, a child's rag doll was smiling up at him. It had a cream face, brown hair, blue eyes and a long blue and white check dress, slightly burned at the lower hem.

Charles reached down to retrieve the doll. To his astonishment, his hand felt nothing, and went straight through it. He quickly snatched back his hand, which was wet with sea water. Yet there below, the doll still smiled incongruously up at him. He tried to pick it up again, with just the same result. There was no doubt: he could see the doll, but it had no substance. It was not there.

"Mike, look at this!" said Charles quickly. Michael slithered crab-like across the boat. He, too, tried to grasp the doll, with no more success than Charles.

The two men stared at the doll, and then at each other.

Michael said, "I guess that applies to everything else we can see. It's not real. The wreckage, the … bodies and things … not real. Which means there's no point trying to rescue anyone, because they don't exist."

"No," said Charles. "Yet I think they probably did exist. In 1939."

"But that's where we are. Sorry, when we are," answered Michael.

"I don't think so," said Charles. "Look at Oremouth."

There to the north lay the resort, glowing in the sun. Michael studied it.

"There's no chimney!" he spluttered. "And I can see the Ferris wheel! Give me those, will you?" And he took the binoculars, which had been hanging round Charles's neck.

"The pillbox is there, too!" exclaimed Michael. "We're back in our own time!"

"I wonder if we ever left it," said Charles. "Maybe we just thought we had."

"Eh?" said Michael, still lagging behind his friend.

Charles said, "look at the sea."

Apart from a dead mackerel, there was nothing floating near them at all. No doll, no wreckage, no bodies. There was no trace of smoke to be seen anywhere. But they did see the lightship and, just leaving it, the Oremouth mail boat. Not the one they had just witnessed being destroyed, but the one they had seen what seemed like years ago, earlier that day, crammed, as it still was, with happy holidaymakers.

Charles continued. "Seems to me there are only

three possibilities. Either we have just shared a weird joint hallucination or dream, and are still sharing it. Or we went temporarily back in time to witness a most dreadful and mysterious accident. Or we have just experienced something supernatural. Take your choice."

"They're all impossible," answered Michael. He thought for a few moments, then said, "and we don't know for sure that we are in 1969, do we? The wind's getting up. Let's try sailing back to the beach and find out."

The mail boat passed them as they began. Michael waved, and this time some passengers waved back. Charles turned the Wayfarer bows-on to the wake, and the dinghy pitched up and down over it with a wonderfully comforting familiarity.

Few sailors were ever as grateful as Charles and Michael were that day to return to shore, or find such a flood of comfort and relief to see the same launching trolley they had left on the beach, the same cars parked along the road, and the same beachfront clock confirming they had been away just two hours. Few would have bought a newspaper solely to find what year it was. And fewer still would have returned from such a short voyage burdened with an experience so incredible that they both knew they could never relate it to any other living soul.

Sitting in the same Vista Bar from which he and Michael had admired Oremouth's views, Charles wondered whether to break his forty-year silence about the mail boat. In a moment of weakness, he had agreed to accompany his son, daughter-in-law and grandchildren on a holiday to Oremouth, and now he found himself forced into a corner.

"Kylie and Simon would love you to come out in a boat with us tomorrow" Alex said, earlier in the day. Charles had avoided the problem then, and again at lunch. But Alex persisted, and bearded his father for a third time in the Vista Bar that evening.

Charles stared blankly out of the window towards the estuary, sipping his whisky and wondering whether to tell his son the secret he had kept for decades. In the fading light, he absently observed the views he had admired all those years ago. Despite their beauty, he was unable to find the strength to appreciate them. As with much in life, beauty and tragedy frequently dance together, as though every credit has to be matched with a debit, and every good balanced by an evil. As he had done many times before, Charles thought back to what he and Michael had witnessed, and to the still unexplained mystery of how they had been able to. He thought of the mail boat, the awful black coaster and the blood-freezing screams of those who knew they were going to die. He thought of Michael, and the fate that had befallen him.

Charles jerked himself back to the present. His son and grandchildren were pressing and he could no longer avoid giving an answer. With his free hand, he brushed his grey hair sideways across his forehead and came to a decision.

"No," he said with finality. "I will not come with you. You'll be fine without me."

His son was curious, and would not accept Charles's refusal without an explanation. He persisted.

"What's the problem? We almost had to drag you to Oremouth, yet it is absolutely beautiful here. You wouldn't explain your reluctance and now you take issue with a fishing trip with the kids. What's up?"

"Oh, nothing. You know, I don't really like boats much. Make me sick. No sea legs."

Alex had heard this before.

"Look, Dad. You've said that dozens of times. And it's true I can't recall you ever having been out in a boat. But I do remember you told me once that you used to sail dinghies, so you must have liked boats then."

"Well, that was a long time ago," replied Charles. "Things change."

"Come on, Dad. Give. You've got a reason and I want to know what it is. I can't just tell the children you don't want to go without saying why. You know what they're like. They'll either think you don't love them anymore or that you're scared."

"Scared?" repeated Charles, and laughed. He should have resisted coming. He paused and wondered what to tell his inquisitive son. Should he risk it?

Maybe it was Dutch courage from the whisky, but Charles suddenly made up his mind. Perhaps at his age it would not matter if he told his tale. Nobody now could use the information to portray him as unstable. He had secured his position in life.

"I'm going to tell you something I've never told anyone else before. But first, I'd like you to promise me you will keep what you hear to yourself, or I won't tell you. Is that a deal? You'll have to say I just wasn't up to the trip and not give the real reason."

Alex grinned. "Alright, Dad," he said. "If it makes you happy, I'll keep your secrets."

Charles knew he had no choice but to believe his

son, and began his story. He nodded towards the photograph of Oremouth, taken from the sea, which had been the starting point for his experience in 1969. He had been rather surprised to see the photograph still hanging on the bar wall when he first came into the room.

"The picture over there is Oremouth in 1939. The problem is, I've seen that view of it before."

"Of course you have. You've been propping up the bar here for the last week."

"That wasn't what I meant," said Charles, slowly. "That wasn't what I meant at all. And there's another thing."

"What's that?" asked Alex.

"What do you see down there?" Charles pointed towards the south-west over the estuary mouth.

His son followed Charles's finger.

"There's something flashing," he said.

"There used to be a lightship there," replied Charles, "but they replaced it about thirty years ago with a modern navigation buoy. Cheaper, I suppose. No crew." He sipped his whisky again.

"Well, ten years before that, about a year before you were born and just before I married your mother, I came here on holiday with a friend of mine, Michael Hobbs. I was old-fashioned. Your mother and I never went on holidays together before our wedding. Unlike you."

Charles looked quizzically at his son. Alex had no intention of being directed down that road and replied, "as you said, things change."

Charles continued. "We decided we wanted to look at the view in the photograph from where it was taken and to visit the lightship. We owned a dinghy, you see."

Alex nearly clapped his hands. "I knew you hadn't always disliked boats," he chortled.

Charles ignored him, and told his story.

Alex listened in silence, until Charles reached the point when he and Michael had returned to Oremouth.

"That," said Alex, "is a very elaborate reason not to go fishing."

"Yes," said Charles, "but unfortunately there's a bit more."

"It's a pretty good fairy tale so far," grinned Alex, "and I'm longing to hear the rest."

Oh dear! He had brought this mockery upon himself, thought Charles. He should never have been so weak as to return to Oremouth. But he had gone too far now.

Charles bought more drinks and resumed his seat and his tale.

"As Michael found the barman here had been around for a long time, I asked the fellow about the Oremouth mail boat. I told him I'd heard there had been some kind of a disaster. I had to wait until Michael wasn't there. He and I never discussed the affair after we got back to the hotel that day, not ever. I knew he was too upset about it, so the subject wasn't raised. Anyway, I asked the barman if there had been a disaster."

"And had there?" asked Alex.

"Yes. In July 1939, the boat taking mail to the lightship and laden with trippers exploded for no apparent reason. The boat disappeared on a bright sunny day in a flat calm. Twenty-five people died, not far from the lightship. There were many witnesses, including four men on the lightship, but none had seen anything that could account for the explosion. It was, predictably, known as the Oremouth mail boat disaster.

"There was an investigation, but it was inconclusive, partly because so few bits of the mail boat were recovered and partly because the Second World War started very soon afterwards and there were bigger fish to fry in Oremouth. Pardon the pun. The photograph on yonder wall was taken by one of the investigators, which is why it's of such high quality – it was done by a professional using some of the best kit of the day."

"I noted the barman mentioned nothing about any other vessel being involved. There were some other odd things as well. You know I mentioned the coaster's jack, the flag at the stern?"

"Yes," said Alex.

"It was the Dutch flag. And there was something else."

"What was that?"

"As you can imagine, I was beyond curious about the whole thing. So I eventually went to the newspaper library at Colindale and looked up every press report I could find about the incident. They confirmed the barman's story, and made no mention of any other vessel. The reports said the mail boat's captain was a man of thirty years' experience who had previously captained sea-going cargo ships all over the world. His name was Jan de Vries."

"So what?" asked Alex.

"Have you never heard of the Flying Dutchman?" replied his father.

"Vaguely. Fill me in."

"I must have failed in your education somewhere," said Charles with mock regret. "The Flying Dutchman is a marine ghost. There are different versions of the story, but they mainly revolve around a drunken Dutch sea captain who tried to force his ship round Cape Horn, and sank, about three hundred years ago. He has been seen since from time to time, usually in southern latitudes and usually in storms. But occasionally there have been reports of sightings in other parts of the world, not in storms and also in ships other than his old square rigger. The name applies to the captain, not the ship. At least, that's what I've picked up."

"And you think that's what you saw?" smirked Alex.

"On balance, yes. It was either something like that, or a joint hallucination, or time travel."

"Or booze and an over-active imagination," said Alex. "You must have been dreaming. You could easily have read about the disaster and then your mind played on it."

"And Michael's mind, at the same time?"

"You could have dreamed he was there. You told me the subject was never discussed afterwards. That must have been because he wasn't there, experienced nothing and knew nothing. And you didn't mention anything to him partly because it wasn't clear what had really happened and partly because recounting it would upset him. If you see what I mean."

Charles merely said "Hmm."

His son continued, "also, if the coaster you saw was a ghost, how could it have caused an explosion? What was there on a mail boat to explode anyway?"

"Well," said Charles, "there would be the fuel.

And there was a war coming. Maybe it had other things aboard; maybe something in the supplies for the lightship. The boat did explode. All the reports agreed on that."

"True, but there must have been a physical cause: a fuel leak or something, or a collision with a real ship, not a spectral one. But even if the coaster had been real, how did it disappear so dramatically? Besides, they would have found its wreck when they were investigating."

"I have wondered about these things myself, many times," sighed Charles. "I've had forty years of wondering. Never came to any firm conclusion, though. I settled on the ghost story as the most likely explanation from an unlikely range of alternatives."

"Except the one I think it was," said Alex. "You dreamed or imagined it all. On the whole," he continued, "it was a good thing you didn't tell anyone else. They'd have thought you mad."

"I knew that," replied Charles. "I never did tell anyone. But I haven't quite finished the story."

"Go on, then," said Alex, indulgently.

"Working against your dream theory, Michael had taken a lot of photographs. There were no digital cameras in those days. All his pictures were on film and had to be developed. No mobile phones, either, of course. When the pictures came back from the chemist, he posted them to me. There were some very good ones of Oremouth. Modern Oremouth, with its Ferris wheel and no chimney. And there were some others of Oremouth, but not quite so good."

Charles paused for a sip of whisky.

"Were they of modern Oremouth as well?" asked Alex. "You said earlier that Michael had taken some pictures of Oremouth when you thought you were in 1939."

"They were just the same as the others," admitted his father. "Modern Oremouth. They were very poorly composed though, which fits with them being taken whilst Michael was upset and disoriented. There were also some which just showed empty sea and sky."

"It also fits with you having dreamt the whole thing," said Alex. "Maybe you just dozed off whilst your friend was taking his snaps. If he had experienced the same thing as you, he would have mentioned it at some time or other."

"Why? I didn't. He didn't have much time to, either."

"What do you mean?"

"He killed himself a few weeks later, just after I came back from honeymoon with your mother."

"Oh," said Alex.

"He was on a North Sea ferry," continued his father. "According to the many witnesses, he was on deck and they heard him screaming "Keep away! Keep away!" whilst pointing out to sea. Then he shouted "he's going to hit us! He's going to hit us!" ran back to the stern as far as he could and jumped overboard. They never found his body."

"What was he pointing at? Did anyone say?"

"No-one else could see anything other than open sea. There are always other vessels about in the southern North Sea, but that day there was nothing close. The ferry was going from Harwich to the Hook of Holland."

"Your Dutch association again," observed Alex.

"Yes," said Charles, who sipped more whisky.

"You might sneer, but I don't think it was a dream, and I don't believe that Michael didn't experience it with me."

He paused, and Alex said nothing. Charles coughed.

"One recurrent feature of Flying Dutchman stories is that seeing him is a curse: an omen of death," he added.

"You're still here, though."

"A statement of the obvious," said his father. "But Michael isn't."

"Hmm," said Alex. They remained silent for a few moments. Then Alex said, "playing along with this for a while, perhaps he did tell someone about it. Perhaps that's part of your alleged curse."

"What do you mean?" asked his father.

"Well, at least some people who see the Flying Dutchman must live long enough to tell others the story, or it could not be perpetuated. If the curse operated immediately, the story would die out. As the story has not died out, therefore the curse cannot operate until the witness has spilled the beans."

"And maybe Michael did spill them to someone. Yes, I can see your logic."

Charles paused, and then paled a little.

"I hadn't thought of that. Now I wish I hadn't told you," he said.

"What, because you think the curse is going to hit you after all these years because you've just told me the story? It's nonsense, Dad. You dreamed the whole thing."

"OK," Alex added, "it is odd, the way your friend died. But he could have been drinking, or just flipped. There's no evidence at all for what you think you saw."

"No," said his father, doubtfully. "Not a shred."

Alex drained the last of his whisky and put his glass down. It was time to stop this nonsense.

"You haven't put me off," he said, "I'm going fishing tomorrow with the kids, even if you're not. But now I'm off to bed. See you at breakfast?"

His father nodded, and sat for a while longer in the Vista Bar, nursing the remains of his drink, feeling more than a little disturbed. No evidence, Alex had rightly said. But could it really have been a dream, very vivid, but a dream nevertheless, whilst Michael had been taking his photographs, or even at some other time? Charles began to wonder if Alex might have shaken his conviction that he had seen ghosts all those years ago. But he eventually went to bed with a heavy heart and a thundering headache, thinking he would probably never know for certain.

'Fishing trip' was a rather grandiose description for a planned hour and a half in a small boat, trailing hooks baited with small pieces of mackerel, trying to attract other mackerel.

"Fish cannibals," thought Alex, when the boatman told him and his family how to bait their hooks. After that, all they and a few others had to do was hold onto their lines whilst the boat cruised around Oremouth's inshore waters, each feeling for a slight tug on their line to signify a fish had taken the bait.

Unexpectedly, Charles had not come down for breakfast before Alex was dragged away from the table by his family. "Don't disturb him," said Alex's wife. "We can tell him all about it later."

Alex regretted his father had not come with them.

He would have enjoyed it, Alex was sure, with excellent weather and what was proving to be a very good haul of mackerel. After forty-five minutes on the boat, Alex's family had between them collected ten wriggling fish.

The boatman, knowing most holidaymakers could do nothing useful with their catch, suggested they might give the fish to him, or to any other person on the boat who might like them. Alex, still fishing, was debating this with his children when he felt another tug on his line. He started pulling it in.

"Oh, look, Dad," said his daughter, staring over the stern as the business end of Alex's line came into view. "That's not a fish. Someone must have lost it."

Alex finished pulling in his catch, which to his surprise seemed to have no weight at all. He lifted it out of the water beneath the side of the boat and held it dangling from the line gripped in his right hand.

He stared at it with rapidly growing unease. It was a sodden child's rag doll, which slowly revolved like a wind-spun corpse on a gibbet. Beneath the still-baited hook entangled in its brown hair, Alex could see a smiling cream face, blue eyes and a long blue and white check dress, slightly burned at the lower hem.

Behind him, the boatman coughed. "We're going back to the beach," he said. "There's a mist coming in."

THE GIRL ON THE TRAIN

"That just proves my point," said my wife, "about that programme last night. You just can't avoid life – it happens."

She was right, of course. Darned annoying, a wife can be. You argue a perfectly good case for this, that or the other but, despite all the logic and facts, she states the opposite is true. And then fate muscles in on her side and shows you, the poor hubby, to be a prize-winning drongo.

'That programme' was a TV drama about a middle-aged man who took a late-night train home. He found himself in a carriage where the only other occupant was a young woman. Two stops into the journey, a pair of rough and noisy young men in their twenties boarded his carriage, and promptly set about teasing and taunting the woman. Our would-be hero first tried to make himself invisible and then, as the taunting got worse, summoned enough courage to tell the men to leave the woman alone. He was told, with some rather graphic threats, to … well, I won't repeat the exact terminology, but its intent was perfectly clear and he lapsed into silence. Shortly afterwards, he got off the train. The next day, he shame-facedly saw a police placard on the station platform seeking information about a rape that had taken place on his train the night before.

My wife asked me what I would have done in the traveller's position. Well, I'm an overweight 50-year-old, and have never been what you might call 'physical.' And since a car accident some years ago, I only have one arm. I told her I didn't fancy a beating by two toughs half my age, or winding up with a knife between the ribs. Did she fancy being widowed as a consequence of my public-spiritedness on behalf of a woman neither of us knew? She said she was disappointed: what if she had been that girl? I could always find a conductor, she remarked, or think of some other way to help the woman without fear. She added a lot more besides, particularly about the lack of community spirit these days.

Well, you can't win arguments like that, so I didn't try, and we left it there.

Next day, April 3rd, I went to work as usual. Commuting to London by train is a dreary occupation at the best of times, and on this particular day times were not at their best. It was raining like fury. The train was late, and only half its normal length. Umpteen hundred people, with mixed irritability and resignation, were crammed into the available carriages.

At this point I should tell you these events occurred before the advent of the more comfortable trains running on that line today, which have air conditioning, carpets and toilets which work more than fifty percent of the time. With the old trains, on a wet day the floors would be covered with cold rainwater from passengers' shoes and umbrellas, the windows would stream with heavy condensation and the atmosphere would be thick with the stale breath and microbes exhaled by hundreds of miserable people. Ventilation meant opening a window, incurring the wrath of everyone nearby and freezing the entire carriageload to boot.

Unluckier commuters sometimes had to suffer thirty miles of this, mostly standing up. But I was better off than most: the reward for my long journey, getting on near the Kent coast, was that I always got a seat. And I usually kept it, even when the train was short. I gave up standing for women, as I was brought up to do, after one young specimen some years earlier had called me a pig for doing so. After that, I decided I would stand only for women older than me. The mechanism works pretty well: the older you get, the less you stand. But on this journey, the mechanism let me down, in an odd and, as it turned out, rather unnerving way.

I had been reading a newspaper, and wasn't really aware what was going on around me. Even with all those people in close proximity, I have a knack of insulating myself from them. But suddenly, I was reminded of their existence by a heavy thump from the aisle between the seats, immediately on my right. I jolted back into social consciousness and saw, right next to me, a young woman prone and motionless on the floor.

As far as I could see, the girl had fainted. How had she managed to fall down, I wondered facetiously, amidst so many people? But she had achieved it, and I became aware no-one nearby was doing anything about her. They were looking in silence, but no-one moved or spoke. By this time, the train had stopped at Sevenoaks station, and I realised with a flash of inspiration that dealing with a lifeless young woman would be a sight easier at a station than in the middle of nowhere.

I looked for a communication cord – you know, the red chains on the older carriages that used to run into London, that you pulled to stop the train, and were fined fifty pounds for pulling if you did it after a night on the tiles. Of course, I wasn't near one. Useless. I could see one, though, over a door about five yards away. The train had not yet started to leave Sevenoaks, the last stop before London, over half an hour distant. Even more people had piled into the carriage and getting through that press of bodies would have been nigh on impossible. I don't know what came over me, but there were two men standing near the door, and without conscious thought I shouted down the carriage, "pull that chain!" in a voice like a sergeant-major after an assertiveness course.

It was as though my instinctive command had broken a spell, and all the waxworks in Madame Tussaud's suddenly decided to dance. One of the men near the door pulled the chain. Almost immediately, two railwaymen appeared through the door beneath it. The crowd cleared round the girl, who was waking up. At the same time, someone claiming to be a first-aider materialised from goodness-knows-where and started to examine the girl. I learned something about authority that day.

After looking at her, the first-aider declared loudly

that the girl had merely fainted and then suggested she might like a seat. I immediately felt guilty. I knew the girl must have been standing to have ended up where she did, and I remorsefully recalled my approach to standing for women on trains. So I got up, and the first-aider watched as the girl groggily deposited herself in my former seat. The girl had a bruise near her right temple, with a sort of blotchy reddish-blue colour. I pointed it out to the self-professed first-aider, who said the girl must have done it when she fell, but that it didn't look particularly bad as bruises went.

Having observed this little drama to satisfy themselves no-one had been messing about, the railwaymen did whatever railwaymen did to those old trains when someone had used the alarm, and the train resumed its journey to London. I remained standing near the girl, who lolled silently in her seat with her eyes closed, perspiring heavily and looking very pale. Apart from these two features and the bruise, she was rather good-looking. Very late teens or early twenties, I thought, slim, and probably quite well-off judging from her clothes, which had about them the slightly aggressive quality some professional women seem to like. There was something distantly familiar about her, but I couldn't put my finger on it. On her lap rested a large and expensive-looking black leather bag, which I hadn't noticed before, with a full-length zip fastener, which was unzipped.

As the train whizzed through miles of suburban sprawl, it never occurred to me that, so far, I had only experienced the first instalment of my involvement with this unfortunate lady. Eventually the train clattered over the murky River Thames into Charing

Cross station and stopped. From commuter trains of that vintage, with exit doors next to every seat, the hundreds of people who had shared an unhealthy hour or two of their lives in a confined space together could vanish within seconds of arrival. And that day was no exception. Soon there were just two people in the once-crowded carriage.

I sat down. I did not like the look of the girl. Her bruise had spread, and there was a swelling of some size, extending out of sight beyond her hairline. The sweating and paleness had not diminished; if anything, they were worse. I began considering the mercurial nature of Charing Cross station. To a healthy commuter, in a bustling crowd, it is a familiar and essential channel through which one must pass twice a day. To someone ill and alone it can be, as the impersonal London railway termini all can, a threatening and hostile place. London abounds with predators, alert for every opportunity to prey upon the weak. And this sick young woman qualified as a target. I decided to see what she would do.

I did not have long to wait, as she soon tottered off the train without noticing me at all. Then she quickly found a platform seat, sat down again and, leaning back, closed her eyes. I realised I couldn't leave her there, but felt a selfish urge not to get any more entangled than I already was. I had a job to get to, and was already late. But the previous evening's TV drama and ensuing conversation floated back into my consciousness. The girl could be my wife … Perhaps I could ferry her to her employers and leave them to sort out the rest.

Yes, that would be the best approach. I spoke. "Hello. I was with you on the train, and can see you're not well. Tell me where you work and I'll take you there, so your colleagues will be able to help."

There was no reply. Instead, the girl pointed upwards, at the station roof. What did she mean? Then I remembered; there was a large office above the station entirely used by one company. And I knew that the entrance was just round the corner, in Villiers Street. What luck!

I said, "I'll take you." The girl shook her head, and fumbled in the black bag. She pulled out a plastic carrier bag, which I noticed was from a supermarket which had closed down a couple of years back. Before I could say anything else, she vomited copiously into it. Then she held it shakily out towards me.

I cannot honestly say that this greatly pleased me. I could have walked off and left the girl to fend for herself. I could have deposited the bag on the floor, where it would have instantly disgorged its contents. But I also reckoned, if I did nothing within a few seconds, the girl would drop the wretched bag and soak both of us with vomit, so I took it and looked round for inspiration.

Sometimes I think there is no God in heaven, but on that occasion there certainly was. Twenty yards away was one of those mobile litter carts station janitors use, loaded with a large plastic bin bag. To this unlikely blessing, at arm's length, I carried my unwanted cargo. The bin bag was half empty. Gratefully, I rapidly jettisoned the carrier into it and went back to the girl, who was still sitting silently, eyes closed, pale, and sweating.

I said, "come on, now. Let me take you to your office. They'll look after you." The girl's eyes opened and she stared straight at me. Her eyes were bright blue, I remember, and they made me shiver. But I held out my arm. She took it, gripping my coat, and rose unsteadily to her feet. We walked slowly along the platform towards the barrier. On the way, we passed a janitor pushing a litter cart in the other direction. He smiled at us as we went by.

I turned a little to glance guiltily at the janitor, and as I did so the girl's hand slipped along my solitary arm and gripped mine. I jumped. Her hand was ice-cold and clammy too. I knew then she needed rapid attention from her associates, and hastened as best I could out of the station to her office entrance. Luckily, the automated barriers weren't working, and we were able to walk straight out without using tickets. I didn't think the girl would have been able to stand for the time it could take to find hers.

The office was the headquarters of a publishing company. There was a couch near the security desk, and I left the girl sitting on it whilst I went to explain to the security officer what the problem was. The only other person there was a sandwich deliveryman, and I had to wait a couple of minutes whilst the guard dealt with him. When the sandwich seller had gone, the guard turned to me.

"Can I 'elp you?" I outlined to him what was wrong and what needed doing with the girl.

As you will probably have guessed by now, I related this story to my wife, knowing she would crow at least a little after our disagreement over the TV programme about the rape. She had listened in silence up to now, but could contain herself no longer, and made the observation with which I started this narrative.

"Yes," I said, rather irritably, "you have a point, but I haven't got to the end. There's a bit more yet."

"I'm all ears," retorted my wife, in rather a gloating tone, I thought. I let it go and resumed my story.

Well, the security officer looked at me in silence for a few seconds. Then, very much a Cockney, he said, "wot girl?"

"That one over there, on the couch" I replied, turning to point her out. To my surprise, she wasn't there.

Rather annoyed, I turned back and said, "she must have gone in anyway, with her security pass."

"No sir, no-one's gone in. An' anyway, you wuz alone when you came in."

"Nonsense. As I told you, I've just spent a very unusual hour or so with this young woman. I doubt she could have gone far in any direction in her state, and she wouldn't have gone outside again."

"I told you, sir. There wuzn't no-one wiv you when you came in. Look." The security man turned to a CCTV monitor beside him. "I'll wind the tape back."

Well, I can't explain it. The tape showed me coming into the foyer, right enough, with my arm stuck out as though I was father of the bride escorting my daughter up the aisle. But there wasn't anyone holding it.

"Bloody hell," I said, and leaned heavily on the counter. Then I moved and sat down on the couch.

The guard eyed me curiously. Then he asked, "want some water?" I said I did, and he disappeared into a side room. I wondered if he was thinking I was mad. I wondered if I was, too. But it turned out the guard wasn't thinking that at all.

He returned after a couple of minutes with a plastic cup of water, and gave it to me. "Fing is," he said, "I've only worked 'ere for a year, but when I came I wuz told about the job by Derek Burton, anuvver guard. An' I remember that 'e told me about a girl wot worked 'ere wot came in one day sayin' she 'ad a bloke wiv 'er when she didn't, like you just did but the uvver way rahnd. Derek still works 'ere, an' 'e'd be interested in this, so I've told 'im about you on the blower an' 'e's comin' over."

I drank the water. Derek can't have been far away, for by the time I'd finished it, he had arrived.

Derek came through the same door guard No. 1 had used to get the water and make his telephone call. When he saw me, he stopped and stared. Then he, too, sat down, behind the counter.

"What's up, mate?" asked guard No.1.

"'E's only got one arm," said Derek.

"Yes," I said, "I lost the other in a car accident twenty years ago."

"She said 'e only 'ad one arm," said Derek.

"Who said?" I asked.

"The girl. The girl said that, five years ago. The girl said it."

I looked at him. So did guard No.1. Then Derek spoke again.

"It wuz exactly five years ago. Today, April 3rd, is my son's fifth birthday an' it wuz the day 'e wuz born that it 'appened. There wuz a girl wot worked 'ere, young, early twenties, trainee accountant. She came in 'ere, staggered in to be honest, sayin' she'd 'ad a fall on the train an' that the man wiv 'er 'ad 'elped 'er, so could I let 'im in to 'elp 'er upstairs. But there wuzn't a man wiv 'er. I didn't see no-one. I could see she'd 'ad a bump on the 'ead, an' I fought she wuz imaginin' fings. She wuz in a bit of a state. But she insisted the man should go wiv 'er. 'E'd been so kind, she said, particularly wiv 'im 'avin' only one arm. But before we could get any further, she passed out, an' we carried 'er into that room over there. I checked later on the tape: there wuzn't any man."

Guard No. 1 and I looked at Derek in amazement. For a few moments there was silence. Then I said, "what happened to her?"

"She died there," said Derek. "Brain 'aemorrhage, they said. Caused by a bump on the 'ead."

CHANGING LANES

"You'd better pull into the next service area," said Helen, "or there will probably be an accident."

"It's twenty miles," replied Mike. "About fifteen minutes. Can she last that long?"

Katie, his daughter, said nothing, but squirmed uncomfortably against her mother in the back of the Volvo.

Helen said, "just hurry up, that's all."

They were driving to the Lakes for a summer break. Keen fell-walkers, Helen and Mike had originally met on a walking holiday at Boot, a tiny Cumbrian village with spectacular scenery to look at, walk through, or, for the more energetic, over. Boot also offered a narrow-gauge railway, with a castle not far away. It was quite close to the coast, although that was rather desolate, windswept, and the site of a nuclear waste reprocessing plant.

Nearby, too, was Scafell Mountain, where Mike had proposed marriage to Helen as they sat overlooking Wastwater Lake, sparkling below in the afternoon sun. It was a beautiful place and the day had been perfect.

But Katie's arrival had curtailed Mike's and Helen's fell-walking for a few years, and it was only now that Katie had reached eight years of age that they thought they might gently introduce her to the world they loved.

Despite his wife's urging, Mike resisted the temptation to rush to the service area. With nine points on his licence, he was not taking any chances, and stuck rigidly to under 70 mph. He drove on. Helen said nothing more, and Katie stopped squirming.

"Pass me on the outside, you moron!" Mike suddenly exclaimed, as his eyes flicked back from the mirror.

"What's the matter?" asked Helen.

"That guy behind," said Mike, "flashing me aggressively to get out of the way. He came out of nowhere."

As Helen looked round, an obsolete and battered black Transit van, one of the more powerful models, drew level with her on the inside lane, only about three feet away. Through its open windows, at high volume, boomed rock band Status Quo's unmistakeable 'Whatever you want.' The driver had long greasy black hair tied back in a pony tail. He wore an old black leather jacket with studs and chains and his face was hardly visible behind a full black moustache and beard, with green-lensed mirror sunglasses seemingly clamped to his head. A huge death's head ring jutted from the third finger of his right hand, which dangled lazily out of the window in the slipstream. Tattooed on the back of the podgy hand was the word 'ACID.' The only incongruous feature was that the driver's vehicle was a van, not a motorcycle.

Helen was absorbing these details of the unexpected arrival when the driver suddenly turned and looked straight at her for what seemed a very long time. She could not take her eyes off him, and her blood froze. Slowly, the van driver raised his otherwise unemployed hand and drew it across his throat from left to right.

Transfixed, Helen continued to stare. As she did so, the van accelerated hard and then cut sharply in front of them. Its brake lights came on. Helen screamed.

Rather as alert cyclists sometimes sense without any tangible reason that a car is about to pull out in front of them, Mike was somehow expecting this eventuality. His foot hit the car's brake almost before the other driver hit the van's. He felt the vibration of the anti-lock system, and it was probably that semi-forgotten part of the car's defences that stopped him hitting the back of the van.

The van accelerated again. The podgy right hand, with ring, was raised out of the window, an insulting finger erected in Mike's direction. As Mike's right foot now lacked the strength to depress either brake or throttle, the car drifted on at its much reduced speed, while the van disappeared in the distance, trailing a cloud of blue oil smoke.

It was fortunate for Mike and his family there had been nothing else behind to shunt into them. He did not stop, but commanded his shaking right foot to steel itself again. Crossing to the inside lane, he continued to drive slowly for a few minutes, the silence in the car broken only by Katie crying as her mother hugged her tightly.

Perhaps to prevent alarming her daughter any further, Helen did not make the obvious remark that they had all nearly been killed. Instead, the pressure of her combined fear, anger and relief found a different safety valve.

"That was your crazy fault," she snapped at Mike. "You and your stupid arrogance. You always do that."

"What?" said Mike, perplexed. "What arrogance? What did I do?" Still calming himself from the incident, he was not ready to connect with what he had often considered to be his wife's elliptical reasoning.

"You always stay in the middle lane even when the others are empty. I've heard you say a thousand times British practice is wrong. Weaving from lane to lane is dangerous, you say. Look at that idiot crossing three lanes to get to the inside, you say. We should do what the Yanks do and stay in lane except to overtake, you say. Well you may be right about bigger roads with more lanes, but we're not in America and this road has only three lanes. You were bang in the middle and I'm not surprised that Neanderthal was angry."

"You're not excusing him, are you? He had no reason to do what he did. He nearly killed us!"

Mike did not have his wife's sensitivity to juvenile emotions. Clearly distressed, Katie renewed her wailing.

Helen merely said "idiot!" and turned again to comfort her daughter.

Mike knew enough to leave the matter there. He drove on silently, his alarm and resentment at the unjustified abuse becoming gradually less. Something of his former composure had returned by the time the sign announcing 'Moreton Bridge Services' came into sight. He certainly needed a break. Mindful also of the possible accident Helen had referred to, and grateful that, despite the unsettling events, he had received no report of it happening, Mike quickly pulled into the service area, parked, and switched off the engine.

All three passengers had the same thing in mind. Mike, still not totally calm, said over his shoulder, "see you in the coffee shop," and stalked ahead into the men's room.

His wife shepherded Katie through the other door. As it closed behind them, Katie said, "Mummy, I think I'm going to be sick," and promptly was, before Helen could get out of range or propel her daughter into a cubicle.

With the experience of all husbands, Mike was not surprised to be back on the main floor of the service area before his wife. He sat down at the edge of the coffee shop and waited.

Mike looked around, taking in the coffee shop clock, which said ten past two, and then the crowd of people there. After the mauling Helen had just given him, he was feeling a little sorry for himself, and began reflecting on the loneliness of the Moreton Bridge service area. About forty people were milling around and not one would view a conversational overture by him with anything other than the deepest suspicion, even if they felt alone themselves.

Before his marriage he had often travelled about, stopping during journeys in places just like this. Somehow, they always induced in him the feeling of being quite alone in the world. He was fifty, and he and Helen had married late. Most of the people he was watching were about twenty years younger. Don't believe a word you hear about younger people being more caring these days, Mike thought. They are at least as self-centred and suspicious as we were before them.

Where does a society like that leave a couple without children, Mike wondered? When one of them died, who would befriend the survivor? What was the future for them? Ever-increasing isolation, against the background noise of billions of younger people who don't give a damn about them? Mike smugly thanked his luck he had a daughter and, despite the verbal mauling, a wife.

The name Moreton Bridge Services seemed vaguely familiar. Mike searched the recesses of his memory. Yes, that was it. The Moreton Bridge robbery some years back. Half a million pounds in used twenties and one of the guards had been killed, run over by the robbers as they made their escape. The gang had driven their van through a normally closed access gate off the motorway onto the ordinary road network and vanished. As the gate had been unlocked with no signs of being forced, there had been speculation it had been an inside job. Mike idly wondered how much joy the robbers had out of the money and whether they ever felt guilty about the guard's death.

At this point, the smell of the coffee finally succeeded in penetrating Mike's reverie, and he started to walk towards the counter. Then he realised he had left his wallet in the car, and without that there could be no coffee. He went back to the Volvo.

With his wallet safely in his pocket, Mike started back to the building, when he suddenly had a feeling of nausea. For a while, his head swam a little, and he had the impression of being alone on a mountain-top, looking down at the sun glinting up at him from the surface of a lake far below. Then the nausea and vision began to leave him. As his head cleared, Mike could hear receding from him the insistent strains of 'Whatever you want.' He looked up and saw a familiar black van moving away across the car park, leaving a trail of misty blue oil smoke behind.

Funny, thought Mike. Where had that come from? He had not noticed the offensive vehicle when parking earlier, but there were a lot of cars about and he had been distracted. Glad the van was departing and not approaching, he started back to the coffee shop. Somewhere nearby, a siren sounded, but stopped almost as soon as he noticed it.

Mike need not have bothered with his wallet, because he no longer wanted any coffee. What he did want was his wife and daughter, so that they could press on with their journey.

Mike was used to Helen taking her time in the Ladies: it was a cliché. He sat again in the coffee shop, and waited. He heard a woman complaining about her coffee being cold. A child whined. Somebody had left a newspaper on the table, front page up. Mike glanced down and read it. Nothing much of interest there. The coffee machines hissed. There was a buzz of conversation around him. Mike dreamily began to see the sunlit lake again. Then someone dropped some crockery somewhere in the background, and he abruptly refocused.

It suddenly seemed to Mike that his spouse and daughter had been away a lot longer than usual. As he was normally quite good at judging time, it surprised him he could not confidently assess how long it was since he had last seen them. He checked his watch.

"Damn!" thought Mike, as he stared in amazement at his wrist. The watch crystal was smashed, with the second hand jammed against a piece of it. The watch had stopped at eighteen minutes past two.

Mike was upset. He was fond of the watch, but it was now useless. Wondering what caused the damage without him noticing, he mourned it silently for a few seconds before remembering his wife and daughter were still absent. He looked round and his eye fell again on the coffee shop clock.

It showed ten to three.

That couldn't be right, he thought. He had not done anything that would take forty minutes since he last saw the clock.

He totted up the time in his mind.

"Say, what, three or four minutes in the coffee shop and another three or four to get my wallet and come back here. Scan the paper. That's another three or four minutes. So, about ten to fifteen minutes. What happened to the rest?"

Mike considered this for a few seconds before his concern about Helen and Katie blotted out all else. If it had been ten past two when he first came into the coffee shop, it must be three-quarters of an hour since he last saw them. That was on the long side for even Helen to stay in the Ladies' room, with or without Katie. Where were they? Had something gone wrong? Mike stood up and went towards the entrance to the Ladies toilet, hoping to catch them coming out. There was no sign of them.

Mike began to pace up and down. He looked around. Apart from the coffee shop, there was a W H

Smiths, another shop devoted exclusively to the sale of cuddly toys, a pair of fruit machines, a tourist information desk and, slightly further off, a Burger King. There were also steps and a lift up to a bridge crossing the motorway.

Mike felt a peculiar mixture of anger and worry. Helen and Katie must surely have finished by now. He must have missed them, but if so, why hadn't they met him in the coffee shop? Maybe Helen had gone into Smiths.

In Smiths, he could find neither Helen nor Katie. Mike kicked himself. Of course! The toy shop. They must be in there. That would be a perfect place to take his little girl.

But they were not in the toy shop either.

Mike was now getting very worried. They couldn't still be in the Ladies, could they? But he could not go in and look. Perhaps he could ask another woman to check for him. No, that would make him look a fool – it really was the nuclear option. And how could another woman check locked cubicles anyway - shout out their names? Perhaps he should ask some of the people milling around the area. Again, something held him back. He must have another final look round. But they could be anywhere, over the bridge, anywhere …

Mike suddenly remembered the siren. It had stopped outside, hadn't it? Why? Had it been an ambulance? Could it be anything to do with Helen and Katie? An accident? Mike rushed outside into the car park.

There was no sign of an ambulance. Nor was there any sign of Helen, nor of Katie. There were just parked cars, one or two people coming and going, and an empty police car. Maybe that had sounded the siren. Mike, now almost beside himself with worry, wondered if his wife had returned to the Volvo. He ran helter-skelter towards it.

Mike stopped just in front of his car. There was a security guard there, standing next to a damp patch of sand on the tarmac and looking at him intently. The guard was uniformed and had a golden pony tail swept tightly back into an elastic band. Mike looked at the sand and then met the man's gaze, with horrible, horrible thoughts in his mind.

"Good afternoon, sir," said the guard.

Mike could contain himself no longer. A cascade of words tumbled out of him.

"I, I, I'm looking for my wife and daughter. They just went to the Ladies, but that was ages ago, and I've lost them. I can't find them anywhere and I wondered if they'd come back to the car. You haven't seen them, have you? A woman in her early forties, about five-six, fair and slim, with a little eight-year old girl with dark hair and a blue dress? I've gotta find them. Where on earth could they have got to?"

The man looked at Mike for a few seconds, as though he was turning the descriptions over in his mind. Then he said, "I have seen them. May I ask you to come with me?"

"Why? What has happened?"

"They are perfectly alright now," said the security man. "If you come with me, I will take you to them."

Mike inwardly sighed with relief to learn Helen and Katie were fine, but hesitated with confusion about what had happened, why the man was involved at all, and the need to go anywhere with him.

"Why should I trust you?" asked Mike.

"There's no reason," replied the man. "But there has been an incident, and it is my job to tie up the loose ends, as it were. Will you come?"

Mike hesitated again. There was something very odd about the situation. Something definitely not right. But, on the other hand … Mike was desperate to find Helen and Katie, and maybe this fellow did know something: he was clearly official. And what harm could befall him here, with people all around?

"All right," said Mike, reluctantly. "I'll come."

The man turned to walk away from the Volvo, and Mike began to follow. Then he stopped again.

"What do you mean; they are alright 'now'?" asked Mike. "For God's sake, tell me what's happened!"

"That will become clear in a few minutes. I can understand your impatience and concern, but the passage of just a little more time will remove all necessity for me to explain anything."

"Tell me, tell me!" Mike yammered at the man. But he received no answer. The man kept walking.

Mike had no choice. He followed the pony-tailed guard in silence, desperately worried, towards a Portakabin sitting at the edge of the car park and labelled 'Security.'

Helen had not been expecting the unpleasant little package that, with messy accuracy, Katie delivered just after they entered the Ladies. She ruefully observed whilst cleaning up both herself and Katie, that a little vomit went a long way, rather as a tiny spillage of red wine seems to spread everywhere. She lost track of the time she took cleaning it and its fragrance off their clothes, before drying everything off on noisy and temperamental hand dryers.

When they finally went back into the main part of the service area, Helen, having heard her husband's suggestion of a rendezvous, made straight for the coffee shop. In view of the time she had spent, she confidently expected him to have finished a coffee and Danish without waiting for her, and that, in ignorance of Katie's condition, he would press for a return to the car to complete the rest of their journey. She resolved to take a firm line and insist on water for Katie, if she wanted any, and a coffee for herself whilst she discussed with Mike how to get to the Lakes without triggering further car sickness in their daughter.

To her surprise, Mike was not there. Helen looked around, and saw the same features her husband had seen a little while earlier. Her thought processes followed a similar pattern to his as, first with irritation at Mike, then with anger and then with rising alarm, she inspected Smiths, the cuddly toy shop and Burger King, all without success.

As she left each of these establishments, Helen's concern rose by several degrees. By the time she had checked Burger King, she was getting frantic. Then she cursed herself for a fool. Of course! Call him on his mobile!

Helen dug her phone from the depths of her bag and rang Mike. There was no answer. Then the network's voicemail system came on, the syrupy woman's voice instructing Helen to leave a message after the tone even more annoying than usual. Mike must have switched his phone off.

"It's Helen. Where the hell are you?" she barked into the phone, and cut the call off.

A vague thought crossed her mind: why hadn't

Mike called her? That would mean his phone should be on and that hers should either have rung or be showing an incoming message. But, subconsciously, Helen was getting past the stage of rational analysis and she did not want to consider other possibilities.

Helen was standing near the tourist information desk, where an underemployed young man had noticed her distress.

"Can I help you, madam?" he inquired.

Helen whipped round and looked at him.

"I'm looking for my husband. He should have been waiting for me here ages ago. You must have seen him, you must!"

"There are lots of men here," said the young man, politely, "and I've only just come on shift. But I'll do my best. What does he look like?"

"Look like? Oh, Lord, he's, well … He's six feet, dark hair … Wait! Wait! I've got a picture!"

Helen remembered the photograph of her husband, which she usually carried. She ferreted around furiously in her bag, and finally pulled out a blue plastic wallet with a transparent panel, behind which was a photograph of Mike. A set of car keys fell out as Helen extracted the wallet.

"Here, have a look." Helen thrust the wallet at the young man, and picked up her keys, hooking her left hand little finger through the ring, as she often did.

"Nah," said the young man, "haven't seen him." He paused before giving the wallet back, and hesitated. There was something else he wanted to say. The outgoing shift employee had told him there had been an accident in the car park which had been swiftly dealt with by the service area's staff and the occupants of a police BMW which happened to be there at the time. The young man wondered if he should tell Helen. Not knowing what the effect of his message would be, he lacked the courage, but still wanted to help as much as he could.

"There's a security office on the other side of the car park," he said. "They might be able to help you. They deal with lost persons and ... accidents, that sort of thing."

He handed Mike's photograph back to Helen.

The young man was not adept at concealing the truth, and Helen spotted the weakness immediately.

"Accidents? What accidents? Has there been one? Has there?"

"Well ...," began the young man, but before he could finish Helen had grabbed Katie by the arm and started for the exit.

Half way to the security office on the other side of the car park, Helen suddenly felt nauseous and giddy. She had the strange and vivid impression of being with Mike and Katie on a mountain-top, looking at the sun sparkling on a lake below. Then the nausea and the panorama were gone and she could hear the fading tune of 'Whatever you want.' She looked up and saw a black van receding from her in a haze of blue smoke.

Helen wondered briefly where the van had come from, but the other matter on her mind crowded the thought out and she pressed on, still dragging Katie, into the security office.

Inside, there were two men, both in uniform. One was sitting down at his desk, writing, and did not look up or acknowledge Helen's arrival in any way. The second man, who sported a golden pony tail restrained by an elastic band, was standing looking at her.

"Good afternoon, madam," said the standing security man, as the other guard continued writing.

"The tourist desk sent me here. I've lost my husband. Six feet, dark hair – I've got a picture. He went to the Gents what … ? I dunno, could have been …" Helen paused. Strangely, she could not accurately get a feel for the time that had passed since she last saw her husband.

"Well, it was a long time ago and I've not seen him since. The man said you might help. I don't know what to do. I've looked all over and can't find him anywhere. Has anything happened? Where is he? Can you look in the Gents for me?"

The sitting guard continued to write, completely ignoring the drama unfolding in front of him.

The standing man said, "I have seen him. May I ask you to come with me?"

"Why? What has happened?" Helen demanded.

The standing man ignored Helen's question. Instead, he said, "come with me and you will be able to see him." Then, looking at her left hand, added, "but you won't have to wait like he did. And neither of you will need those keys again."

He let the implications of his remark sink in. Then, noting Helen's eyes shift towards the seated guard, he added "don't waste your time with him. He's writing up what happened to your husband while his mate's outside dealing with what has just happened to you. He can't see or hear us."

Through the security office window, Helen, speechless, heard the sounds of 'Whatever you want' approaching. They grew louder and louder until, after what seemed to Helen an eternity, the vehicle from

which they emanated drew up outside. Beckoning
Helen to follow, the security man walked towards it.

COME TO MUMMY

"Come and find me!"

Melanie Pemberton, aged ten, looked towards the woman in the wide-brimmed hat, who beckoned invitingly at the entrance to Barton Manor's maze. Hide-and-seek in her new home's maze. What fun! Melanie ran for the entrance, her pink dress bobbing, as the woman vanished between two of the maze's eight-foot cypress walls.

"Mummy, where are you?" The woman's head peeped alluringly round the far corner of the oppressive corridor.

"I'm coming, I'm coming! Wait for me!" The little girl continued running round the corner, to face a choice of four more verdant passages, quivering in the strengthening breeze. For a few seconds, she stopped, uncertain, seeking her guide. The figure flitted across a corridor-end, and Melanie ran again, happily giggling, towards her.

"Here I come!" she pealed. A few raindrops spattered lightly in her face. Along the grassy path she flew, to a second junction.

Right, left, straight ahead, left again, and right. Melanie buried herself deeper in the labyrinth as the wind rose, chasing the elusive lady in the wide-brimmed hat.

"Come and find me." The words undulated on the wind along the swaying avenue. Gusts ruffled the branches in waves, as though giant vertical fingers were sliding invisibly, unstoppably, along the hedges, caressing them as a mother strokes her child's hair. Despite the warmth of running, Melanie paid the wind the shiver-tribute it demanded.

"Come and find me." Obediently following, Melanie emerged without warning into the clearing at the centre of the maze, and slowed, mystified, to a halt. She looked round for her mother. There was no-one there. There was no woman. She looked at the darkening sky, the scudding clouds, felt the wind, sensed the oncoming storm, and suddenly felt alone and afraid. Where was Mummy? She began to cry, tears mingling with the still precursory raindrops.

"Mummy, Mummy, where are you?"

"Come and find me," she heard, from the middle of the clearing.

She looked towards the sound, towards a rectangular fishpond, enclosed behind a low parapet much patterned with lichen and encompassing a smooth plaque simply declaring '1860.' A shining black obelisk stood nearby, as tall as the hedges. Was that her mother, peeping out from behind?

"There you are! Found you!"

Cheered, Melanie ran to the obelisk. She looked all round it, but saw, on all sides, only the waving green cypress walls of the clearing, and the deceiving, dank green corridors that led from it.

"Come and find me." The voice wafted again from the direction of the pool, but Melanie, turning, could see no-one. She ran to the parapet and looked over into the water, its dark surface ruffled and rippling in the cold wind, and pockmarked with rain. What did she see moving below? Fish? No. Her own reflection? Transfixed, she leaned over further for a better view.

From the verandah steps, Melanie's mother called, anxiously, "Melanie, where are you? Come to Mummy, darling." She strained to catch an answer, but all she heard was the rising wind, and the patter of raindrops on her wide-brimmed hat.

She called again, "Melanie, it's time for tea. Iced buns and orange. Where are you?" The rain spat and the wind echoed "Where?"

Yet, what was that, at the maze entrance, that flash of pink fifty yards away?

"Melanie, come here!" But the elfin figure vanished into the dark green opening. "Come and find me" floated mockingly on the air behind it. Following to the maze, Melanie's mother strode this way and that, along the whispering green avenues, up one cul-de-sac after another, ever faster as the squall's full force broke. The wet, hostile cypresses were impenetrable, and she could see neither through nor under them. She plunged on, in vain calling "Melanie, Melanie, stop!" But only "Come and find me" greeted her ears until, by chance, she blundered panting into the sombre hub of the maze.

Through the pool's unquiet surface, Melanie could see only a distorted, indistinct image. Dead white, shimmering and glowing in the depths, it grew slowly wider as it seemed to float upwards ever closer to the girl, now immobile in unwary fascination.

Suddenly, the water smoothed over, as though a miniature storm's eye were hovering over the pool, and Melanie stared down aghast at a female face not hers, and, although of a young woman, not her mother's. With it, reflected next to her own, was a man's face under a flat Army cap. Too late, in terror she started backwards from the parapet, but before she could turn away her head was clamped on top and under her jaw, by two cold, vice-like hands. She could not look round. She could not open her mouth to scream. Struggling, Melanie was forced downwards towards the face, that submerged, grinning face. A new invitation, "Come to Mummy," penetrated her fated consciousness. She saw, rising inexorably to meet her, two white, weed-wrapped arms. She felt them icily enfold her as they dragged her down, down, down in an eternal embrace, to their parental bosom.

As she burst into the clearing, Melanie's mother slipped on the wet grass. She fell with an image in her mind of a tall man in khaki uniform and cap, gazing triumphantly at her from the pool's rim. She looked up from the ground, but there was no man, only the pool, the obelisk, and a rainstorm driven by the pitiless, wailing wind. In all-consuming alarm, she looked about her, but to no avail. And then she heard, faintly, seemingly from the direction of the pool, but from infinitely beyond, "she's ours."

Melanie's mother stumbled towards the pool. Her wide eyes searched the waters beneath, which, disturbed and rain-pocked at first, smoothed again under her gaze as they had under her daughter's.

Behind her, as she stared, incredulous, at the swirling, coalescing and fading forms in the waters of the pool, the inscription on the glistening obelisk read, 'In memory of Captain Rupert Pemberton, killed in action at Passchendaele, 21st July, 1917, aged 30 years, and of Rachel, his beloved wife, drowned without issue, aged 29 years, 15th November, 1917.'

DEAD END

The road glinted as the September sun emerged feebly from a scudding cloud, and Don Beavis stopped his Mercedes. Wet roads could suddenly dazzle a driver heading into a low mid-afternoon sun. He ferreted out a pair of polarizing sunglasses and resumed his journey.

Don wanted to make Fort William before nightfall. He had dawdled somewhat since leaving Perth earlier that day, and followed some interesting-looking detours off the main road. He was following one now, narrow and single-carriageway, which, according to his satnav, would return to his main route some miles ahead via a village named Cragganside. But the day was ageing, and this would be his last deviation.

Next day, Don planned to go south from Fort William to Oban, where he was to meet the manager of one of his three hotels. Then he would take the ferry to Craignure on the Isle of Mull and drive to Tobermory, where he and Barbara had a holiday home. She would be there with Alastair, Douglas and

Fiona, and Don was looking forward to a solid business-free week with Barbara and their children. Earlier in the year would have been better, but, Don reflected, the Western world was divided between the overworked and the unemployed, and he preferred to be in the former category. That meant work coming first, and holidays having to wait.

The road twisted, rose and dipped through the Scottish countryside. On his right was a pine forest, a plantation, and on his left open moorland falling away to a river, with mountains beyond. Squalls of rain alternated with sunnier periods, and there was a strong wind blowing.

Don was enjoying himself, planning his forthcoming family week whilst bowling along in the comfort of his brand-new saloon. Whisper-quiet and automatic, it had a formidable range of gadgets and extras, from air conditioning and programmable leather seats to rain-sensitive wipers. With a built-in satellite navigation system supplying regularly updated traffic reports, lights that switched themselves on and off depending on external light levels and a very high quality music system, there was not much Don's car did not have. It was a luxurious bubble in which he could travel, perfectly insulated from the world outside.

For most of the afternoon he had felt 'king of the road,' but despite his comforting steel and glass cocoon, Don was beginning to find the desolate countryside rather forbidding. There was little traffic and habitations were few, with considerable distances between settlements, which was unusual by UK standards. He visualized what being marooned there in a blizzard might be like, and decided he did not want to find out.

As another rain shower burst, the road descended sharply into Cragganside, a gloomy-looking place at the bottom of the valley. With no more than a couple of hundred souls, its squat, solid houses huddled together along a single, short main street, which boasted a number of parked cars, none of recent manufacture. There was no-one about, Don noticed, as he cruised through the village. There was a general store, which was shut, and an inn which, as it had a light burning inside, possibly was not. There was also a large rusty green corrugated iron shed. Over the main door was a long and not quite level cream sign, the peeling black lettering of which proudly proclaimed:

'Johnson's Agricultural and Automotive Repairs.'

This was closed as well.

After that, Don was out of the village and back on the narrow open road.

"In two hundred metres, turn left," ordered the female voice of Don's satnav, which he had programmed to take him to Fort William. He had been tempted to turn the thing off earlier because its complaints at unplanned deviations from his previously-planned route had become irritating. But the machine seemed very adaptive, and recalculated the route well enough when he abandoned it. So Don had left it running.

Probably luckily, he reflected, as he arrived at a junction. The narrow road forked into two equally narrow options. There was no signpost. Don sighed and stopped, studying the roads. Like the one he was on, neither seemed much used. They were both asphalted, but both had a sprinkling of fallen leaves from the deciduous trees that eked out a meagre existence from the rocky soil in the valley's lower reaches. Don wondered whether Cragganside's residents went in and out of their village mainly by the way he had entered it, and not this side.

The Mercedes' wipers stopped, sensing the rain had ceased again. This time, though, the squall was not replaced by a watery sun. The sky remained overcast, with clouds of myriad grey hues speeding across it. Some dead leaves blew past in front of him. Don removed his sunglasses and then took the left fork as his electronic dominatrix had bidden.

At first, the road dipped a little and curved to the left round a tree-covered knoll. Beyond the bend lay a bridge over the river. Don slowed for the bridge, which was barely wider than the road. He glanced over the low stone parapet to his right at the river only just below, swollen with the recent rain. The river was much broader than it had seemed from the road into Cragganside, and eddies swirled powerfully in the beer-brown water, stained presumably by peat somewhere higher upstream.

Immediately after the bridge, the road began to rise sharply, with a bend to the right round another clump of stunted trees grouped around an outcrop of rough grey rock. As the road continued to climb, the trees thinned out rapidly and were replaced by scrubby grassland. A partly-collapsed dry stone wall snaked away up the hill to the left, and down towards the river on the right. The wall had a gap where the road passed through, on one side of which was a wide wooden gate, closed and in poor condition. On the other was a cattle grid.

Don rumbled over the grid. For a couple of

minutes he drove on through rock-strewn moorland, grassy with large patches of heather still in bloom, some white and some purple. Several sheep were grazing, and one or two wandered brainlessly in front of him, forcing him to slow down to a speed more appropriate to his surroundings than he would have preferred. Then potholes began to appear in the increasingly uneven road, and its edges became more ragged. Don realized he would have had to slow down even if his way had not been obstructed by suicidal sheep.

A slight doubt crossed his mind that his satnav may have misled him, but 'the voice' had directed him up some very poor and narrow roads before and always been proved right. He pressed on.

Further up the hill, the road followed a long gentle bend round a flat, level area at least a quarter of a mile across and peppered with small knolls and tussocks. It looked very wet. On the far side there was a plantation of pine trees of some sort. After a while, a stony track led off into the forest on the right, whilst the road continued, its condition deteriorating.

The road was now very bad, little more than a track with occasional patches of tarmac. Don was forced to proceed almost at a walking pace. Perhaps that was fortunate, because just after he had rounded another bend, the road suddenly ended. There was a gate, with a muddy and deeply rutted track behind it, blocked by a fallen tree. In front of the gate was a semi-circular area, partly flooded and only just broad enough for a car the size of Don's to turn round without reversing.

Don stopped. His satnav had finally let him down, and he swore at its captive harridan. It dawned on him the road was probably used for planting trees, for logging when they became harvestable, and for not much else at other times. Whatever map the satnav used, it must have assumed the track was part of the road. Perhaps the track did lead through the forest towards Fort William. But it was obviously impossible to find out.

Don stared at the partly flooded area ahead. Where it was not flooded it was uneven, muddy and stony.

"This is ridiculous!" he said to himself, angrily.

He accelerated and swung the car into a tight right-hand circle in the area ahead. Three-quarters of the way round, his nearside front wheel plunged violently downwards. The steering wheel jerked anticlockwise under his grip and the vehicle came to an almost immediate halt, tilting sharply down to the left.

Don's seatbelt saved him from being flung forward against the steering wheel. Luckily, the wheel's airbag did not activate. He swore again, at length. Still cursing, he tried to drive on. But the vehicle would not move. All attempts to drive away forwards or backwards were rewarded by the engine revving, a rasping sound from behind him and a few ineffective lurches.

Don stopped the engine and got out. The ground immediately next to the driver's door was not covered by water. He was able to jump from one dry patch to another, island-hopping, to escape from the flooded area to the road, and view his stricken vehicle from a distance.

He walked round the car as far as he could. There was little doubt. He must have driven into a deep hole hidden under the water, damaging the wheel and probably the suspension and steering too. The wheel was still stuck in the hole, almost completely submerged, and that meant he was stuck as well. Diagonally opposite, his offside rear wheel was in but light contact with the ground. The rasping sound had been the wheel spinning uselessly and grazing the ground beneath it.

Don jumped back to the car and retrieved his coat from the front passenger's seat. In it were his wallet, credit cards and mobile phone. He tried the phone. No signal. He tried the mobile phone built into the car, with the same result. Then he returned to the road and tried again with the handheld phone. Still no signal. He held the phone above his head and walked around trying to find one. But there was none. He looked around. Pine trees everywhere and mountains in the distance. He bitterly thought there was probably no good reason why anyone should wish to provide such a remote place with mobile phone coverage.

Don considered his options. The car's modern gadgets had just been rendered useless in this lonely spot, and he had been abruptly plunged into unknown territory. He could not stay where he was, because it might be weeks before someone else came by. He had not seen a single house since leaving Cragganside. Nor could he call anyone for help. Night was approaching, and the weather was threatening.

Cragganside was his only choice, despite the weather. He would have to walk, even though it must be several miles away. He might even find a mobile signal on the way. But, realistically, he knew the chances of getting his car retrieved that day were slim. It was too late. He would have to find somewhere to stay in Cragganside, and let Barbara and his hotel manager know he was going to be delayed.

Don thought of taking his suitcase. But it was heavy, and he did not fancy lugging that weight several miles, so he decided to leave the case behind in the boot. He buttoned his coat and, from force of habit, locked the car, wondering as he did so what he was locking it against. Then he started walking.

The wind was strong and cold, though after ten minutes' brisk walking Don noticed the latter less. His mind was anyway still focussed on the serious inconvenience of his position and the prospect of a substantial repair bill for the Mercedes. But he was a practical man and never usually dwelt for long on things he could not change. It also occurred to him that running into a pothole might qualify as a collision, and thus be insured.

The forest began to recede from one side of the road, being replaced by a widening strip of rough humpy grassland covered with sheep droppings. A white object partly obscured by one of the humps caught Don's eye, and he walked over to see what it was. When he got close enough, he wished he had not been so curious, for it was a half-decomposed sheep, flyblown and crawling with maggots. He made his way quickly back to the road.

The dead sheep reminded Don that car drivers missed a lot of detail about their surroundings, and he looked around as he walked on, wondering what other things he had not noticed. The most obvious was the sound of the wind. It made the trees rustle, of course, as their branches rubbed against each other. But the wind had its own sounds as well. The sound of it clawing round oneself, tugging at clothing, whipping the hair and resonating in the ears. The sound, half like a whistle and half like a long sigh as it passed through the trees. And the deeper, almost inaudible, undulating roar that seemed to come from everywhere and nowhere and could almost be felt.

Despite the warmth from his exercise, Don shivered at the loneliness and isolation conveyed by these wild, natural sounds. It was one matter to listen to them, as he had many times before, within easy range of a warm house or comfortable car, yet another entirely to hear them in the remoteness of his present predicament. He quickened his step.

The pine marten rather surprised him. At a distance, Don first thought it was just another stone in the road. It was motionless enough. But as he approached he realized the stone was an animal, and that it was looking directly at him, staring him straight in the eye. Don took a few moments to identify the creature as a pine marten. He had seen one before, but they were rare, and that was part of his surprise. The other part arose from the marten's immobile lack of fear. It was clearly alive. Don got close enough to be able to observe its nostrils twitching. Then he backed away, wondering if it could be aggressive.

But the marten continued to stare at him unblinkingly, and did not move. Don stared back for a few seconds before walking rapidly past in a wide circle. It must be ill, he thought. Further down the road, he looked back. The pine marten had turned a hundred and eighty degrees and was still staring straight at him, motionless.

"Odd," thought Don. "It can't be that ill."

Don's thoughts then returned to his immediate challenge, and he left the marten behind. He looked back after about thirty yards, but it had gone.

Don tried his mobile again, still with no luck. He walked on and rounded a bend in the road. On his left was the track he had noticed on the way up, leading off into the forest. Once more he realized how many details car drivers miss. He had seen the track on one side, but not the derelict single-storey house opposite. Don forgave himself though, for the house was quite deeply set back into the forest, surrounded by trees, and although visible directly from the front, was almost impossible to see from the side.

Don studied the roofless, dilapidated ruin and walked over for a closer look. There was what had once been a rudimentary garden to the front, but heather from the surrounding areas had invaded. Here it was mainly white. The building was square, squat and stone-built. Its two small windows gaped at him, any glass they may once have had long gone. The doorway between the vacant windows led into one of two rooms at the front, which in turn had two more empty doorways, one leading to the other front room and the other to the back of the house.

Some of the stone of the walls had tumbled, and what remained was green with damp and moss. Even without its roof, the house was dark. Everywhere there were sheep droppings and other rubbish. There were no signs of anyone having been there for years. The wind moaned through the surrounding trees, the empty doorways and the forlorn windows. Don felt a tinge of sadness at the unloved nature of the place. Yet, curious, he picked his way across the room and went through the doorway to the house's back rooms.

As he stepped through the doorway, the sadness he had begun to feel swelled to a flood. He was suddenly overwhelmed by senses of infinitely deep sorrow, loss and remorse. He was also dimly aware of something else; an uneasy, unsettling undertone he could not quite place. But Don did not linger long enough to identify what that might be. He quickly returned through the doorway, across the front room and back to the road.

Once outside, all the unwelcome sensations left him, except the sense of unease. He did not like the house, and it occurred to him, before his rational mind dismissed the weird thought, that the house did not like him. He walked rapidly away from it towards Cragganside.

The gale blew and the evening was drawing on. A few spots of drizzle, carried and tossed on the restless wind, dashed Don's face. He drew his coat tighter around himself and quickened his pace. This was not a good place to be in the dark, he thought. The unease he felt in the house permeated him still. No, it would not do to be up here in this wilderness for much longer.

Carried before the wind, a flock of crows flew low overhead as he marched on. The wind gusted and buffeted him. He was now out of the forest, with moorland and sheep for company. Their fleeces were being roughly massaged by the wind as it carried their bleats away. Something screeched loudly nearby. Don whipped round, but saw nothing. One of the crows perhaps. Certainly not a sheep.

Don was now back to the flat, level area he had noted on the way up as being very wet. It was certainly a bog, and quite large, coming close to the road. Don wondered how deep the bog was and whether anyone had ever driven into it. He threw a large stone onto the surface vegetation, which shook for several yards in each direction as the stone sank.

His unease grew as he passed the bog. The desolation he had felt in the ruined house seemed to be returning as well. He approached the dry stone wall and cattle grid with hastening step. The sky was darkening, and the wind tore at him. Some more rain spots blew into his face.

He picked his way carefully over the cattle grid. The grassland beyond rippled and danced as the wind tortured it, visible waves racing across the moor as, in formation, the blades and stalks turned against the light to invisible Aeolian commands. 'The wind passeth over …,' Don recalled, from somewhere in the Bible, he thought. What was the rest of the quotation? He racked his brains. Ah, yes. 'Man is grass: the wind passeth over it and it is gone.' Don knew the quotation was slightly different, but that was the gist of it.

He shuddered. His unease was increasing by the minute. Then, with a cold shock, he realized he felt he was no longer alone. He spun round, searching for signs of other people, but could see no-one. Nonetheless, the impression remained and grew stronger. But he only saw the rippling, waving grass. The grass. There was something different. Don could not at first identify what it was. The grass was the same, but, but … Then Don saw what it was, and his eyes widened. The windblown ripples were forming themselves into semicircular shapes, still moving, still racing before their unseen master. And at the centre of their semicircles was … Don himself. The ripples were all blowing equidistantly away from him, as though he were the stone he had tossed into the bog.

Don stepped backwards involuntarily and almost fell. At the same time, an overwhelming sense of loss, grief, torment and sheer blind terror overcame him. He turned and started to run. He ran crazily, unthinkingly, at impossible speed down the wet hill road through the trees, towards the bridge with its low parapets and the deep, dark, swollen river swirling beneath. He ran and ran, driven on by something unseen and unspeakable behind him. Suddenly, a pine marten ran out in front of him. He tripped, slipped and then tumbled, over and over, down and down, towards the water.

Don did not know exactly how long he had been lying there. He was looking up at the dark grey sky, ringed in the foreground of his vision by treetops. The terror and suffocating grief had gone. All Don could feel was that his back and much of the rest of him were wet and very cold. He was face up in a large puddle about two inches deep at the bottom of a bracken-covered bank, and he had no idea why. He tried to remember how he came to be where he now found himself, but at first all he could recall was that his car had been damaged and he had been walking back to a village called Cragganside. He remembered seeing a derelict house with a garden of white heather, a dead sheep and a pine marten behaving oddly, but that was all.

Apart from the cold and wet, Don was unharmed. He had pitched up sideways against a large boulder in the midst of the trees. It overhung him very slightly, with a downward-facing flat surface close to his face. As he started to get up, his eye was caught by a marking on it. He looked closely in the fading light and could make out a Celtic cross about nine inches in diameter, crudely scratched into the stone and partly obscured by golden lichen. Something else was scratched inside the horizontal of the cross, but much of it was rendered illegible by the lichen. All he could read of the inscription was a mark that looked like another cross, although there was probably more.

Don was in no mood for further investigation. He had to get to Cragganside before nightfall. He had clearly rolled down through the bracken, which was broken and crushed where he had passed. He retraced his tumble and found he had fallen from a muddy track, not the road on which he had started. The track bore traces of footmarks, presumably his own, which ceased where he had tripped. He followed them and found he was back on the road within about fifty yards, just above the bridge.

Don still could not recall why he had left the road and gone down the track. Perhaps, he thought, he had seen something interesting, followed the track to investigate, slipped and then banged his head against the rock. Odd, though, that his head felt fine. There were no aches or bumps as far as he could tell. But night was falling, and he knew he could not stay to muse about what had occurred. He tried again to use his mobile phone. Still no signal.

Don hastened over the bridge and jogged back to Cragganside.

The village looked to Don just as lifeless as when he had driven through it earlier. The only visible chance of warmth, help and accommodation was the Fisherman Inn, whose interior was relatively brightly lit against the now very dark evening.

Drinking inside the small saloon were four men

and a woman, plus another man standing behind the bar and a large woman sitting on a stool next to the till. A warm and welcoming wood fire blazed in a basket grate.

All conversation stopped as Don entered the bar. Quite apart from being a complete stranger in a small and rather isolated village, Don correctly realized he looked dirty, wet and dishevelled. He forced a smile at seven pairs of appraising eyes.

"I've had a small accident," he said to the barman, feeling he should explain his appearance. "No-one else involved, no-one hurt and no damage, except to my car, which won't move."

The barman nodded, but said nothing. Don paused and scanned the shelves behind him.

"Could I have a double MacAllan, please? Then I need to see about sorting out my car."

The barman smiled back at him.

"Sure," he said. "Do you want water with it?"

Don shook his head.

"No, as it comes," he replied. "I need something strong right now."

The barman gave Don his drink. Don paid him and went to stand by the fire, hoping to dry his wet clothing. Then the barman said, "you're in luck about the car."

He grinned in the direction of one of the other drinkers. "Isn't he, Jimmy?"

Leaning on the bar nursing a pint of heavy, Jimmy was a lean, tall man, about thirty-five years old and with dark untidy hair. He wore trainers, dirty jeans and an equally dirty and careworn black sweater, and looked as if he needed a good wash.

"Yep," said Jimmy. "I'm your man. Jimmy

Johnson, at your service."

Don did not think Jimmy Johnson looked the sort of person to whom he wished to entrust his new Mercedes, even in his present circumstances. But he knew he needed help from these people, and had to be careful.

"You must be the chap who owns the green building," he said, thinking of the rusty shed he had now passed twice that day.

"That's me," replied Jimmy.

"Well, thanks for the offer," said Don. "But I've got breakdown insurance. I really ought to call them."

"Won't make any difference," said Jimmy, helpfully. "All those people use me. I'm the only person with a recovery truck for miles around. Still, 'phoning them will mean they pay my charges, rather than you."

Don paused, thinking. There did not seem any way around this.

"Fine," he said, "let's sort it out now." He pulled his mobile out of a pocket.

"No use in that," remarked one of the other men. "There's no mobile signal anywhere in this valley."

The barman ducked behind the bar and retrieved a grimy cream landline phone.

"Try that," he said. "There's no charge."

"Thanks," said Don. He called his wife on the pub's dirty phone and told her what had happened. He also asked her to warn the hotel he had planned to visit the next day about his delay. Then he looked up the breakdown insurer's number on his mobile and called them on the landline.

The conversation, which had ceased on his arrival, resumed whilst he talked with his wife and insurer. He made a few notes on a piece of paper retrieved from his now filthy coat. When he had finished, he put the phone down, and smiled wryly to himself.

"What did they say?" asked Jimmy.

"They said I should call Johnson's Agricultural and Automotive Repairs, of Cragganside, and give them this reference number." He gave the piece of paper to Jimmy, who grinned.

"Right, let's get to it," he said, downing the last of his beer. "Where's the car?"

When Don had finished describing the car's location, and explaining how it got there, Jimmy was silent for a while and then said,

"it'll have to be tomorrow."

"Oh," said Don. "What's the problem?"

"It's a bit too far up there," replied Jimmy. "It'll be as black as pitch and good daylight would be useful for a job like that."

Don considered this, not entirely convinced by Jimmy's sudden volte face. But he did not have much choice. Jimmy was the only pony in the ring. There was nothing to be gained and much to be lost by upsetting him.

"OK," he agreed, adding, "I'll need somewhere to stay."

"I'm sure Rob will help you there," said Jimmy, nodding at the barman. "You're not full up tonight, are you, Rob?"

Some of the other drinkers chuckled softly.

"No," said Rob. "I've got a room you can have."

"I'll pick you up at nine tomorrow morning," said Jimmy. "That OK?"

"Yes, yes," replied Don. "Nine will be fine."

"See ya," said Jimmy. He waved at everyone

generally, and departed.

"You'll be alright with him," said Rob, after Jimmy had gone. "Want another?"

He indicated Don's now empty glass.

"Yes, thanks," said Don. "Same again."

He wondered if Jimmy's postponement of his rescue was a delaying tactic to force him to spend money staying at the inn. But if that were so, why had Jimmy at first suggested doing the job immediately?

"Thanks," Don said, as Rob handed him the refilled glass. He went back to the fire.

"I wonder what changed Jimmy's mind," he asked, out loud. Don grinned at the barman, who did not grin back. There was a pregnant silence in the bar.

"You're still wet," said Rob. "You'll be wanting to dry those clothes properly. You didn't fall into the river, did you?"

"No," replied Don. "A large puddle."

"Bad luck," said Rob, before changing the subject.

"I'll get your room ready." He left the bar to the large woman on the stool. She stood up and leaned on the counter. She waited until Rob had gone and then said,

"Jimmy won't go up there at night. Most people won't. Not at night. Not in the dark."

"How did you come to fall into the puddle?" asked one of the other men, after the slightly embarrassed silence that followed this remark. Don turned towards him.

"I fell down a bank." he said. "Banged myself against a rock and woke up in the puddle." He paused. "But I can't clearly remember much beforehand. Though I do recall a derelict house. Oh, and a pine marten behaving strangely."

"A pine marten?" repeated the man. "You don't often see those."

"Did you go into the house?" asked the female drinker.

"Yes. At least, I think I did," replied Don. There was another short silence.

"And you didn't … er … see anything?" asked the woman inquisitively.

"Like what?" replied Don.

"Anything, you know … unusual." she said.

"No, I don't think so." Don paused before asking, "are you telling me the house is haunted, or something?"

Silences were in plentiful supply that night in the Fisherman Inn. This one lasted about ten seconds. Then the man who had asked how Don had fallen into the puddle spoke.

"There was a family who lived there once. A shepherd called Andrew Laurie and his wife Morag. He was killed on the Somme in 1916, leaving Morag with a three-year-old daughter, Katrine. Morag stayed on up there, tending the sheep and bringing up her daughter. She always wore black, mourning her husband, but always with a sprig of white heather when it was in bloom.

"It's a lonely spot, always was, and I daresay not many folk went by. They don't now, of course, except by accident, like you. The road goes nowhere. The story is that Morag became even fonder of her daughter than mothers normally do. That she became possessive of her. Katrine was, after all, the only person Morag would see from one month to the next.

"Anyway, the girl was schooled here in Cragganside. She would walk all the way from the house and then back again every school day. And of course, at school she met other youngsters. One of them was Finlay McKenzie, a farmer's son from the other side of the village."

He paused and sipped his beer.

"Well, the pair became childhood sweethearts, and it lasted after they left school. Finlay worked for his father and Katrine helped her mother, but the two would meet and so on. Finlay would go to the house and take Katrine out walking with him. About 1930, I think, things were getting serious between them."

"1931," corrected the large woman behind the bar. "That was the year it happened."

"Yes, Annie, but they must have got serious before then." replied the narrator. A murmur of agreement circulated round the bar. Don realized the obvious: this story was widely known. These people, he thought, probably inflicted it upon every newcomer to Cragganside.

"Anyway," the narrator continued, "they wanted to marry, but there was a problem. Finlay made it known that Katrine had said yes but that her mother wouldn't have it. She didn't want to lose her sole companion and her help with the sheep. There were constant rows."

He paused for another sip, then continued.

"That's all we know for sure. What happened next was the subject of a police investigation which never got anywhere. One misty day, Finlay went up to see his sweetheart and neither of them has ever been seen since."

"Ah, a mystery," said Don, who was warming up very pleasantly next to the fire.

"Yes, but it doesn't end there. There were a

number of theories about the tragedy. Morag, the mother, said that her daughter had eloped with Finlay. Morag had been looking after the sheep, she said, and when she got back home there was no-one there and she never saw either Finlay or Katrine again. But no-one saw them go and no-one ever reported them arriving anywhere else. Some folk thought the couple had eloped as Morag said. Others thought Morag had killed them in a jealous rage or that they had killed themselves, while some believed there had been an accident."

"What sort of accident?" asked Don.

"Well, Finlay used to walk up there. There's a bog about a third of a mile across, known as the Moss. It's dangerous, and has claimed many sheep over the years. The road bends right round it. You'd have gone along past there earlier. Finlay, of course, knew the area very well and knew there was a way through the Moss which cut the corner off the bend and saved him a longer journey each time he visited Katrine. She knew the same route, of course. The theory is maybe one of them lost their way in the mist and ended up in the bog. The other heard screams, went to help and met the same fate."

"Well," said Don. "Elopement would explain why there were no bodies. But if there were any in the bog, wouldn't they have been recovered?"

"The police did their best with the Moss. But it's very big and difficult to deal with, and they found nothing. They also said they could not be certain there were no bodies."

"I see," said Don. "So Morag could have thrown the couple into the Moss, couldn't she?"

"Sure. She could have if she had killed them. And

she could have if they had killed themselves as thwarted lovers opposed by a jealous mother. If that had happened, depending on how they did it, Morag might well have disposed of them in the bog and concocted the elopement story to avoid being accused of their murder."

"So," asked Don, "it was all inconclusive?"

"Yes. No-one discovered what really happened. Morag stayed up there on her own almost as a recluse, and became increasingly unhinged according to those who did see her. Anyway, she died in 1943 and the truth went with her."

The narrator stopped, and there was another of the Fisherman's short silences.

"I gather there's more," said Don.

"Yes. Soon after Morag died, folk began to report seeing her, dressed in her habitual black, with her sprig of white heather, at various points along the road. They sometimes say they suddenly feel deeply sad for no apparent reason, even when they haven't seen anything. Most stories say she stands at the edge of the trees a little way above the bridge, beckoning to the person who sees her. Not surprisingly, she's known as Black Morag."

The story-teller paused. Then he said,

"That's all, really."

"And, that's why Jimmy won't go up there at night?" asked Don.

"You'd have to ask him," was the reply.

"Sad story," said Don. "Whichever way you look at it."

Silence briefly descended again.

"Your room is ready," announced Rob as he returned to the bar. Don swallowed the remainder of his drink.

"Thanks. I think I'll go and clean up as far as I can. Do you have anywhere I can finish drying my clothes?"

Rob nodded.

"I'll show you. There's a separate bathroom. Come this way. And I daresay you'll be wanting some supper."

"Yes, please," said Don, as Rob led him towards a door leading out of the bar. Then he thanked the narrator for the tale of Black Morag and went upstairs, deep in thought.

Jimmy was as good as his word, arriving next morning in his recovery wagon exactly at 9.00 a.m. Don was waiting for him, having just enjoyed a large breakfast which Rob had described as 'Full Scottish.' In England, the same meal was invariably described as 'Full English.'

"The deal is," said Jimmy, "your insurer will pay me to take you to the nearest dealer for your car's make. There's one at Perth and one at Inverness. As there's not much between them, I can take you to either."

"Oh," said Don. "Is there nothing near Fort William?"

"No," replied Jimmy. "Glasgow's the next nearest but it's too far."

"Perth, then," said Don. "I moved there only three months ago."

He settled the bill with Rob, and thanked him. Then he clambered into the cab of Jimmy's lorry.

The weather was much better than the day before, with some sunshine. It did not take very long for

Jimmy to winch the stricken Mercedes onto his lorry and for the two men to start back towards Cragganside. Then Don said,

"do you mind if I show you something?"

"What's that?"

"Something I saw yesterday after I had fallen down the bank. I think you'll find it interesting, after what I heard last night."

"What did you hear last night?" asked Jimmy, curiously.

"After you'd gone, they told me all about Black Morag."

"Did they?" replied Jimmy.

"Yes. About her and about Finlay and Katrine disappearing without warning. Then it struck me last night after supper. When I fell down the bank, I fetched up against a rock. It had a cross scratched into it and there was something written on it which I couldn't make out."

"So?"

"I reckon it's a makeshift tombstone," said Don.

"Eh?" Jimmy looked sharply at him for a couple of seconds.

"I'll show you, if you stop here." said Don. They were now approaching the bridge, and Don could see the track he had run down the previous evening.

Jimmy stopped the lorry.

"Am I mad?" he asked, mainly of himself. "Alright, let's have a look."

He and Don descended from the lorry. Don led him along the track and down the bank to the large grey rock. There in front of it was the puddle Don had fallen into.

"I can't see anything," said Jimmy.

"No, you can't," replied Don. "Not from here. But you see just above the puddle, there's a flat in the rock that faces downwards. You can't see anything unless you're down low, as I was last night."

He dropped down onto his haunches in front of the puddle and twisted his head down and round to get a better view.

"There it is. Take a look."

Jimmy did so. After a few seconds, he said,

"Well, it's odd, right enough. I can see the cross, but the rest is covered up." He paused, and thought.

"The rock's hard. It would take a lot for someone to scratch into it, particularly down there at that angle. They'd have to have a very good reason."

"Wouldn't they just," said Don. "Like a grave for someone very well loved?"

Jimmy stared at the rock. Then he said,

"I'll get something to shift the water and scrape the stone clean so we can read it."

He bounded up the bank and returned five minutes later equipped for his task. He soon emptied the puddle, using a shovel. Then he lay on a small duckboard he had brought and scraped at the rock with a short piece of wood, wiping away the scrapings with a damp rag. Don waited.

"K + F," said Jimmy, standing up. "That's what it says."

The two men looked down at the rock.

"Oh my God," said Jimmy.

"Yes," said Don. "I thought it might say something like that."

They stared again at the rock for a few moments.

"Are you thinking what I'm thinking?" asked Jimmy.

"You mean … ?"

"Well, if it is them, shouldn't we find out for certain?"

"It could be just a memorial," said Don. "Maybe they're in the Moss."

"Nah," said Jimmy. "She'd have made a memorial up there nearer to them. No, they must be here. Let's think." He paused.

"She'd have buried them directly in front of the cross. And not very deep – it's stony soil. I wonder how far back, though."

"No more than a few feet, I would say" said Don. "Why not dig a narrow trench starting at the rock and work straight back for, say, six feet?"

They found the first bones within ten minutes, about eighteen inches under the now drained puddle. They needed to do no more. They returned to Cragganside and reported their find to the police.

The discovery caused quite a commotion, which meant Don had to spend another night at the Fisherman. He was the centre of even more attention than he had aroused the previous evening, reporting to the incredulous population of the bar that Finlay and Katrine could finally be accorded all the proper ceremonies.

Rob said, "perhaps this'll mean the end of Black Morag as well. Perhaps she'll settle now."

"If you believe in her," replied Don. "Anyway, I'll be away upstairs. It's been quite a day." And he left the bar.

Jimmy and Don arrived at the dealer's in Perth early the following afternoon, and unloaded the damaged car. Don went to retrieve his suitcase before accepting Jimmy's offer to drive him home, and opened the boot.

On top of his suitcase was a sprig of white heather.

OASIS

Gerald Hughes had not occupied the flat very long. It was a temporary arrangement. His divorce from Felicity turned acrimonious after lawyers got involved. Forced to leave their London house, which needed to be sold to release equity, Gerald found himself in the middle of legal trench warfare. In the end, the only common ground was gladness that their only child, Natasha, had left home the previous year, although they were not glad she was living on benefits in a grimy flat in Peckham with an equally grimy boyfriend.

Though difficult to believe now, he had been fond of Felicity once. But there had always been a part of him that kept distant from her. Even from the very beginning of his marriage, in moments of brutal honesty, he had known she was never going to be the love of his life. He just did not have that depth of feeling. Like many couples, they coasted along amicably enough for years. Initially, they had not been unhappy and he became accustomed to the routine of their life together.

But when the marriage dissolved, the end was a mess. Gerald found the combined strain of separation, moving and lawyers overwhelming. He constantly felt almost suicidally anxious, and developed the habit of sitting for long periods staring at the floor, chin resting on chest, hands clasped on lap. His sleep was disturbed by bad dreams. An overpowering sense of loss and regret for something he could never identify would awaken and assail him at around six every morning. He had suffered this from time to time throughout his life. The divorce merely made it worse.

Gerald's doctor prescribed antidepressants. These helped his daytime symptoms, but the restless dreams of loss and remorse and the early morning gloom remained almost unmitigated. Maybe those would diminish too, in time, he thought. But he did not like taking drugs.

Location mattered little to Gerald. For years he had worked from home as a website designer, and he could live almost anywhere. 'Almost,' because his likely share of the divorce settlement meant another London house was out of the question. He needed to look somewhere cheaper. He always thought living in the West Country might be pleasant, but he also liked the buzz of towns, even if his introspective nature meant he seldom made friends. For some reason, he felt drawn towards Exeter and, after exploring the area, it felt comfortable and welcoming. So Exeter was where he decided to start his new life.

The flat Gerald found, above a carpet store, with other flats to the left, right and above, was cheap to rent. It would do well enough whilst the divorce battle dragged on and until he could buy himself somewhere suitable. He moved in.

Unfortunately, Gerald quickly discovered living in the flat was going to be a problem. His work required concentration and a clear head. This demanded silence and a good night's sleep, which even at the best of times he found difficult to achieve. With the divorce proceedings a constant source of worry, and having to restart his life, these were not the best of times.

Silence proved to be a commodity in short supply within his new environment. With delivery vans coming and going, a ventilator fan at the rear of the building and the subdued murmur of conversation periodically seeping up through Gerald's floor, the carpet shop was quite noisy during the day. The shop's closure at 5.30 p.m. each evening (4.00 p.m. on Sundays) should have helped, but its quietness then permitted other noises to penetrate his little world.

A family in one of the flats to the side had two bulky children under ten, whose undisciplined screaming and shouting seemed to Gerald to have the armour-piercing qualities of a depleted uranium tank shell. Occasionally, the shouts faded, only to be replaced by the sound of a television booming through the wall.

With a gentle request for a diminution of the racket, Gerald mentioned the problem to the children's obese mother, who reminded him of a barrel. She responded with an abusive assertion of her children's rights to express themselves.

Gerald retired hurt, bitterly thinking the world would be a much better place if its citizens gave as much weight to their duties towards others as they did to their own imagined 'rights.' He also wondered whether the Barrel's assertions were an attempt to excuse herself for not exercising control over her young thugs.

Next day, he was rewarded by television noises much louder than before, and of longer duration. The Barrel's children never seemed to attend school.

The noise problem wore him down. Despite the antidepressants, his daytime anxiety began to return and he often found himself sitting in the flat with his chin on his chest, hands clasped in front of him, just staring at nothing. The bad dreams and early morning despondency motored on at full strength.

Gerald realised he would have to stay out of the flat as much as he could. Working there was almost impossible. So he decided to take a risk. He longed to move into a detached house, and wanted to find one as quickly as possible. Ideally, he should have waited until the London house sold and his divorce was finalised, but the noisy flat focussed his mind on the need for quiet and he felt impelled to make progress towards finding a permanent home.

Detached properties were more expensive, and Gerald was forced to consider spending more than he had anticipated, as well as sooner than originally envisaged. It was not usually in his character to be impulsive, but he felt compelled to gamble on having enough cash in time. All this weighed heavily on him, further aggravating his despondency.

He inspected, and rejected, a number of possible candidates for his future abode. Then an online search revealed the availability of a house which seemed to match his requirements perfectly. Located in a cul-de-sac described by the agent, Bigley & Co., as 'sought-after,' it was detached, with two bedrooms, a manageable garden and a garage, with no upward chain. It almost seemed to leap at him off the screen. In small print at the bottom of the particulars, the property was further described as 'in need of renovation and priced accordingly.'

In fact, Gerald thought the price very attractive, even allowing for the property's condition. He knew what would happen, though. With a description like that, the house would be subject to hot competition from couples eager to 'improve and move.' As a potential cash buyer, he would have an advantage, but he would have to be quick. Bigley & Co.'s office was nearby, and he went round immediately.

"Can I help you, sir?" enquired the steely, aging blonde, mechanically. A bottle blonde, thought Gerald, with jaded complexion and crow's feet around eyes hardened by years of experience in her cut-throat occupation. The sort who would, as a matter of course, disdainfully say, "we've nothing in that price range, sir," irrespective of the customer's expressed price preference. A badge clipped to her lapel read 'Maureen Chivers.'

Gerald fished a printout of the particulars from his inside jacket pocket.

"Yes," he said, showing Maureen the paper. "This house. May I take a look?"

He half-expected Maureen to say the property was either sold or under offer, and was pleasantly surprised when she smiled at him and said,

"Ah. Egremont. Yes, of course you can. When would suit you?"

"When can you show me round?" asked Gerald, hardly believing his luck. "Today or tomorrow? I'm available at almost any time."

"It's empty, so you can visit immediately if you like." Maureen paused for a few seconds and looked downwards at her nails. "But you'll have to go on your own. We're very busy, and there's no-one available at present."

She looked up again, smiling.

Gerald did not consider for long. He could look round at his leisure, without an estate agent like Maureen breathing down his neck trying to divert his attention from the less attractive features of the place. He jumped at the opportunity.

Before releasing the keys, Maureen insisted Gerald should complete a short form, and briefly disappeared into a back room to find one. Gerald looked around the office. Despite Maureen's claim, he was the only customer. There were three other staff members present, none of them doing much as far as he could tell. Lazy beggars, he thought.

The form demanded his name, address, the type of property he was interested in and a few other details.

"Do you ever get any trouble giving out keys to people you don't know?" Gerald asked, as he handed the completed form back to Maureen.

Maureen looked down at her desktop, and rooted around in a drawer underneath.

"I'm a good judge of people," she said, "and I don't think there will be any difficulty with Egremont."

She handed Gerald a set of keys, each labelled to show which door it should unlock.

"Can you bring them back within, let's say, two hours?" she asked.

"Fine," said Gerald, "what's the address?"

Maureen told him, and he left the office. He got back into his car and sat for a while, feeling low again. He loathed house-hunting, and dealing with people like Maureen. Hard as flint, thought Gerald. He looked at the unknown people milling about in the unknown street, all those busy, shuffling, happy people. He thought of the prospect of buying a house in an unknown town, and for a few seconds felt very alone. Then, almost as quickly as it had come, the feeling was gone, replaced by sudden confidence that he was doing the right thing.

The street map Maureen had given him was a jumble of little roads. Gerald drove past rows of depressing 1960s utilitarian buildings. Before the War, Exeter had been a jewel, its architecture considered second only to that of Bath in the South West of England. He could almost visualise how it had been. But German bombs had destroyed most of the city's historic core during the vengeful Baedeker raids of 1942. Gerald was sad to see almost no attempt by later town planners to recreate the city's former beauty. He mourned the lost opportunity, as he failed to find any view of the cathedral's spectacular Gothic architecture or Norman towers along the dreary roads he travelled. For a moment, he felt enraged. Then his attention returned to the busy road, and the turning he must make to find the property he sought.

Egremont stood at the end of a pleasant cul-de-sac, set back from the road behind an overgrown lawn, with some overhanging trees on the left and a garage and some weedy flower borders on the right. It looked as if it dated from the 1920s or 30s. Gerald idly thought Egremont must have witnessed, and survived, the Luftwaffe's destructive handiwork.

He sat in his car looking around. There were four other houses nearby, all occupied by the look of them, and all detached, well-maintained and smart. A good area, then. Maybe the agent was right to say it was 'sought after.'

Egremont itself, looking a little tired and in need of some decorative attention, was not a particularly uplifting sight. The short driveway was green with moss. There was a path across the lawn to the front door, running like the Grand Canyon through the long grass and covered with dead leaves. Two large bushes stood, one each side of the front door, bearing small flowers. Planted in the middle of one side of the lawn was a white post, with a 'For Sale' sign hanging on drunkenly by one nail, displaying Bigley's address and telephone number.

Gerald walked up the path and gazed in turn through the two curtainless ground floor front windows, which stared blankly down the cul-de-sac. Inside, he could see worn-out carpet and peeling wallpaper, but little else.

The key labelled 'front door' proved unequal to its assigned task, and Gerald eventually gained access through the front door using a similar key tagged 'back door.' He stepped into a hallway rather wider than he expected for a small house.

As he entered he was greeted by the slightly acrid smell older houses acquire after long periods of disuse and lack of airing. On looking down, he noticed a dirty doormat bearing the woven warning 'Cave canem.' Gerald thought by the time a visitor read the warning, placed where it was, it would be too late to escape the hurtling dog.

Egremont did not take long to inspect. It

contained no furniture or furnishings except old carpets in every room, excluding the kitchen. There, the floor was covered in very worn and dated wine-coloured linoleum, which contrasted garishly with the dirty yellow-painted cupboards lining the walls. Gerald was reminded of the 'blood-and-custard' livery of railway coaches from a bygone age.

Throughout, fittings and décor seemed consistent with the tastes of several generations ago. Gerald tested the light switches, which worked, and the taps, which did not. But overall, nothing justified the statement that Egremont needed renovation, which Gerald found odd. Given estate agents' ability to understate every drawback, such a description normally indicated a building was just about to collapse. Perhaps a survey would reveal something.

To Gerald, the house felt pleasant and comfortable, almost familiar. It was also a good size for his now reduced requirements.

"This would be just right," he said to himself, half out loud. "Unless the survey turns up some problems, I wouldn't need to do anything except decorate."

He went out through the back door, using the key labelled 'front door,' and examined the garden and the garage.

The back garden was in the same neglected state as the front, but a little spade work and inspiration would soon sort things out. He walked to the bottom of the garden, which was not very far, turned, and inspected Egremont from the rear. Then he inspected the sides. There seemed nothing untoward about the building. There were no cracks in the brickwork, the pointing seemed in good shape, and there appeared to be no tiles missing from the roof, nor were there any signs of damp or other difficulties. The garage measured up equally well, and from glimpses over the fences and hedges he could discern no reason beyond them to deter him from proceeding further.

Gerald completed his circumnavigation of the house in the front garden. Standing at the end of the drive, looking at him, was a stocky, elderly man with a tweed cloth cap, a red face and, on a lead, a large black dog of indeterminate breed.

Gerald deduced Dog Man might be a neighbour, wondering what he was doing, and that he might know something about the house. He went down the drive.

"Good afternoon," said Gerald. "I'm Gerald Hughes. I've come from Bigley & Co., to look round the place." He nodded towards the semi-collapsed 'For Sale' board.

"Ah, I thought as much," answered Dog Man. "They're always sending people. You all have to pass my house on the way in."

"Really? How long has it been empty?"

Dog Man pondered briefly. "A couple of years I guess," he said. "The last occupant was old Bill Grant, but he died in a home two Septembers ago. It'll be his family who've been trying to sell."

"I wouldn't have thought they'd have had much trouble," said Gerald. "You said there were a lot of people looking at it."

The dog edged closer to his right leg.

"Yes," said the man, prodding the dog with his foot. "Get away from there," he rapped.

"Eh?" Gerald had not noticed the dog's advance.

"Oh, sorry. Prince here was eyeing up your leg. Now, where was I?" The man paused.

"Oh, yes. Well, lots of people have looked at the place, all young ones wanting to chop it about and build extensions as far as I can tell. If you don't mind my saying, you'd be the oldest, much more in keeping with the rest of us in the close. Perhaps we're why the others weren't interested: too many old fogies around!" Dog Man laughed.

"Mind you," he added, "I did hear a number of them say the place smelt bad. One couple said it was like a mixture of drains and rotten cabbage. Probably, being closed up all the time is the problem. Anyway, must be going. Prince is getting restless."

And Dog Man continued walking his pet.

Gerald went back into Egremont through the front door, then stopped in surprise. He was standing on the doormat just inside. Coming in again from the fresh air, the smell hit him. But not the one Dog Man had described. He was completely unprepared for the fragrance enfolding him on the threshold.

Gerald expected the unaired-building miasma he detected on first arrival, and there was certainly a trace of it. But, far from Dog Man's drains and cabbage, the most prominent smell was jasmine. Gerald had always particularly liked the smell of jasmine, and he looked around to find its source.

Only the bushes around the front door could account for the scent. He studied them, sniffing their rather puny flowers, but could not make out much of a smell. The blooms could be responsible for the aroma, he supposed. He did not know what the bushes were, but he was sure they were not jasmine. Over the years he had come across one or two plants producing a scent resembling jasmine. Maybe that was it.

Gerald went back into Egremont and explored each room again. Now conscious of other prospective buyers, he came to a quick decision. If there was a problem with drains or anything else causing a smell, a survey ought to reveal the cause, especially if the surveyor was directed to look out for the problem, and it could be fixed. The place suited him perfectly, and already he felt relaxed at the thought of it becoming his home. He would offer the asking price.

Using the wrongly-labelled keys, he locked up and went back to Bigley & Co.

Maureen's broad smile on hearing the news managed, for a few seconds, to soften even her hard eyes. Gerald thought she might just have been beautiful once.

"I'll take it off the market," she said, and thus began the tedious business of arranging a house purchase.

Still in his noisy flat, and having added to his sources of anxiety by starting to buy Egremont, Gerald was for a while very unsettled indeed. But there were good signs his life was about to turn a corner. To his great relief, the divorce was finally settled. Other satisfactory news followed. He received a surprisingly favourable survey report on Egremont. Nothing suggested bad smells or any other significant fault. The gamble there would be enough cash for the deal also paid off, when the London house sold for a good price.

Having procrastinated slightly to allow his share of the sale proceeds to arrive, Gerald was now able to complete his cash purchase of Egremont relatively quickly. He then wasted no time commissioning builders to do some minor repairs and major decorations, including updating the 'blood-and-custard' kitchen. They quoted a month for the work.

After finding Egremont, Gerald kept out of the flat during the daytime by exploring Exeter and its surroundings. Then he switched to ordering carpets and monitoring the builders who, against all his expectations, proved model workmen who stuck to their timetable. They seemed to like working in the house, and on a number of occasions remarked how pleasant the place was.

Gerald began to feel a little more relaxed than before. Unfortunately, almost as soon as the major sources of irritation in his life disappeared, an unavoidable new one began to afflict him.

Previously, he had experienced no trouble with the flat above. But, a few days after his builders started work, a new occupant, a young woman, arrived upstairs.

Whatever the new arrival did for a living kept her out of her flat from noon, until she returned soon after midnight every night. The return was always marked by music being played in the room above Gerald's bedroom. Her preference was mainly rap but, oddly, included one song by Dolly Parton, whose 'Jolene' began to entertain Gerald through the ceiling in the small hours.

At first, he found Miss Midnight, as he dubbed her, more cooperative than the foul-mouthed Barrel and her devil-spawn next door. After suffering a few unwanted early morning concerts, he asked her to turn the music down, and for a while she did.

But after a few days, Miss Midnight's music returned to its previous agonising volume. Gerald endured 'Jolene' and rap for a couple of nights, before knocking on her door again to reiterate his objections, this time in stronger terms than before.

This secured relative silence for a longer period than his first, more diplomatic, approach produced. He was just able to sleep. However, after about a week, Miss Midnight restored her music to a volume which made sleep impossible.

Perhaps it was to do with all the change and upset. Perhaps it was a side–effect of his antidepressants. Perhaps it was impotent rage against the selfishness of his neighbours. Perhaps it was because he hated rap and was not very keen on 'Jolene.' Perhaps it was all of these things. But, as Gerald lay awake in bed at half past one, forced to listen to 'Jolene' for what seemed the millionth time, he suddenly lost all reason. Something snapped in his head. The injustice of the noise was just too much, and he decided to fix the problem once and for all.

He flew out of bed. He tore open his door and raced up the stairs in bare feet to the floor above. There, he pounded wildly on Miss Midnight's door.

Why Miss Midnight opened it remained forever a mystery both to him and to her. But she did, and before she could speak, Gerald pushed violently past her into the flat, knocking her hard against the wall, shouting obscenities at her. A CD player, still playing at high volume, stood on a small table. He pushed the table over with the underside of his right foot, and the player hit the floor with a squawk and stopped playing. He then picked the thing up and smashed it down hard.

Miss Midnight was staggering to her feet near the door, blood trickling down her nose. Gerald rushed past her, out of her flat, down the stairs and into his own, slamming his door shut.

Gerald looked down at his foot, which was hurting from violent contact with the table. He went into his bathroom and bathed it in hot water. Suddenly, his anger left him. Justice had been served. He had actually done something positive about a perceived evil, and it felt good.

This feeling of achievement progressed to a state of unnatural serenity. Calmly, he reasoned Miss Midnight would call the police. As she should. It was a matter for the police. He must be ready for them. He knew they would want to take him away. He changed out of the nightshirt he always wore in preference to pyjamas, and donned his day clothes. He smartened himself up and packed a small case, as though he was going away for a holiday. Then he sat and waited.

The police did come. They had been called both by Miss Midnight and by another upstairs neighbour. And they did take Gerald away. At first they were predictably firm, but his quiet, matter-of-fact acceptance that he should be arrested, and his readiness to go, proved both disarming and unusual. Without any fuss, he was led gently away and driven to the police station.

In the presence of a sergeant and a constable, Gerald was made to turn out his pockets and his case. When the sergeant saw the packet of antidepressants, he became cautious.

"What are those?" he asked, even though he already knew.

Gerald told him. The sergeant studied Gerald, tapping the desk with his pen.

"So you've got a problem, have you, Sir?"

"Yes," admitted Gerald. "But these control it." He paused. "Most of the time."

"Prescription drugs, aren't they?" asked the policeman.

"Yes."

The sergeant had mistakenly taken insufficient notice of signs indicating mental problems in someone under arrest before. The lawyers made hay with him. He did not want to go through that again.

"I'm going to call a doctor," he said, motioning the constable to take Gerald to a cell.

Alone in the cold cell, awaiting the doctor's arrival, Gerald felt his mood change and his serenity evaporate. The overpowering sense of injustice that sparked his attack on Miss Midnight's CD player returned, reinforced now by the additional humiliation of being locked up for tackling the unprovoked sonic abuse inflicted upon him. The unfairness of being put in a cell raced round in his mind until Gerald returned to boiling point.

He heard voices outside, a key turned in the lock. The sergeant led another man into the cell and closed the door.

The policeman moved to the side to allow the other, younger, man to come forward, saying as he did so,

"This is Doctor Jameson."

Without warning, Gerald lunged at the doctor. Dr. Jameson was fortunately on the alert for unpredictable behaviour. He recoiled rapidly and fetched up against the cell door behind him, far enough away for Gerald's outstretched and clawed hands to miss. He received nothing more than a slight scratch near his Adam's apple from Gerald's right middle finger, and a mild bump on the back of his head.

An approved social worker was found, and Gerald's reward was to be incarcerated in a secure hospital against his will under Section 4 of the Mental Health Act, following a process known as 'sectioning.' Initially he was detained for three days, but this was extended to four weeks whilst the extent of his disturbance was investigated.

During this period, his medication was adjusted, and the results were eventually good enough to convince the doctors no further detention on medical grounds was required. Miss Midnight dropped her complaint and Gerald was told that, apart from his stay in hospital, no further action would be taken against him.

Before Gerald's final release, the builders finished readying Egremont for him to move in. Gerald's doctors believed he should do so quickly, but worried the stress might rekindle his aggressive behaviour. So they allowed him out on leave provided he was accompanied by his nearest relative.

Gerald considered his rather limited options. His nearest relative was his daughter, Natasha. She was very close to her mother, and took her mother's side over the divorce. She was also prickly and devious, with a well-developed selfish streak. Gerald had provided for her as any father should, but there had been trouble between them from time to time. He had never really considered her as being 'of' him; more 'with' him. He dithered for a while, but was forced to realise there was little choice. So he took the plunge, and telephoned his daughter.

Gerald was glad Natasha readily agreed to help. Her assistance enabled him to quickly vacate the repellent flat and move his possessions into Egremont, with such ease that his doctors allowed him permanently back into the community. Natasha also persuaded Miss Midnight to accept the very generous restitution he offered for the damage he had caused. Gerald offered reparation worth more than the combined value of the CD player and table, as that seemed the right thing to do, despite thinking Miss Midnight was a thoughtless and ill-mannered young woman.

Had Miss Midnight behaved properly, Gerald ruefully told his daughter, he would never have attacked her and would not be in his current position. It was always the way, he said. Those pro-actively and directly infringing the rights of others often get away with it, whilst their victims who react and respond get punished.

Natasha's help began to restore Gerald's faith in natural justice. He gave her a key to Egremont, where she stayed until the morning his sectioning came to an end.

Gerald decided he would keep up the momentum of his renewed acquaintanceship with Natasha, and get her out of the awful London hovel she lived in, by inviting her to visit him more often. Even her boyfriend, Newt, would be welcome. Gerald started on this course immediately by issuing two invitations.

Since boyhood, Gerald had been intrigued by stories about King Arthur, and thought it would be pleasant for his first significant outing after moving house to visit Tintagel, in Cornwall, some sixty miles away. Tintagel boasted a cliff-top hotel, very close to a castle with strong Arthurian associations. He wondered if Natasha and her partner might like to join him as his guests, for two nights in the hotel. It would get them out of London, he said. They could have some fun, good food and sea air, all at his expense.

Natasha said they would be very happy to accept. Gerald then asked if they would also like to be his guests over Christmas in another hotel, which he would gladly arrange. Natasha accepted, and he felt pleased to be establishing some normal family relations.

Natasha did a lot of thinking on the train journey back to London. The moment her father telephoned, she sniffed the possibility of an opportunity. She did not know what the opportunity might be, but she knew fortune often sprang from the misfortune of others. So she had jumped at the chance to help him, to be the loving daughter after all his troubles.

Natasha was very close to her mother, whom she encouraged throughout the adulterous affair that eventually led to divorce. Natasha viewed Gerald solely as a provider and, in view of her circumstances, an unsuccessful one. She despised him, and they had often quarrelled in the few years since she had left university.

But now, Natasha knew a lot more about her father's position. She knew he owned a decent little house outright, even if it did smell a bit of cabbage, and Miss Midnight had been colourfully informative about his behaviour. Natasha thought hard about her own seedy London accommodation. Now she and Newt were to have further access to Gerald, and two holidays, at no cost to themselves. Slowly, the germ of an idea began to form in her mind that might, just might, yield considerable benefit.

Gerald was delighted with Egremont. The builders had done a good job. He had been very lucky to find such a competent firm. His initial concern that they might string the job out, as builders often do, proved unfounded. The boss even told him they enjoyed working on Egremont. Unlike many of their projects, he said, nothing went wrong. There were no unexpected snags.

Gerald had asked the builders to look for possible causes of bad smells, but they found none. The only things of interest they did find came from under the kitchen floor: a fountain pen of indeterminate age and an old framed photograph of a young couple, which they put in a Jiffy bag in the garage. Otherwise, there was nothing.

After booking the Tintagel hotel and Natasha and Newt's Christmas treat, almost the first thing Gerald did after his daughter returned to London was to invite a feng shui consultant, Simon Bruce, to visit him. He was curious about feng shui, having heard it was to do with arranging buildings and their contents, 'balancing energy' for the maximum happiness of the occupants. Perhaps he should have considered it before the builders arrived. But balancing energy between Egremont as it now was and the little furniture he possessed should not, he thought, be beyond the consultant's ability.

Other than Natasha and the builders, Simon Bruce was Gerald's first visitor to Egremont. When, on the agreed day, Gerald answered the consultant's knock at the door, he observed a small man, looking at the unknown bushes near the door. They still bore the flowers Gerald thought responsible for the scent of jasmine which regularly pervaded most of the building.

"Mr. Bruce?" asked Gerald. His visitor turned towards him. He sported a dark goatee beard and swept-back dark hair, and wore a black open-necked shirt under a black suit.

The visitor said, "good qi."

"And to you," replied Gerald, smiling.

"No," said Mr. Bruce. "Good qi."

"Pardon?" said Gerald. A feng shui consultant might be expected to behave unusually, but, even so, Gerald was slightly taken aback.

"You don't need me," said the visitor. "This house has good qi and is very good for you already."

"Aren't you going to come in?" inquired Gerald.

"No," said the consultant. "The house does not want me, and you will be happy with it as it is."

"But you haven't seen inside!" remonstrated Gerald.

"I don't need to. I can tell from here," replied the strange visitor.

He turned to leave. As he did so, he said, over his shoulder, "there's no charge."

Gerald stared, bemused, at his visitor's receding back.

"Thank you," he said lamely, and closed the door.

Gerald found his reluctant visitor was right. Whenever Gerald was at home, he was happy. Nothing seemed out of place. All the fixtures and fittings worked well. The plumbing now behaved faultlessly. Everything fitted like a glove. He had not even suffered the usual difficulties arranging his broadband connection, which was essential for his work. And the fragrance of jasmine from those durable bushes, everywhere in the house except his bathroom and bedroom at the back, delighted him whenever it was present.

Gerald rapidly fell in love with Egremont. He felt safe and secure almost for the first time in his life. Whether it was his new environment, with its sharp contrast to the hostile atmospheres he had so recently endured, or whether it was his adjusted medication, he could not tell. But his bad dreams disappeared. He no longer awoke early with a sense of irreparable loss, nor did he feel crushed by the weight of the world.

Feeling good, Gerald began to wonder whether, as the causes of his depression had passed, he may no longer need antidepressants. The doctors had told him not to stop using them, as stopping suddenly could produce serious side-effects. Antidepressants were not Smarties, one doctor explained, but powerful psychiatric drugs which needed treating with respect. Yet Gerald longed to be free of the pills, reasoning that if he stopped taking them and suffered side-effects, he could always restart them. He decided to take the chance.

To his relief, and to some extent surprise, he experienced no sudden side-effects, and life in his new home continued in a very happy vein.

After two weeks busying himself to ensure everything at Egremont was exactly to his taste, the time came to visit Tintagel with Natasha and Newt. He had already posted them a little money and their railway tickets, which he bought online. Now he picked the couple up at Exeter Central railway station and together they drove to Tintagel.

Gerald had met Newt once before. Other than thinking him unkempt, Gerald found him rather wishy-washy. He wondered if such men were drawn to powerful characters like his daughter, and vice-versa. Newt turned out to have a keen interest in Arthurian legends which, Gerald reflected, was probably why Natasha accepted what must have seemed to her a slightly unusual invitation. The common interest lubricated conversation in the car, with even Natasha chiming in, and the journey passed quickly.

As it was late in the year, seaside hotel rooms were relatively plentiful and the rates reasonable. Gerald had been able to secure two rooms overlooking the sea, although he and his guests would have to wait until daylight to enjoy the view. After settling in, all three met for drinks in an otherwise deserted bar.

Gerald arrived feeling tired. His earlier flow of conversation dried up, and he contributed little to the evening, either in the bar or at dinner. Immediately following the meal, he made his apologies and retired to his room, where he read a magazine for half an hour before going to bed.

Natasha watched her father leave the dining room, then, turning to Newt, said, "as I told you, all we've got to do is be friendly. I know you think he's a prat, and so do I, but he could be our meal ticket. Don't forget, he's got no-one else he can turn to. That's why he asked me to get him out of the booby hatch. Humour him. Put up with the old idiot. There are chances here for us; I can smell them. I reckon, if we stay close, we'll soon find out what they are. He owes me."

Newt grinned at her, and they moved back to the bar. There, they spent more of Gerald's money before taking further supplies of alcohol into the hotel's Games Room, where they played snooker for a couple of hours. Confident though they were of gaining from the situation, neither of them guessed quite how soon their path would become clear.

Gerald did not sleep well. His bad dreams returned and he found himself awake just as day was breaking, feeling completely bereft, regretting something nameless, and horribly alone. He knew that, once awake and in a low mood, the only remedy was to get up and try shaking it off.

He blamed himself for going to bed too soon after dinner. He should have let the meal settle. Then he would have slept better. But it was too late to worry now.

He looked out over the sea. There was a clear blue sky: it was going to be a beautiful day. He opened the window, felt a gentle breeze on his cheek, and listened to the sea breaking on the rocks at the foot of the cliffs. Over to the left were the remains of the castle. Yes, it would be good to look around here. The views were spectacular and timeless.

After showering and dressing, Gerald went down to an early breakfast, which the hotel was starting to serve. Although he cursed himself for going to bed too soon after dinner, he nevertheless felt very hungry. Guessing Natasha and Newt spent the previous evening drinking after he left them, he was not surprised they were not in evidence, and surmised they would probably want little more than coffee anyway.

Gerald, however, indulged heavily in a full cooked breakfast, the sort which normally produces a feeling of near-invincibility for the rest of the day. Yet, as he ate, he found himself reflecting gloomily on his solitude. He ought to be enjoying this, and with someone else. But there was no-one, except a disinterested-looking waitress. He finished his meal and went into a large lounge, where daily newspapers were neatly laid out on a long table. He picked one up and sat down to read.

"Can I help you, Sir?"

Gerald lifted his head and looked at the waitress. He realised that, for goodness knows how long, he had been sitting with his chin on his chest and his hands clasped, just as he used to do before he moved into Egremont.

"What?" said Gerald in a disconnected fashion.

"I'm sorry, Sir" replied the waitress. "You dropped your paper some time ago, and I wondered if there was anything wrong."

She stooped to pick up the newspaper.

"Leave me alone, will you?" snapped Gerald.

Bent almost double, the waitress turned her head to look at him, taken aback.

"I'm sorry, Sir. I was just …" she started.

"Never mind what you were just doing. Just go."

The waitress straightened, leaving the paper where it was, and began retreating towards the door, red-faced and upset.

Realising he been unjustifiably rude, Gerald, disgusted with himself, said loudly,

"Wait! I'm sorry."

The waitress stopped.

"That was unforgivable," said Gerald. "I do

apologise. Will you accept this?"

From his wallet he pulled a twenty-pound note, which he waved at the waitress. She hesitated, then said, "no, sir. I'll accept your apology, but not your money," before retreating from the room, head held high.

The episode made Gerald even more gloomy. There was still no sign of his daughter and her friend. He decided to go outside for some fresh air and to look at the sea. He would spend about half an hour meandering, then check again whether Natasha had managed to get up, before visiting the castle he so wanted to see.

Outside the hotel, at the rear, the dishevelled and overgrown remains of a garden sloped down towards the cliff top. Gerald navigated his way through the weeds, wondering why such a good hotel paid no attention to its grounds. Before long, he found himself standing on top of a large flat rock, looking down an almost sheer cliff face to the pounding sea far below.

In the crisp cloudless daylight, the sea was a limpid blue-green, its restless surface flecked with white foam. The wind had risen, and powerful bulging swells crashed onto the rocks, throwing up occasional prominences of spume and leaving thick borders of white foam behind, which survived only long enough to be washed away and replaced by the next inrush. It was the same everywhere along the coast, as far as Gerald could see.

He stared downwards. The scene was peculiarly familiar, but he did not know why; maybe because he had read such a lot about Tintagel's wildness, and it had now become real. He thought about Felicity and the life they had shared until her adultery and everything that followed. All gone, now. He thought about the divorce, the awful flat, the hospital, his loneliness. Then his mind wandered to thoughts of King Arthur, and he felt the eternity of his majestic surroundings seeping into him. What a place this would be to draw a line, to be relieved of the losses and disappointments of the world, to become part of the ages. He looked down at the beckoning waves, as inviting as a warm blue swimming pool.

"Good, isn't it?" boomed a voice to his left.

Gerald whipped round, wrenched from his contemplations. Standing not two yards away and gazing out to sea was a man in his thirties, wearing a baggy and worn dark suit of a rather outdated style, his left hand clamping a bedraggled trilby onto his head in the strengthening wind.

Gerald eyed the man for a few seconds. He wore a soiled dark blue tie over a dirty white shirt, and his feet were encased in old black Oxfords with wide cracks through the uppers just behind the toecaps. His right hand carried a well-used black leather briefcase, with the initials 'G. B.' embossed on it in thin, patchy gold leaf.

"Yes," said Gerald. "It's really, well, frightening, I suppose."

"Spectacular," replied the newcomer, in a strong Devonian burr. "To my mind, there's nothing like it anywhere in the world." He turned towards Gerald, who wondered if there might be something distantly familiar about the man.

"I've come from the hotel," continued the stranger. Your car's blocking someone in and they want you to move it. I heard them talking in

119

Reception. I thought I'd seen someone come down here. I wanted to look at the sea anyway, so I said I'd tell you."

"Right," said Gerald. "Right. Thank you. I'd better do that, then." He started back up towards the hotel, picking his way through the neglected garden.

"Strange," he thought. "I don't remember parking next to anyone last night. I didn't think there were many cars about." But he had been tired the night before, and it was dark when he arrived. He could well have parked carelessly without noticing an exit or another vehicle.

He went round to the front of the hotel, to move his car. It was standing as he left it, nosed up to within a few inches of the hotel wall, and blocking nothing. There were no other vehicles anywhere near, and no sign of any exit or entrance.

"Flipping nerve," said Gerald, angrily. "A hoax!" He felt his face reddening and his annoyance rising at the thought.

He stalked into the hotel, straight to Reception, where a young receptionist was studying her computer.

"I'll be with you in a moment," she said.

"You'll be with me now!" barked Gerald. "It's absolutely disgraceful to be messed about like this and then ignored. Why did you send that man to bring me here with a cock and bull story about my car blocking someone in? Tell me that!"

The receptionist stared at him in alarm. "I, I, I didn't send anyone for a-anything," she stammered.

"You must have, a few minutes ago," replied Gerald.

"No. I've been here two hours. There's been

nothing about cars or …"

"You're lying!" shouted Gerald. "Young people these days! If you were my daughter I'd …" He moved forward sharply towards the receptionist. She jumped involuntarily away from him, and the counter held him back.

"Dad!" Sharp and shrill, Natasha's voice rang out across the foyer. "Stop it! What the hell are you doing?" Gerald spun round to see his daughter and Newt staring at him from the bottom step of the stairs they had just descended from the floor above.

"This lying witch sent someone to get me to move my car as a joke! You can't enjoy yourself anywhere these days without someone upsetting things. 'Find out what John's doing and stop him' That's the attitude! Well, I'm not having it! I'm going to find the man who did it!"

Gerald stormed out of the hotel, leaving Natasha and Newt to calm the receptionist and apologise on his behalf.

Outside, Gerald searched in vain for any sign of the man in the trilby. As he blundered about, his unreason began to leave him. He sat down on a dilapidated bench, and wept.

Half an hour later, Newt found him still sitting there, staring at the ground with his chin down on his chest and his hands clasped in front of him.

"'Ello, mate," said Newt. Gerald did not respond.

"Hey, Gerry!" Newt tried again. "You OK?"

"I don't know," said Gerald, without looking up. "Fed up, tired … this place. I don't know what came over me. What an idiot."

"Yep," replied Newt.

"It must have been some silly prankster," Gerald

said, regretting being bamboozled by his incongruously-dressed cliff top companion. Then he asked, "where's Tash?"

"Packing. Says we can't stay 'ere no more."

Gerald nodded slowly. "I suppose not," he said, sadly.

"Will you be able to drive?" asked Newt. Gerald nodded again, and the pair went back into the hotel through a back door.

Gerald packed his things and joined his daughter and Newt in Reception. He was the only member of the party with the means to pay for their stay. He did this with a credit card whilst mumbling apologies at the hotel manager, who had replaced the distressed receptionist. Apart from the bare minimum necessary to complete the transaction, the manager said nothing.

Then Gerald retrieved a cheque book from his overcoat pocket, put it on the counter, and asked the manager,

"What is the receptionist's name? I want to write her a cheque as an apology."

The manager considered for a moment.

"Jane Treloar."

Gerald completed a cheque and handed it to the manager.

"It won't bounce," said Gerald, as the manager's eyes widened on seeing the cheque was made out for five hundred pounds.

Gerald could feel those eyes boring into his back as he and his guests left the hotel.

"That was a lot of money," remarked Natasha, quietly.

"Was it?" asked Gerald.

Nothing more was said about the incident, and they drove back to Exeter in silence, Gerald reflecting bitterly on what had happened and Newt not knowing what to think.

Natasha faced no such quandary. As soon as she witnessed her father in the hotel's Reception, her course of action became obvious. She now knew what she was going to do, and spent the journey quietly turning the plan over in her mind to check for imperfections.

The episode fuelled Gerald's depression. He could not understand his bad behaviour. It was a further symptom something was really wrong with him. He wondered whether suddenly stopping the antidepressants might have produced a delayed effect. Maybe the stuff stayed in the bloodstream for a couple of weeks before wearing off. Perhaps he should start taking the pills again.

Approaching Exeter Central after more than two hours without speaking, he suddenly enquired,

"You're still coming for Christmas, aren't you? I've booked the hotel."

Sitting in the back with Natasha, Newt only managed to say, "well …," before Natasha overrode him, jabbing him gently and invisibly in the ribs with her elbow.

"Of course, Dad. We'd love to, wouldn't we, Newt? We'll just have to make sure you don't block anyone's car in!" She laughed.

"Er … great." Newt had picked up the message, but did not sound convinced. Gerald ignored the inflection in his voice.

"Good," said Gerald, and, with rather subdued farewells, deposited his guests outside the station.

Natasha and Newt watched Gerald drive away. Then Natasha said,

"I know what to do now. But there are too many people about. I'll tell you when we get home."

Despite repeated attempts by Newt to prise information out of her, Natasha refused to say anything more about her father until they were safely back in their flat. The moment their door closed, Newt said,

"Right. You've got a plan. So, gimme! It had better be good after all this."

Natasha said, "I'm not sure you'll like it."

"Try me."

"Well, we're stuck, aren't we? I hate this place. It's a dirty, damp dump, and the neighbourhood's worse. I shouldn't be living in a sink estate. It's noisy and dangerous, and this flat is about the only place the thugs out there haven't turned over. We're both on benefits, while my fool of a father is sitting pretty in the West Country. He owes me. He owes me big time. But he's never so much as lifted a finger to get me out of here."

"So? What're you goin' to do?"

"We're going to get him locked up."

"Eh? How are you goin' to do that?"

"We, Newt, we. We're going to do it. Or, rather, we are going to help him do it to himself."

"How?"

"You saw how he went on at the receptionist. He'd have hit her if it hadn't been for the counter. It was much the same with the other one. You know, the girl with the music over his bedroom. Only then a CD player got it. He's unstable. With only a slight shove, he goes over the edge. He only escaped prosecution last time by the skin of his teeth. If he does it again, they'll throw the book at him."

"So we're goin' to shove him, are we? How do you do that?" Newt was not cottoning on as fast as Natasha hoped to the possibilities before them.

"Look, if the counter hadn't stopped him getting at the receptionist, after what he did before he'd probably be under lock and key now, and they wouldn't let him out again for a long time. And there's another thing."

"What?"

"Well, you know I got up before you this morning?"

Newt nodded.

"I went down to get a paper from the lounge. I was just outside, and looked in. There he was, with a waitress."

"Oh, yeah? What was 'e doin' wiv 'er?" asked Newt, grinning lasciviously.

"Nothing like that. No, he looked like he'd dozed off and dropped his paper. She wanted to pick it up, and boy, did she get it in the neck."

"Right."

"He was completely out of order. Way over the top. Then he offered her money by way of saying sorry. She wouldn't have it. Then I left. He didn't see me."

"So?"

"Well, it wasn't as bad as the other times, but he's gone for young women three times now. We're going to make it four."

"Who's the lucky girl, then?" smirked Newt.

"Me. We're going to get him to attack me."

There was a short silence. Then Newt said,

"You must be crazy."

"No. You'll be there to stop him if it gets too violent. I'll be OK."

"Look, let's go back a bit," said Newt. "Suppose we do get him locked up. How do we benefit?"

"If he gets put away for assaulting his own daughter, after what he did before, he'll be away for a long time. It makes no difference whether it's prison or a hospital. It could be for ages, maybe indefinite. So he won't need the house, will he?"

Newt thought for a moment, then said,

"OK. But he could still stop us stayin' in it. You know, give it to a lawyer or somethin'."

"Ah, that's the clever bit. I think he'll ask us to stay while he's away."

"Why?"

"Think what he did with the other three. Each time, he felt guilty, and tried to do something about it by giving money. Over the odds for a CD player in the first case, twenty pounds or something with the waitress and then a cheque for five hundred for Jane what's-her-face. Chances are he'll feel guilty about me, and then I can offer to stay in his house to keep it aired. With luck I'll get a cheque as well."

Newt considered this, then asked,

"How will you wind him up, girl? And where?"

"No sweat. I can get him going about the divorce. And where's easy. In that hotel he's got us into for Christmas. I'll get him to go for me with lots of people around."

Newt thought again.

"Sounds OK."

"Then, when the cops come, you can tell them about the receptionist and the girl with the music.

And I'll tell them he stopped his medication despite being told not to – which he has."

"Blimey!" said Newt. "What a nut."

"They'll check the records and, bingo! He'll be banged up for ages. And he'll be so remorseful about me he'll almost give us the house."

By the time they met Gerald again, Natasha and Newt had gone over and over the idea and refined their plan until they thought every possibility had been covered.

As Gerald pulled into his driveway after the disastrous visit to Tintagel, he started feeling better. Egremont was home, and the house almost seemed to smile at him. He went inside, and was immediately greeted by the scent of jasmine. Enfolded in its lovely fragrance, he felt relieved to be back. His new home comforted and cheered him. This was a much better place to be. He put his travelling things away with a lighter heart, his depression vanishing.

Yet there was something irritating him, at the back of his mind, something tantalisingly just out of reach, telling him all was not as it should be. He made himself a hot drink.

Drinking his tea, he started to reflect on the awful day. He felt wrong from the moment he arrived in Tintagel. He shuddered at the recollection of his rudeness to the waitress, and his atrocious behaviour towards the receptionist. Whatever had got into him? Then he dwelt upon his cliff top reverie, and wondered what would have happened if the hoaxer with the bedraggled trilby had not played his stupid prank. But somehow the events of that morning already felt remote, much longer ago than a few hours. He tried, but could not quite manage, to reconstruct his mood even as recently as half an hour ago, before he arrived home.

Yes, that was it. His arrival. The teasing annoyance at the back of his mind was to do with coming home. He must have noticed something was different when he returned.

He went outside down the front garden path and looked around. There seemed nothing amiss. Everything was normal. The lawn, no longer an overgrown meadow, the garage, the flower beds, the trees; everything was there as expected.

Then it struck him that he might have noticed something visible only when coming in, facing the other way. He walked into the cul-de-sac and turned round to view the house. Again, everything looked as it should.

He shook his head and decided to abandon his quest. The answer would probably come to him out of the blue, whilst he was in the bath, or some other time when his thoughts were elsewhere. He walked back to the front door.

And then, just as he was about to step inside, he saw the solution. He stopped in surprise. The unidentified bushes either side of the door were there as always. But there was a key difference, and he instantly knew he was looking at the reason for his puzzlement. There were no flowers on the bushes. The dying year had finally taken its toll, and only stems and leaves remained. "The flowers have gone," he mused. They could not, after all, have been the source of the jasmine fragrance which even now, standing on his threshold, he could still smell; the beautiful smell of jasmine of which he never tired.

He went back inside and started to think. Where was the scent coming from? Part of his fragile mind was happy to be invigorated by the perfume. But his rationale for its source had just been disproved. He began to consider other odd things too.

There were Dog Man's comments about the people who complained Egremont smelled bad. No-one would ever describe jasmine as a bad smell. And why did Simon Bruce, the feng shui man, behave so strangely, not wanting to come in?

If others disliked Egremont, that was their loss, thought Gerald. Personally, he felt nothing but intense contentment in the house. Perhaps feeling good at Egremont was itself an inconsistency, though. He had never really felt at peace anywhere else. Perhaps that was because Egremont's 'qi' was good and lots of happy people had lived there before.

Into his searching mind floated the recollection that his builder had found an old photograph whilst renovating the kitchen. A young couple, the builder said. Gerald had been in hospital when the picture was found and, as yet, had not seen it. There seemed no obvious reason why he should want to see it now, either, but he suddenly felt curious. So he went into the garage, located the Jiffy bag containing the photograph and fountain pen, and brought them back into the house.

Wondering how a framed picture and a pen could have slipped between floorboards, he extracted the photograph. It looked decades old. A smiling couple, holding hands, gazed at him happily out of the cheap wooden frame. Then he nearly jumped through the ceiling. He could not quite believe his eyes. The young man was identical to the cliff top hoaxer at

Tintagel!

For a moment, Gerald felt ice-cold. Was he imagining things? Dumbfounded, he tried steadying his nerves with a large whisky. He looked at the picture again. There was no doubt. A ringer. A dead ringer, he flippantly thought. The day may have been disturbing, but his memory of the cliff top that morning was clear. He wondered whether the photograph held any secrets about its provenance.

A kitchen knife soon prised the back off the frame, and he anxiously looked at the picture's reverse side. On it was written, in pencil, what was presumably the photographer's description: 'Gilbert and Rose Blinkhorn. 17th June, 1933.'

Gerald stared at the inscription in disbelief. The hoaxer's briefcase had been embossed 'G. B.' Gilbert Blinkhorn.

What, wondered Gerald, were the chances of the hoaxer looking like the man in the photograph, and of his initials being the same, of it all being a coincidence? His logic said, 'infinitesimal.' But his logical side also told him there were few other possibilities. Maybe he was hallucinating, or possibly something supernatural was happening.

He wrestled with the improbable alternatives. The possibility of coincidence seemed so slight as to be effectively zero. What about hallucinations? He recalled the doctor's description of his medication as 'powerful psychiatric drugs.' He had stopped taking the pills, against medical advice. Could that be the trouble? After all, no-else had smelled jasmine or seen the hoaxer, as far as he knew. Then Gerald reasoned he had first smelled the now inexplicable scent before stopping the drugs. Nor could the hallucination theory explain Dog Man's tales of bad smells, nor Mr. Bruce's weird reaction to Egremont, unless Gerald had hallucinated them too. He could smell jasmine even now. Could one suffer an hallucination even whilst believing it could be one? Would such awareness destroy the hallucination? Gerald could not work it out.

He then considered whether he was experiencing something supernatural. If so, it was not frightening. He was happy at Egremont. In fact, it was the only place he had ever felt totally at peace. Even now, though shocked, he was neither fearful nor apprehensive, merely curious, which was remarkable for a man suspecting his house might be haunted. What was more, the hoaxer, the man identical to the one in the photograph, may have stopped him jumping off the cliff. So if there were supernatural forces at work, they were not hostile.

Gerald realised he possessed no means to test whether he was suffering from coincidence or hallucination. By definition, a coincidence left no evidence of links between events, because there were none. And hallucinations were, by their nature, untestable by the victim in any reliable way.

But what about the supernatural possibility? Could that be tested? Suppose, he thought, the man on the cliff and the smells were inspired by some supernatural force, could whatever it was be induced to reveal itself? Could he communicate with it? He began to think he already had, that morning on the cliff. But he suspected there must be more to the matter than that.

Although he could foresee no particular reason why a supernatural entity, if it existed in the house, should necessarily be an enemy, he drew back from trying to provoke an encounter. Instead, he made himself a sandwich and sat meditating for a long while, listening to Egremont and smelling it, trying to detect further supernatural signs already present but which he may have missed.

But there was nothing, and he progressed no further with the mystery. Strangely, he still felt completely relaxed despite his environment's new overtones. Presently he went to bed, tired by his poor sleep the night before and confused by the eventful day, wishing for further enlightenment without having the courage to seek it.

He dreamt vividly. He dreamed he was writing a letter, many letters, always to the same person, using an old-style fountain pen. But he did not know and could not read what he was writing, nor to whom. As he wrote, he felt growing despair, but did not know why. He dreamed of Tower Bridge in London, not looking up at it but down from it. He was not at road level, but on the walkway high above. The Pool of London beneath was full of ships. He felt he was in a place of interminable blackness, immediately dominated by overwhelming feelings of remorse and loss. Then he dreamed of Egremont, and the sense of loss ceased. But the remorse, for something unidentified, continued until he saw Tintagel Castle. And then the feeling of remorse left him, too.

He awoke in the dark of early morning, and sat upright in bed. He moved from deep sleep to full wakefulness in an instant. And in that instant, he was certain he knew the answer to his questions of the previous evening. The answer was so incredible he could scarcely believe it, yet something told him he could confirm it. He left his bedroom, and went out onto the small, cold landing. Sure enough, there he was greeted by a strong scent of jasmine. He returned to his bedroom. No smell. He double-checked, going in and out of the room several times. There was no doubt. The fragrance was only outside his room. It had never been inside. He got back into bed. Then he said, loudly,

"I could not let it happen again. I came to myself, and I've atoned now. You have forgiven me, haven't you? I know you have. We are together again, aren't we? Even after all this time? You can say 'Yes' by coming in, or 'No' by leaving completely."

Gerald waited in the silence. Then, suddenly, his bedroom was filled with the smell of jasmine, and he with a sense of deep, deep contentment.

On Christmas Eve, as planned, Gerald collected Natasha and Newt from Exeter Central about four o'clock. They arrived smiling, having disembarked from the busy London train after using the tickets Gerald had provided. A short drive took them to Goodman's Court.

With so little notice, Gerald felt lucky to have secured a booking for Christmas. Goodman's Court had been a Victorian millionaire's fantasy, that became disused immediately its builder died. His family disliked the riot of Gothic rooms, and sold it for conversion into an hotel after the Great War.

Gerald could see why the place might be disliked. Underneath the Christmas adornments and various other decorations, the building was a gloomy granite-grey throughout. Living there before modern central heating must have been like being inside an enormous bone-chilling tomb. Perhaps that accounted for its Christmas vacancies even now. But Gerald put these thoughts aside. He was determined to have a good time, despite his separation from Egremont.

In the short period since understanding why Egremont was so special, Gerald became completely integrated with its haunting ways. Inside Egremont, he would be happy and loved for the rest of his days. After his many disappointing life experiences, that seemed to him a very acceptable future, even if Egremont's benevolence did not extend into the world beyond. Fortunately, his work enabled him to stay indoors most of the time, and supplies could be ordered online and delivered to him. Except for excursions such as this Christmas outing with his daughter, he had little need ever to leave the building, and his new life situation meant he would never need antidepressants again.

Being away from Egremont was going to be a wrench. He did feel a little lonely and rather tired as he checked into Goodman's Court. But he decided he was going to be the perfect companion for his daughter. After all, she and Newt were his guests. Gerald wanted to be bright and cheerful for the evening's festivities.

"Strange place," commented Newt, as he and Natasha entered their room.

"Yes," replied Natasha shortly. "But never mind that. We've got a job to do."

"Right," grunted Newt.

"Now," said Natasha, "let's go over it again. We've got to pick our time, and it's got to be when other people are around. Stick close, and let me take the lead. All you've got to do is haul him off if he gets too aggressive. That's the only risk – apart, of course from the possibility he might not rise to the bait at all. Remember, if you do have to intervene, don't hit him. We don't want complications. And stay sober."

Newt nodded. "OK, babe. No probs."

They found Gerald in the bar. He had come down some time before, and was sitting on his own amongst a growing throng of guests, staring at the floor meditatively, hands interlinked in front of him. On a low glass-topped table beside him there was a glass of whisky, which looked untouched, and a card outlining the evening's events.

"Dad?" Natasha said. There was no answer.

"Dad!" said Natasha again, as she touched Gerald's shoulder.

"What?" Gerald looked up sharply. "Oh, sorry, I was miles away."

He stood up.

"What'll you have to drink?" he enquired of his guests.

Natasha requested a white wine spritzer and Newt a pint of Guinness. Natasha shot a warning glance towards her partner.

When her father returned with their drinks, Natasha asked, "where were you, Dad, when you were miles away just then?"

Gerald paused. Sitting down again, he said,

"Oh, you know. Thinking of times past. Christmases past. Like Dickens, I suppose."

"Dickens?" asked Newt.

"Yes. You know. 'A Christmas Carol?' Scrooge?"

"Oh," said Newt, who fell silent again. Gerald could not tell whether Newt understood or not.

"Sins of the past, woes of the present and their consequences in the future," said Natasha.

"Hey, that sounds good, girl!" said Newt. Gerald said nothing.

"Like with Mum," added Natasha. Gerald stared at her.

"What do you mean?" he barked.

"Oh, nothing. Christmases past. You know. They were good. With Mum."

At that moment, a gong sounded. Conversation died away approximately as fast as the sonorous reverberations of the bronze, to be replaced by the voice of a Master of Ceremonies.

"Ladies and gentlemen …"

The MC announced mulled wine was about to be brought round and that, because of his busy schedule, Santa Claus was expected to make only a brief appearance. Guests would later be invited to join the local church choir singing carols around the hearth in the Great Hall. Dinner would be served at eight, followed by coffee and mince pies in the Drawing Room.

"Brill," said Newt, as the MC finished. Gerald remained silent, as the hubbub of conversation again arose around him.

"Shame Mum's not here, isn't it?" asked Natasha, driving her barb in a little further.

Gerald still said nothing.

"She'd love this, Mum would."

"Shut up about her, would you?" snapped Gerald, beginning to turn pink. Newt was suddenly reminded why he was there, and that he was unlikely to sample the mince pies.

"Why? Feeling guilty you never took her to

anything like this?"

"Stop it! Stop it!" Gerald was now quite red in the face. Nearby, a burly man and his jewel-encrusted wife, in the process of being served mulled wine by a smartly-dressed waiter, turned to look nervously at the trio, wondering what was coming next.

"Go for it, girl!" grinned Newt.

Whether or not she heard him above the background chatter, Natasha drove on mercilessly.

"She always thought you loved someone else, but could never prove it. She never had all of you, she said. That's why she took a lover. Good thing, if you ask me. Useless, she said you were … Ow!"

Natasha screamed as Gerald suddenly leaned forward and slapped her hard across the face. Still sitting, she recoiled involuntarily from him, as deep into the upholstery as she could get. He then lunged at her with both hands outstretched, grabbing her throat.

Although primed, the speed at which the row developed temporarily left Newt motionless. But now he sprang up and started to pull Gerald off the trapped Natasha, aided by the burly man and the waiter. The burly man crooked his arm across Gerald's face and pulled him backwards, forcing him to release Natasha's throat.

Together, the three men hauled the struggling Gerald away. Some other guests and the burly man's wife attended to Natasha, who was now whimpering in the chair with one hand rubbing her bruised throat.

Bundled into an office, Gerald posed no difficulties whatsoever to the waiters appointed by the manager as impromptu guards. By the time two police cars and an ambulance arrived, he was completely calm. It was a repeat of the Miss Midnight event. Gerald felt good at having taken active steps against an attack, empowered rather than sitting back enduring barbs like he always used to do. Added to this was now a sense of acceptance that, of course, he must go with the police. It was rightly their concern.

The ambulance crew pronounced Natasha unscathed, except for superficial bruising round her neck. The burly man, his glittering wife and some others who witnessed the row were questioned by two officers, who took statements. Natasha and Newt were deposited in one police car and Gerald in another. Then the dysfunctional Hughes family was driven away to Exeter police station.

The desk sergeant at Exeter remembered Gerald from the incident with Miss Midnight. Once again, Gerald was detained in a cell whilst a doctor was summoned. In another room, Natasha gave copious details about the evening's events, attacking her father for discontinuing his medication and assaulting her, insisting he should be locked up for her protection and his own good.

This time, when left in his cell, Gerald did not become angry at the injustice he felt he was suffering. Instead, he sank into a well of despair. He had left Egremont, where he was safe and loved, to provide what familial Christmas bonhomie he could for his daughter, and his reward was to be taunted and locked up. He could not understand Natasha's behaviour. Why did he deserve such unkindness?

Away from his sanctuary, he felt unutterably and infinitely desolate. Into his mind's eye came the face of a young woman who loved him all those years ago, who loved him still, and from whom he was now forcibly separated. The vision depressed him severely. He knew he was going to be locked away, maybe for ages, and that he would be kept from her again. The situation was hopeless. Nothing but darkness lay ahead. His newly rebuilt life was in ruins. Pointlessly, he looked around the cell for solace. He found nothing but a concrete bench, bare walls, a locked door, and barred windows.

Dr. Derek Stafford had practised in Exeter for thirty-five years. He was a highly respected physician, particularly known for his meticulous and humane ways. He did not normally do police work these days. But, this Christmas Eve, he agreed to stand in for his colleague, young Dr. Jameson, whose wife had just produced their first baby. As he drove to the police station, he thought that, with luck, he would be there only briefly and be home long before Christmas Eve became Christmas Day.

Remembering Gerald's last sojourn in the station and his attack on Dr. Jameson, the duty sergeant briefed Dr. Stafford fully, and provided two constables for his protection. But there was no need. When they entered Gerald's cell, they found him curled up at the far end of the bench, hugging his knees to his chest and mumbling in disconnected snatches. The doctor watched him for several minutes.

The idea flitted through Dr. Stafford's mind of recommending Gerald be sectioned again without further ado. He could leave the detailed task of examining the man to others and get home quickly. Instead, Stafford sighed. Here was a miserable sight to behold. Conscientiously, he decided to try to get the unhappy man to communicate with him, even though the end result was likely to be the same. He had managed to start productive dialogue with many difficult patients over the years, and thought that as long as there was a reasonable chance of getting something useful out of this one, he should try.

Not wanting to intimidate Gerald unduly, Dr. Stafford told the constables he only needed one for protection. He then sat down on the bench next to Gerald to assess the mumbling and whether it contained any useful information. The remaining policeman stood near the cell door, watchful and silent. Gerald muttered on. After a while, Dr. Stafford decided his course of action.

"Who is Rose?" he asked, softly. Gerald had uttered the name several times.

Gerald remained curled up on the bench. He said nothing.

"My name is Derek Stafford," said the medical man. "I'm a doctor. I would like to help you."

There was still no response. Stafford paused, and tried again.

"Tell me, who is Rose?"

Still curled up, Gerald mumbled, "lives with me."

"Is she your wife?"

"Yes, no, yes. Rose."

"So it's Rose Hughes?"

"Rose, Rose. Blinkhorn."

Dr. Stafford stared at Gerald. Had he heard aright?

"Rose Blinkhorn?" he repeated.

Gerald wittered, "Blinkhorn, Blinkhorn, Gilbert, Gerald, Rose, jasmine. Together. Blinkhorn."

For a few moments, Dr. Stafford was silent. Then he turned to the policeman and asked, "do you know where this man lives, and how long he has lived there?" The policeman consulted Gerald's file and told him.

"Where was he before?" asked the doctor. The policeman told him that, too.

Dr. Stafford thought hard. In the background, Gerald was still muttering.

"Blinkhorn, Blinkhorn, Gilbert, Gerald, Rose, jasmine. Together. Blinkhorn."

This was very strange, thought Stafford. Very strange indeed. He cast his mind back thirty years. A Rose Blinkhorn was one of his patients until she died of pneumonia in her seventies. A gentle lady. Dr. Stafford had liked visiting her in the few years their paths crossed and enjoyed their chats over cups of tea. He particularly remembered teasing Rose by calling her 'my little hybrid,' because she always wore a jasmine perfume.

"A Rose with the scent of jasmine," he quipped soon after they met. "You're a hybrid!"

Rose told him a good deal about herself, and he recalled she had once been married, but the husband died before the War. Gilbert? It could have been. Here Dr. Stafford's memory failed him. But he had never forgotten Rose and her lovely perfume. Nor did one forget a name like Blinkhorn. Even the address sounded right.

What was going on? It must be coincidence. How could this man know? Was he a relative of Rose, or did he have some prior knowledge of her? Perhaps he read in some of Egremont's legal documents that a Rose Blinkhorn lived in the property once. But knowing about the scent? That was stretching the bounds of coincidence beyond probability.

The doctor had experienced many strange situations during his career and concluded some things were incapable of rational explanation. Maybe this was just another example. Nonetheless, his professional and human curiosities were aroused: this warranted further attention.

But a more immediate decision was necessary first. The patient was clearly in a bad way. Treatment was required, no matter what the 'Blinkhorn' aspects of the case might mean.

The doctor left Gerald and returned to the desk sergeant. Two young people, a man and a woman, were just leaving. Dr. Stafford paid little attention to the couple, other than noticing the man's bright red socks, with what looked like Christmas trees on them.

"Did Mr. Hughes's daughter go back to his house this evening?" he asked, an idea forming in his mind.

"She's being taken there now, with her partner. That was them, just going out. Why?"

"Oh, no particular reason. Anyway, Mr. Hughes needs psychiatric attention, right away. Another seventy-two hours' emergency under section 4 to start with – you know the drill. As she was the victim, I don't think his daughter's agreement is appropriate. Let's get a social worker instead."

After the time it took phoning around to track down a suitably qualified social worker and completing all the paperwork, Derek Stafford was at the police station for quite a while. By the time he left, it was far too late to call on Gerald's daughter, but Stafford decided he would do so the next morning, even though it would be Christmas Day. This was just too strange to leave hanging. Besides, he thought, Gerald's family would want to resolve the matter as quickly as possible under the circumstances, despite the season.

"I think we've done it!" crowed Natasha, as she unlocked Egremont's front door and entered the hallway. "I think we've really done it!" She punched the air by way of celebration, still holding the key Gerald had given her last time he was detained, for destroying Miss Midnight's CD player.

"Yep," grinned Newt. "He did just what you said he'd do. What a knucklehead!"

"Let's have a drink," said Natasha. "I could certainly do with one. The old beggar must have some booze somewhere." They soon located Gerald's whisky, and sat down to enjoy it.

"I nearly died larfin'," said Newt. "All that stuff about 'Mum would have loved it!' You wound him up good 'an proper."

Then, as an afterthought, he added, "It doesn't hurt much, does it? Your neck, I mean?"

"No, not really. I'll mend. Though you took your time pulling him off."

"It was too bloomin' quick. But no harm done. How long do you reckon they'll shut him away?"

"Could be months. Or years. We're going to have a ball. By tomorrow the stupid old fool will be just like he was with the others, all remorseful. 'I can't think what came over me,' he'll say. 'I am so sorry. Can I write you a cheque?' he'll say. And I'll be ever so nice and say, 'well, alright, if you want to. But would you like me to stay at Egremont whilst you're here, and look after it?' And he'll agree, give me the cheque and be delighted I'm not offended at what he did. Clever, aren't I?"

Newt raised his glass to his partner.

"You did well, girl, you did well. But I'm hungry, what with no mince pies 'an all. What do you reckon he's got in? Let's have a look-see."

Newt and Natasha found Gerald had thought ahead beyond the Christmas break and provisioned Egremont well. There was enough food for at least a week for the two of them in the freezer, or even longer if tinned food was included. Recounting and congratulating themselves on every detail of the plan they had just executed, they set about reducing Gerald's stocks with energy and cheerful enthusiasm. Then, over more whisky, they watched television for a while before cavorting upstairs around midnight in very high spirits.

Christmas morning always has an unearthly feel, and Dr. Stafford felt its impact the moment he stepped out of his car in front of Egremont. No-one was about, even though it was eleven-thirty in the morning. Everything was still; there was almost no sound at all. The normal noise of everyday was absent. No traffic rumbling in the distance. No sounds of anyone doing anything. Yet he felt a sense of imminence. It was as if the world were temporarily holding its breath, awaiting some unknown trigger upon which it would exhale in a cyclone of human noise and activity.

Stafford closed his car door. The sound seemed an affront to the serenity of the morning. He walked up to Egremont's front door and pressed the bellpush.

There was no answer. Stafford was about to push the button again when he noticed the door was slightly ajar. He hesitated, then pushed it further open.

"Halloo?" called the doctor. "Anybody home?" There was no answer. The doctor called again, louder this time, from just inside the hallway.

There was silence, and a few seconds passed. Then, suddenly, Dr. Stafford was overwhelmed with the beautiful fragrance of jasmine, and a thirty-year-old memory told him his question was being answered. He shivered momentarily, but turned and closed the door anyway.

He could not see anyone there, though the uncleared remains of an evening meal in the kitchen showed two people had been in residence very recently.

Dr. Stafford explored further. If Natasha and Newt had arrived only the evening before, they certainly lost no time making a mess.

Halfway up the stairs lay a pair of panties, followed further up by a bra and a man's red sock, with a Christmas tree design. In what was obviously the spare bedroom he saw a double bed, its linen mainly strewn across the floor. A man's watch lay against the skirting board, its face smashed. A bedside table had been overturned, and a whisky bottle, lacking a stopper, lay on the carpet, having disgorged some of its contents. There were also a suitcase and a holdall, both open but only partly unloaded.

Still surrounded by the scent of jasmine, tinged with whisky, Stafford looked around the rest of the house and then sat down in the lounge to reflect.

He sat for about fifteen minutes. Then he said "Hello, my little hybrid."

Half an hour later, Dr. Stafford went back to the police station, and asked to see the statements made by witnesses to the fracas at the Goodman's Court Hotel. He said he was troubled about certain aspects of the case, and viewing the statements was of direct and immediate relevance to the fate of Gerald Hughes, now in a secure hospital.

The duty sergeant, who was not particularly busy, rooted around and found what the doctor requested.

Of particular interest was the statement made by the burly man's wife. She had overheard most of what transpired between Gerald and his guests, and reported Newt's incitement to Natasha: "Go for it, girl!"

Reading these words, Stafford smiled. To someone unconnected to the events, they would have little meaning. The words could have been shouted by a punter to a racehorse. But only if the punter had money riding on it. And Stafford had left Egremont firmly convinced that Natasha and Newt did have money riding on it. Now he could see the evidence.

Stafford spoke to the sergeant again, and told him what he thought Newt's words implied. Then, stretching the truth a little, he said it tallied with his observations of Gerald.

Stafford did not tell the police about Egremont, but they only needed the doctor's nudge to decide further enquiries were necessary.

Back in London, Newt soon cracked when the police called on him. Yes, Natasha knew her father could be provoked into violence, and that he had stopped taking his antidepressants. Yes, she devised a way to use this weakness to get him put away and allow her to live in Egremont at her father's expense. And yes, he, Newt, was sorry about having anything to do with the scheme, or with Egremont. A terrible place, he said.

The interrogating policewoman asked why Egremont was terrible, but all Newt would say was that he did not like it. Natasha was no more forthcoming, except for saying it smelt very bad and that she never wanted to set foot in the dreadful place again. When pushed, she said she regretted treating her father badly, and agreed not to take proceedings against him.

There was little else the policewoman could do. The only sanction she could think of was to caution Natasha and Newt for wasting police time. She was pretty certain, though, that something had frightened the couple very badly in Egremont. So much so, they seemed unwilling even to talk about their experience. Perhaps that was justice.

When Gerald's three days in hospital expired, Dr. Stafford decided to drive him back to Egremont personally. On the way, he told Gerald about knowing Rose and how he had always called her 'my little hybrid.' Gerald listened.

"Ah," was all he said, before lapsing into silence until the car pulled up outside his home.

The doctor went with Gerald to the door.

A fragrance of jasmine welcomed them as Gerald opened it.

"Can you smell that?" he asked.

"Yes," replied the doctor. "Jasmine. Or is it rose?" Then he added,

"You really are home now, aren't you?"

"Yes," said Gerald, who paused. Then he asked,

"Would you like to come in? We would like to offer you some tea."

REMEMBER ME

Remember me, you crawling coward? No? No, don't turn away. Come on, look at me. Perhaps you don't recognise me. I'm not like I was. You saw to that. You had the power then. Now I have it. I'm in the driving seat, and there's nothing you can do, no way to lie or cheat or bully your way out this time.

Pardon? Who am I? I will let you know in my own good time. It would be wrong if you couldn't make the connection between me and what is going to happen to you. Otherwise the concepts of crime and punishment, cause and effect, would not have been properly served. Maybe you suspect who I am, which is why you are cowering in the corner, trying to claw your way out backwards through the wall. Or perhaps it's my appearance. Either way, you know I haven't come here just for idle amusement. I'm in deadly earnest. You can sense it, can't you?

Go on, scream again. And again, if you like. I've got plenty of time. You haven't, of course, but please be my guest. It's my pleasure. Believe me, it really is my pleasure to hear you scream. There's no audience other than me now. None of the gullible innocents or lazy deadbeats who were your cheerleaders. There is no-one to hear you and won't be until it is too late for you. By the time anyone arrives, you won't be making any sounds audible to them. So scream on, scream for all you are worth. It is music to my ears, nourishment for my clay.

That reminds me. I interrupted your cooking. I do apologise. But I couldn't resist: you provided the perfect opportunity, stepping out of the kitchen, for me to, ah … entertain you in here. Ham, eggs and chips. Lovely. But not relevant to me any more, nor, with one delightful exception, to you. Besides, you are unlikely to have much taste for earthly things now you have met a result of your former handiwork.

You know one of the odd things about our situation? Even through your screaming and fear and retching, you can still hear me. You cannot blot me out, not like you did before. I used to scream too. I yelled from my very soul about the wrongs you committed against me, and screamed against the injustice of your fearful lies. "No more!" I screamed. "Stop!" I screamed until my soul was exhausted, crushed by your unprovoked evil until my former, gentle, easy, happy self became a mangled, embittered wreck. No-one bothered to listen to me then. You made certain of that. Now it is your turn.

You know why you're trapped here, don't you? No? No, you really don't! I suppose I could expect nothing else from someone who relentlessly enjoys destroying people. Like a killer cornering his victim, thrusting a knife into their guts again and again, you have taken a positive delight, almost a sexual pleasure, in causing pain. The sort of delight I am now beginning to experience for myself. A spreading glow of perverted satisfaction, in anticipation of a final explosion of pleasure at the end.

I can sense you still cannot understand why you are in this position, why you are trapped. So let me help. Have I trapped you? No answer?

Well, let me have a little fun. The answer is both yes and no! You are trapped partly by your own fear because you cannot bring yourself to squeeze past me, having in the process to get even closer to me or perhaps to touch me. I'm not the most beautiful object you've ever seen, now, am I? And let me tell you a little secret. You could not move anyway. Go on, try!

Ha! I told you, I have the power now. And as you used yours, so will I use mine. You cannot move because your immobility is my will. Your limbs are like water. But for the time being all your other bodily functions remain operational, particularly those necessary for you to fully savour the prospects immediately before you.

So, yes, I have trapped you. Though I was able to do so only because you first trapped yourself. All that time ago. Let me get a little closer …

How did you engineer your own downfall? You really don't know? It's obvious; at least it is to me. You broke the Golden Rule which keeps human society tolerable. Most religions have it in one form or another, and it is reflected in most secular codes of conduct. I think the Jews and Christians express it best: 'Love your neighbour as yourself.' Or 'Do-as-you-would-be done-by,' as Charles Kingsley put it in 'The Water Babies.' You didn't observe these strictures, did you? Your first, second and last thoughts were always for yourself. As they are now. And you are approaching the time when your thoughts really will be your last, at least in your current form.

You constantly ignored the Golden Rule because it collides with a maxim far more convenient to earthly human advancement: 'Do what thou wilt shall be the whole of the law' is ... was ... your style.

Kingsley's tale also included 'Be-done-by-as-you-did,' which, in a rather amplified and modified form, is now to be your fate. We have a little time left, and I want you to feel complete terror for as long as possible. By the way, there's no point wondering why I am not following the Golden Rule myself. Since you destroyed me and my soul withered under your torment, I have become dead to love; there is none in my current existence. No, I am not here for love. I am here to take ownership of your soul as something on which I can feed for eternity. And I am here for revenge. Served cold, from my viewpoint. It will look a little different from yours.

I am glad to note the smell in the room. In addition to vomiting over yourself, your terror has very satisfyingly caused you to lose control of other bodily functions. You disgusting, revolting creature. Your outer nature, befouled with repellent mess, is beginning to resemble your filthy inner soul. You still find it impossible not to attend to my words, though. That's good.

Now, before we reach the natural conclusion of my visit, I would like to explain what your lack of love has set in train, first for me and then for you. I owe you as much. Wait. Do I mean what I say? Do I owe you? Perhaps not. Perhaps I just want to extend your agony of fear just as you enjoyed extending my torment. It is a risk: you might possibly derive further pleasure from the story, but, given your repulsive state and growing realisation of your fate, I think that highly unlikely.

Redundancy, it was eventually called, your destruction of my life's work and character. You had the power to destroy everything about me, or not to. I'm not going to repeat the details we both know … I don't believe it! You still don't know who I am, do you? I understand you might have difficulty telling who I am from what you see, but how many others did you destroy, that you cannot identify me from what I have said? Let me help. I'm Edward Rains. Or, at least, I was. Remember me? Oh, yes, I see I've connected now!

For the good of the organisation, you said. A lie, of course. It was all fuelled by self-promotion on your part, copiously spiced with lashings of malice. But your ego bungled it! Only because you were so hard-hearted did your organisation have to pay me so-called compensation. 'Your' organisation? What am I saying? You, a newcomer, knew nothing of it. It was not yours, it was mine! I knew it, loved it, had shaped and developed it.

If only the old Chairman had not stood down. He was not duped by your endless flaunting of rich relatives. Nor was he deceived by your slippery charms or Janus-faced comments delivered during those oh-so-generous intimate little dinners you held for dullards on the Board. He told me these things before he, and I, died.

With your advance, there was going to be no

recognition for me, with more than a decade of unstinting loyal service. "Here's a cheque for the bare minimum. Now get lost." That was your approach. You were so sure of yourself, so keen to get rid of me you broke almost every rule there was, written or unwritten. You cared not for my humanity: you viewed me as beneath worth.

As a starter, you falsely accused me of theft to try to get me to quit without you having to pay me a penny. Just to refresh your memory, it was theft of a laptop I took home to work on as part of the dedicated service I provided to the firm, which your predecessor had specifically encouraged me to do. But I didn't rise to the bait, did I? I didn't quit in disgust and anger. Instead, I let everybody know what you had tried to do. At first they laughed at you, and then they warned you, didn't they? And you hated me for it.

Then you tried to get me to break the law – twice. Remember? Verbally instructing me to hire an illegal immigrant, and then urging me to falsify records to help the company evade tax. But I wouldn't, would I? So the immigrant remained unemployed, the company had to pay its due tax, and you could not accuse me of misconduct. You hated me for that too, didn't you? I wouldn't give you any lawful reason to get rid of me, so you tried it unlawfully and I took 'your organisation' to the cleaners in court, didn't I? I loathed doing it, but you left me no choice.

"You'll look back in six months and say it was the best thing that ever happened to you," remarked one of my colleagues, hoping such comfortable sentiments would enable him to accept your actions. Yet for me it proved one of the least accurate comments ever made. I never found another job. In these times of upside-down thinking and youth-worship, the odds were never with an educated but redundant middle-aged man like me. And your highly effective network ensured they were lengthened even more. You put the word about, quietly. You know how it's done. "Yes, a good worker, a nice man, but …" Even a judicious silence, or an inflection of the voice, can do the trick, as you are well aware. You were a good networker, but those people would not recognise you now, as the hideous, fouled thing you really are. Still good at your own PR?

As for my story, you can guess much of the rest. The money ran out, despite my frugality. Every day I awoke early, in a black pit of depression which grew ever deeper, devoid of any hope. With increasing despair came closer acquaintance with the bottle, which compounded the problem. I lost my house, and my self-respect. One morning, I took my wife and our teenage son for a drive, still intoxicated from the night before. I hit the abutment of a bridge, and the car turned over and caught fire.

It's pretty, isn't it, what fire does to you? Do you like it? In a curiously detached way - an out-of-the-body experience, I believe they call it - I watched what happened to me. The way my skin peeled off and charred. The way my fat dripped out in the heat and caught fire itself, as though I was meat on a barbecue, with the flesh blackening and sizzling and separating from the bone, just before the fire people put the blaze out. The way the same things happened to my beautiful wife and son. But I needn't go on. You have seen the result. And you have smelled the burnt flesh and the decay which follows before what is left of you is finally … disposed of, shall we say? Shall I come closer …? Don't gulp.

And now for you, with your futile tears and pleading. They do not move me. Forgive the mixed metaphors, but you are unfinished business – a loose end I have come to tie up and a toy for my present and future amusement. You are going to experience a similar fate to mine. In addition to the fragrance of you befouling yourself, I can smell smoke, and I know you smell it too. Oh, dear! I fear I must have detained you too long, and your chip pan must have ignited. And still you cannot move to do anything about it. But I will keep the smoke from this room. You are going to die, tormenter mine, the same way I died, in searing agony, in flames, not by anti-climactic suffocation. And, through the flames, immune to them now, I am going to watch you blister, burn and writhe, and applaud your corpse twisting and contorting in the heat. I feel I am scaling the pinnacle of ecstasy I mentioned earlier, and cannot contain myself much longer.

Your torment will not stop at death. Oh, no. Death is merely a transition, a moving from there to here. You are going to become like me. And you are also going to learn there is seniority in my sphere. As I am frequently visited by others outranking me who wish to, ah … take their pleasure of me, so, in a form of love perverted by the realms whence I now come, will I periodically visit you to indulge my tastes.

Remember me? Oh, yes. You'll remember me alright, and I'll remember you. To the end of time, we'll never forget.

But look! The flames are all around … burning, burning, burning. I release your limbs for my greater enjoyment. You run, but there is no escape. You are too late! Scream, lady, scream and burn and die! Yes, yes! Ah … what bliss! What delight!

RIVERSIDE AFTERNOON

They parked their borrowed Ford in front of the old footpath sign and got out. 'Waterbury 2 miles' it read, pointing downriver along the path to their left. In the other direction, the sign indicated 'Bridgethorpe 4 miles.' Suspended from the sign by a loop of thin white cord was a battered wooden board, also white and made in the shape of a broad arrowhead. It pointed slightly upwards across a narrow bridge to the other bank. The two friends could just make out the word 'Verona' on the arrow in very faded cracked brown paint and they thought it might be fun to go and have a look.

Chirpily, they started over the bridge, which was little more than two feet wide, with wooden rails on each side. The rails were carved with repeated small images of what looked like a crocodile with an elephant's trunk, but the girls were more intent on deciding their route than on admiring bridge decorations, however unusual they were.

The path on the other side of the bridge looked

almost swampy, which, due to the heavy rain of the last twenty-four hours, was unsurprising. Danielle and Tallulah (predictably known to everyone as Dani and Tally) peered up and down the river, hoping to see Verona. But the river, about twenty yards wide, meandered sinuously through a marshy valley and had dense, tall, willowy bushes all along it with several spindly trees in the foreground. Nothing could be seen of anything that could be described as 'Verona.' Whether it was a place or a building, there was no clue. The footpath sign, with its suspended board, the bridge, their car and the spire of a distant church, barely visible through the trees and over the bushes downriver, were the only man-made objects that could be seen in any direction.

"Someplace in Italy, isn't it?" asked Dani.

"Yeah, I think so. Dunno. Not much use if it is. Why doesn't the sign say 'Verona 700 miles' or something?" said Tally. "I think it's got a football team, though."

Slightly disappointed, Tally and Dani quickly lost interest in Verona. Dani leaned on the rail gazing downstream, whilst Tally retraced her steps to the riverbank.

Flatmates, the two students had decided that, with the rain gone, they would drive out of town this warm Sunday to find some fresher air and gentle exercise. They had been at the university since the previous autumn, but had only just heard about the river, and wanted to explore. Rivers offered the possibility of swimming, and picnics, and interesting dates with boyfriends. Boats, maybe.

But transport was a problem. So Tally had told the

Ford's owner she desperately needed a car to visit her father in hospital. Would it be possible? A huge favour, especially as the car was so new, but … And, of course her urgency, youth and beguiling femininity easily won the day.

As Dani leaned on the rail, Tally looked at her with a tinge of envy. Dani was slim, with fairish tousled hair and a very good figure, which she knew how to flatter. Today, she had put on low-slung tight jeans with broad vertical red and black stripes, which gave her a mild clownish appearance, and which displayed a trace of 'builder's cleavage' when she sat down. Above a generous breadth of tanned bare midriff, she wore an almost fluorescent bright blue figure-hugging T-shirt, the sort that would have revealed the lines of any garment worn beneath it, had there been one. If she had possessed any superfluous bulges, they would all have shown. The composition was completed by short gold ankle socks and flimsy gold-coloured shoes with heels rather too high for muddy river banks.

Tally did have superfluous bulges. But she rather ill-advisedly followed Dani's sartorial style – jeans, with the legs cut raggedly short, showing some calf, the same fashionable naked expanse of mid-section flesh, white and convex in her case, and a short-sleeved top. Her choice of colours was scarcely more restrained, but her clothes were looser and her shoes definitely sensible.

The path along the left-hand river bank seemed much drier than the other. Tally said, "Waterbury would be a round trip of four miles, which we might do. You know, have a coffee there and come back. But eight is too far."

Dani agreed, so Waterbury it was. Dani abandoned

the bridge, and they started to follow the river downstream.

In good humour, they went at a fast clip, chatting about uni, forthcoming exams and the excesses of the previous evening's party. The path wound onwards, following the wandering river past the trees and into the bushes which lined the path and stretched back into the marsh.

After a while, the drift of their conversation triggered a thought in Dani's mind.

"Oh," she said. "I've just remembered about Wayne. Mind if I make a call?"

Without waiting for an answer, Dani retrieved a mobile phone from her shoulder bag, and called an entry in its address book, labelled 'Wayne.' Wayne had first appeared on Dani's radar two weeks earlier.

"Hi, it's Dani – cool party last night, wasn't it?" The answer can have been little longer than a grunt, as Dani quickly followed up on her opening question.

"Yeah, well, I said I'd call so we could fix a date for … yeah, that's right! Wicked!"

She giggled lasciviously. There was a pause.

"No, I can't do Friday. My Mum's coming up to see me." This was untrue. Friday was the day she had arranged to see Zac, Wayne's senior in her acquaintance by one week and two days. But Dani was an accomplished two-timer. In fact, two represented a minimum for her, and Wayne was a beginner who for his own protection needed to learn several chapters of tricks about the mating game.

Dani's conversation about what, where and when continued for long enough to persuade Tally that she too might make a call, so as not to be left out of the fun. She called the owner of the car. Could she borrow it for a few more days, as her father was worse than she had thought and she would have to stay with him?

The day was still, and there was no-one else about. It seemed even warmer than it had been. The river flowed silently and quite swiftly, though not as fast as Tally and Dani walked. Its oil-smooth water showed occasional eddies and transient shallow furrows, the sort that indicate powerful currents and some depth. The sun glinted silently on the troubled surface.

Chatting nineteen to the dozen, mostly about boys now and completely disinterested in the flowing water, the two girls continued their excursion to Waterbury. After about fifteen minutes, they rounded a bend in the river and saw what looked like a large bungalow. The building, set back some distance from the opposite bank, dominated the land in a stretch of the river devoid of the otherwise omnipresent bushes. It was a rather unusual sight, with several striking features, and the girls broke off their conversation to look.

The house seemed to be floating in mid-air. Peering across the river, they realised the effect was a result of the house having been built on slender stilts and that its floor was about four feet above the ground. There was a verandah all around it with a stairway down to ground level. Near the bottom of this, they noticed, were about a dozen people, most of whom were moving around slowly, apparently without any purpose. One man, however, was standing still and he looked directly at Tally and Dani. Tally studied him for a few moments, and found his unwavering gaze unnerving, although he was too far away for her to be able to tell much about him.

But what had stopped the girls in their tracks was the building's other peculiarity. It was bizarrely and extraordinarily ornate. Every wall space, from top to bottom, was heavily carved and painted in a mixture of bright colours and unusual patterns, and peppered with what looked like many doors. Being across the river, which was much wider at this point, the fine details of the house and its retinue were indistinct, but even so it was clearly a very different structure to any Tally or Dani had previously encountered.

Near the water's edge, supported on a post driven into the ground, was a white signboard with writing on it.

"Can you read that board?" asked Dani. "I can't make it out."

"A bit, I think" replied her companion, and paused while she screwed up her eyes against the sun.

"V," she finally stated. "The first letter is V, but I can't read …Oh, what a muppet! It must be 'Verona,' like on the signpost. That was on a white board as well."

"I know," said Dani. "Let's ask them. We can shout across the river." And without waiting for Tally's answer, she cupped her hands around her mouth and shouted "Hellooooo!" in the direction of the strange house.

There was no reply. In the sultry quiet of the afternoon there was no competing sound, yet Dani's overture had produced no result whatsoever. She looked at Tally.

"Let's both try," she said, and they both proceeded to bellow "Hellooooo!" in unison at the opposite bank.

There was still no result. No answer came, and

none of the people near the house showed any sign of having heard them. And the staring man just continued to stare, unmoving.

"Rude beggars," said Tally, angrily. "Let's not waste our breath on them again."

And, after studying the weird building for a few moments more, Tally and Dani resumed their trek downriver.

In the sticky heat, they walked on in silence for a while, thinking about the house. Then Tally said, "funny we've never heard about that place, it being so odd. Wayne and his mate – what was his name? Oh, yeah, Kev. Wayne and Kev told us about the river, but they never mentioned the house. You'd have thought they would have said something, wouldn't you?"

"Yeah, maybe," replied Dani, "but they'd had a skinful by then, and were doing well to remember the river, let alone anything else!"

But Tally continued to wonder about the house, and fell silent. The day continued very warm and still, but the sky had darkened a little, not with discernible clouds in an otherwise friendly blue, but with a grey haze, which had grown slowly thicker. No birds sang. No insects buzzed. The windless air was heavy, and the river sped greasily but silently onwards. In the silence, Dani studied the river, and wondered whether it was not just a little faster, and just a little higher than it had been before.

The bushes bordering the riverbank had now grown much thicker, and pressed in upon the bank, forcing the young women to walk in single file, with Dani ahead. In places, they brushed the bushes to get past.

They had walked on for a further five minutes or so when Dani stopped so suddenly her friend nearly cannoned into her.

"Did you hear that?" whispered Dani.

"What, you prat?" hissed her friend, whose mind had been on the disconcerting house. "You nearly got us both in the flippin' river!"

"Listen!" commanded Dani, again in a whisper. They both listened, and looked around, stock-still. The day was definitely darker now, and the sky had become a uniform dark grey. All they could see was the river and the bushes on both sides of it. The river looked very full, but neither of them gave it much heed. The silence was overpowering.

And then, they heard rustling in the thick bushes ahead. It was faint at first, but got slowly louder, as though whatever was making it was coming towards them.

Forgetting her whisper, Dani said "There!" The rustling stopped. For what seemed an age they both waited, alert, listening, hardly daring to breathe. Then the rustling started again, and got a little closer.

Tally had been thinking about the house and the staring man. She had been thinking about the isolation of the riverbank, and about the clothes she and Dani were wearing. Suddenly, it all came together.

"Who's there?" she rapped out sharply to the bushes. The rustling stopped again.

"There's someone there!" she gasped. "It must be one of them – the man who stared! Maybe it's him, or there could be others about!"

"Eh?" Dani looked at her, alarmed at her friend's fear, but slower to grasp the nature of their situation herself.

"The house, stupid, the house! That odd man who stared at us!" Tally had simultaneously reached both a conclusion and a decision.

"We've gotta get back," she rapped. "He's after us. In your getup he can see everything you've got and I'm not much better."

Dani suddenly connected and, an instant ahead of Tally, turned to run. As she did so, she shrieked with pain and fell across the path, narrowly missing a collision with her friend. Whereupon a fox jumped onto the riverbank out of the bushes of which they had been terrified, eyed the colourful and chaotic pair for a split second, and then bolted towards Waterbury as though the hounds of hell were at his heels.

Tally, who had seen the fox just after her friend fell, did not know whether to be relieved they were not threatened by rape or other violence, or embarrassed to have been frightened by an animal more scared than they had been. But there was no time for thinking as her immediate concern was for Dani, who was lying on one elbow on the muddy path not far above the now clearly rising river, gazing at her right ankle.

"It was a flippin' fox," said Tally, as she started to refocus on their changed circumstances. "No-one there at all. What a pair of … hullo, what's that?"

She too gazed at Dani's ankle. Dani's tight jeans finished a few inches above her short ankle socks, and in the gap, running right around Dani's tanned lower right calf, was a red ring, bleeding slightly all the way round.

"I thought one of your heels had gone," said Tally. "I told you they weren't any good for walks like this."

"Well my heels didn't cause that cut, did they?" grunted Dani, who winced with pain.

"What does it feel like?" asked Tally.

"What do you think, you moron?" Dani silently cursed herself. "No, I'm sorry, I didn't mean that. I'm shaken, that's all. It hurts. My ankle aches like I don't know what, and there's a stinging from the cut."

Tally studied the cut in more detail.

"Hmm. It's odd. It's like a wire has bitten into your leg all the way round. Not very deep, but enough to make it bleed. Did you see anything like that?"

"Maybe. I don't remember."

"I wonder what could have done it?" mused Tally, as she looked around for a culprit. There was nothing. The path, relatively smooth at that point, offered no clue. Neither did the short slope down from the path into the river, nor the other slope down into the bushes. There was no obvious reason why Dani should have fallen.

"Could have been fishing line, left lying around. Maybe you got caught in some. It's very strong and might do that. But there's no sign of any now, so maybe you kicked it into the river as you went down." Dani said nothing. Tally thought about her hypothesis, but did not find it very convincing. How could fishing line, tight enough around a human leg to cut it, be so easily thrown off? Besides, it needed to have been fixed to something firm to draw it tight. And in some kind of a loop to start with.

"Never mind that," said Dani. "Whatever are we going to do about getting home?"

"Let's have a look at your ankle," said Tally. "Can you get your shoe and sock off?"

With some grimacing on Dani's part, the two of

them gingerly managed to achieve this and surveyed the injured foot in more detail.

It was not pretty to look at. Beneath the mysterious ring, Dani's ankle was swelling and turning some very strange colours, and a rapid experiment convinced the two young women that Dani was not going to be able to walk anywhere.

"I don't think I could carry you very far," said Tally.

"I'm not going to let you try," retorted Dani. "But you might try acting as a crutch. You know, I could lean on you so I could hold my foot off the ground. Like a sort of three-legged race."

She thought a bit more. "And before you say it, I'm not going to be able to hop all the way back, either! Or swim, for that matter."

The human crutch idea did not work, mainly because the required hopping action proved too much for Dani's uninjured leg after only a few steps. Even had it not done so the bushes, which had forced them to walk single file over a significant proportion of their outward journey, would have prevented it.

Tally said, "we'll have to get help. We've got mobiles, haven't we?"

"How would help get here?" asked Dani. "There's no road. And if you asked for an air ambulance, where would it land? There's only the river, these blasted bushes and a lot of marsh on the other side of them as far as I know."

"They have choppers with winches on them, don't they? They might have boats, too."

Tally made the call. The operator, a man, asked what had happened and where they were, and Tally explained as accurately as she could. The man seemed very efficient, and within a few minutes Tally had been convinced that their rescue would be performed by a helicopter equipped with a winch, just as she had surmised, and that the chopper would take only twenty minutes to arrive.

Tally and Dani settled down to wait, with Tally propping Dani up as best she could.

"I'm supposed to be meeting Gary tonight," Dani said. "It doesn't look like I'm going to make that, does it? What time is it, anyway?"

Tally looked at her phone.

"Five thirty-nine," she said. "And, no, it looks like you and Gary will have to wait for another night for your fun."

"I'll call him and give him some excuse. I know! You told me how you got the car. I'll tell him I'm staying with you because your father is very ill and you need the support. I don't want him to know I've been such a fool."

Dani fished her mobile out of her now rather dirty shoulder bag, and keyed a call to Gary. Tally privately wondered at Dani's logic. How could Dani possibly avoid later public revelation that she had been lifted off a riverbank by a helicopter? And wasn't it better to be thought a fool than not to let people know about an emergency? But Dani's first instinct was always to dissemble and to sort out any mess later, usually with further inaccuracies.

"Damn," said Dani. She turned the phone off and on, and tried again.

After a few seconds, Dani repeated what was displayed on her mobile screen.

"No network service," she said, and paused. "Odd that we could get through to the rescue people."

"I've heard about that," said Tally. "You can sometimes do it when you've got low signal strength. Y'know, you can call them but not anyone else. Besides, we used my phone. You're on a different network, aren't you? What's your signal strength?"

Dani looked.

"That's weird," she said. "It's full strength. I ought to be able to get through, like I did to Wayne earlier." Then she asked, "what about yours?"

Tally checked her own mobile.

"Full strength," she reported.

"Well why don't you call Gary and give me the phone? I'll give you the number."

This Tally did. But the result was the same. 'No service,' was displayed on the phone.

"Looks like Gary will just have to wonder where you are," said Tally. "Maybe it's just his number that's the problem."

So they both tried other numbers, but the results were always the same. No service. Then Dani mis-hit a key in her address book, and called Tally's phone by mistake.

Tally's phone rang.

They were silent for a while after this. It did not make sense. They could talk to each other on their mobiles, which did not help, or to the emergency services. But not to anyone else, even though they had both managed it not very much earlier.

"Atmospherics?" pondered Tally out loud.

"Eh?"

"Well, the weather's funny, isn't it? Look at it. Maybe it's that."

"Um," said Dani, and the pair fell silent for a while.

As long as Dani was not trying to move, her foot merely throbbed, but now that help was at hand it did not dominate her thoughts. She turned to other problems.

"I've ruined these jeans. Look at them! They're soaked in mud and stuff. And my shoes! I had to tell Chris I'd been robbed of a week's cash to get him to buy them for me."

"Mine aren't much better," replied Tally absently, looking at the river. She paused, and then said, "I don't like the look of that very much."

"What?" asked Dani.

"The river," retorted Tally.

They both looked at it.

"It's higher than it was," said Dani nervously. "I thought so earlier."

"It must have been all that rain yesterday," mused Tally. "Perhaps it rained a lot higher upstream as well, and now it's coming down here."

There was no doubt the river was rising. Its turbid waters slid rapidly past them, puckered by swirls and currents that spoke of menacing depths and hidden power. It was now emitting occasional gurgles as it sucked at its banks, but otherwise the dark and oppressive late afternoon was completely silent. Apart from the strange house and the equally strange people near it, they had seen no-one on their walk. Yet Tally almost sensed they were not alone, that the river was a living thing, watching, waiting, moving ever forward to claim them.

She shivered, despite the heat, and turned towards the bushes that edged the path along the bank, so close that if they moved they would almost push the girls into the water. Her unease about the river began extending to them. Were they concealing anything in their blank, unmoving silence? They seemed to Tally to overshadow her as she sprawled on the bank, rather as she envisaged the imagined earlier rapist might have overshadowed and leaned over her before, before …

Tally shook her head and consciously brought herself back under control, looking along the path instead of at the bushes or the river. Yes, they were in a fix, but help was coming very soon and getting nervy was not going to help. She was almost calm again when a vivid recollection suddenly stabbed her mind. Something she'd seen in the bushes, but had not immediately registered. What was it? What could have … ?

Although constrained by having to support Dani, Tally snapped her head round towards the bushes again. Yes, she was right! The bushes closest to her were rooted in the earth of the slope down from the riverbank path, but beyond that they all stood in the water of the marsh, lower than the now raised water level in the river. Subconsciously, Tally's brain computed what this meant. The riverbank they were lying on was, in effect, a dam, with the water rising on one side. If the water rose too high, it would flood over the top and maybe breach the bank, releasing huge quantities of water into the marsh. And they would go with it, washed into the bushes or the marsh with goodness-knew-what consequences.

"Where's the flippin' chopper?" Dani's harsh question interrupted Tally's watery speculation. "I've just checked – it's been forty minutes since we called. They said twenty, so where is it? I'm getting scared."

Tally listened. There was no sound at all except

sporadic chuckles from the river as it washed and lapped against its banks. A helicopter looking for them would have been audible from miles away in that silence. She checked the time on her mobile. Six-twenty. Dani was right. Where was their salvation?

Tally called the emergency services again. This time, she got a woman operator, who listened to Tally's rushed explanation of the previous call, of where she and Dani were and of what had happened to them. Then the operator lazily asked, "when did you say you called?"

Something about the bored officiousness of this question told Tally she was talking to a jobsworth in a comfortable office, who had not listened to her and was either unaware of, or indifferent to, the danger she was in. Tally felt she was being treated as an annoyance only just qualifying as worthy of attention. She also felt something had gone wrong.

Tally disciplined herself. Icily and precisely, through gritted teeth, she said, "I told you. About forty minutes ago."

There was a pause at the other end. Then the operator said, "the computer has no record of your call."

It was probably the worst statement the operator could have made. Tally's tightly-controlled self-discipline collapsed. She launched a barrage of furious abuse about computers, the emergency services, and the operator, causing collateral damage to a number of other innocent targets as well.

The operator may have toyed with the idea of cutting Tally off, or threatening her with punitive action for wasting the emergency services' time, but Tally's tirade served instead to push her trained side out of its evening slumber. The operator at last began to respond in the correct manner to a caller who was obviously scared and in a dangerous position. She waited until Tally ran out of steam and then apologised for what had clearly been an error. She told Tally to wait for a short time whilst she arranged matters.

After a few minutes, which seemed like a century to the now thoroughly terrified Tally, the operator resumed the call. She told Tally a helicopter would indeed come for them, but that as it would take nearly an hour to get there, the police would also come in a boat from Bridgethorpe, which they thought might be quicker. The operator also said she had no idea where the earlier quotation of twenty minutes had come from, then commented it was odd Tally should have spoken to a man before, as there were no men on shift.

The outlined plan seemed the best solution available. Tally, who had formed a low opinion of the woman's competence, ignored her final comment and merely said "Right. Thanks." And the call ended.

Though still scared, Tally had been calmed just enough by the new hope of rescue to explain to Dani the details of what was planned.

Very quietly, Dani said, "I don't think we've got an hour," and pointed towards the river. In the time it had taken Tally to make the phone call, it looked as though it had risen another inch. The river now seemed very close to the top of the bank. In the suffocating stillness, Tally stared at it. Then she said, "higher ground. There must be some higher ground. Didn't the bank have higher bits than here, further back?"

"I, I, I can't remember! I've gotta do something! I've gotta get out of here!" Dani was losing it, and struggled against the still supportive Tally to stand up. She got part of the way up and then screamed in agony and collapsed back against her friend. Then she fell apart completely and started crying like a child, calling for her mother and trying to cuddle Tally like a soft toy.

Tally, though very frightened herself, retained her composure. The only chance was for her to find a higher part of the bank and then somehow get Dani there and hope that it was high enough to give their rescuers enough time to find them. But that meant leaving Dani where she was.

Tally knew she had to go, and fast. Without her, Dani would be scared beyond expression and might roll into river, but if she stayed they would both be in certain serious trouble.

"I'm going to find a higher bit and then get you there even if I have to drag you," she said, as she struggled to disentangle herself from Dani. But Dani clung to Tally like a barnacle, and Tally had to use all her strength to force herself away, leaving Dani whimpering in pain and fear on the muddy path.

Tally stood up. Which way should she go? Back towards Bridgethorpe or on towards Waterbury? She needed higher ground, or a tree. Yes, a tree would do. She was sure she could drag Dani, even screaming in pain, towards and maybe even part of the way up one. She looked towards Waterbury. Nothing but bushes. But she felt sure she had seen a tree amongst all the bushes they had passed, and equally sure there had been higher parts of the bank.

Tally ran for all she was worth back towards

Bridgethorpe. And ran, and ran, through the thick, sultry air, slipping and sliding along the riverbank. The bank was absolutely level, and she passed no trees, just the blank, threatening bushes. Not built for speed, and not fit, Tally stopped for breath, her head down and her arms acting as struts, supporting her upper body on her knees.

After about half a minute of fierce breathing, Tally looked up. She was opposite the coloured, carved house with many doors. Verona. It still had its accompanying crowd. Tally was just about to try shouting across the river again for help when she thought she saw on one person what looked like a flash of almost luminous blue above vaguely red trousers.

Dani? It couldn't be. It didn't make sense. She shouted her friend's name wildly across the now dangerously swollen river, shouted and shouted. But there was no answer, except the gurgling of the rushing river.

Now completely out of her wits, Tally ran on until she had to stop again for breath. Panting wildly, she propped herself up on her knees with her head down. Out of the corner of her eye, she again caught a flash of blue over red, this time a vague, almost formless figure in the river, just discernible as human. But when she looked full at it, there was nothing, just the eddying waters.

The small part of her rational mind which Tally still retained told her it could not be her friend. If Dani had fallen in the river, she would have been carried the other way, downstream, not up. It was impossible, just impossible.

And again, Tally ran. Her feet were now wet from

river water beginning to spill over the bank. She could not properly see what she was running on, but still she raced frantically ahead until, as her last recollection, something gripped her round the leg and she fell headlong into the flooding river.

When Tally awoke, she was lying on her back on a long cushion. At first, as her eyes opened, she saw nothing except a dark, uniformly grey sky. For a while she stared upwards whilst some kind of mental focus returned to her.

One by one, she became aware of the features of her new environment. Firstly, she was cold and soaking wet and her right leg was hurting. Secondly, wherever she was did not stay still. It rocked from side to side and jerked a little backwards and forwards. And she could hear a new sound, a regular plish-plash of, of … what was it? Of course, oars! She was in a boat.

Tally raised her head and looked at her painful leg. Below her foreshortened jeans, a red ring ran all around the lower calf, bleeding slightly. She sat up to look more closely at it and noticed that a young Indian man was sitting looking at her intently. Behind him, with his back to her, was another man, rowing.

Recollection of what had gone before suddenly returned to Tally, like the unwelcome intrusion of reality upon waking from a pleasant dream.

"Where's my friend? Where's Dani?" she barked.

"We are going to her now," said the man, not in a particularly friendly voice, but in one that was somehow rather familiar.

"Thank God!" said Tally, suddenly relieved of a weight of fear and responsibility. "So the police got here before the helicopter?"

The man did not reply, but continued studying her in silence, as a butterfly collector might examine an insect impaled on a pin. His colleague rowed on.

Not entirely comfortable with the man's gaze, Tally looked round. The boat was heading downriver. Just ahead, off the starboard bow, she saw the crazy house on stilts, with its colours, carvings, doors and silent attendants. She also saw the white signboard she had tried to read earlier, but from Tally's position in the boat, it was still too far away to read, and at too sharp an angle.

Then she noticed that the boat was painted white, the same as the board. She began to look at it more closely. She saw it was heavily carved, with many small images of what looked like a crocodile with an elephant's trunk.

"You're not the police, are you?" All Tally's former terror returned in an instant.

"No," replied the man.

"Who are you? What are doing with me? Where are we going?" Tally recoiled from the man as far as she could, against the side of the boat. An inkling of the truth flashed into her mind.

"Are we going to Verona?"

"Yes," replied the man, "or, to be accurate, to what you think is Verona. But you have read the name wrong. The house is named after its owner."

Tally suddenly realised where she had heard the man's voice before. It was the voice of the first emergency service operator. Although open-mouthed with fear, she found she could no longer speak. The man continued, "it is owned by Varuna. He is Hindu, and very old, and I am his servant. He is god of oceans and rivers, and keeper of the souls of people who have drowned. Varuna also sets snares for liars or, to be exact, authorises me to do so. They make marks like that." He pointed to the red ring on Tally's leg.

Somewhere, ever so far away, Tally could hear the sound of a helicopter.

READ THE SMALL PRINT

That Barry Allardyce never intended to become a debt collector was hardly unusual. The abiding wish from an early age to become the torment of those in financial difficulty, or mercilessly hunt down crooks intent on defrauding finance companies, is granted to a relatively small minority.

But Barry had never purposefully aspired to become anything in particular. Dark-haired and thin with sparrow-like legs, he was neither good-looking nor bad, and though not unintelligent, was not focussed enough for academic stardom. He left school as early as he could and took the first available job, stacking shelves in a supermarket. That post lasted six months and was followed within the next three years by two others. For a while, he worked as an assistant in a bike shop and then as an evening cashier in a filling station.

Reading one of the local papers on sale in the latter one day, Barry noticed an advertisement for a trainee credit controller with a nearby firm,

Greengrass Factors. They required someone numerate and used to dealing with the public, and stated training would be given to the right candidate who, they claimed, need not have any previous experience of credit control.

Barry knew jobs requiring no previous experience and offering training for the unskilled were generally ones no-one wanted as there was often something unappealing about them. But the pay was better than his current emolument and he could easily walk from his lodgings to the address given in the advertisement, so he called the quoted telephone number.

Greengrass Factors bought credit accounts from other companies, supplying cash in exchange for rights to their debtors' liabilities and interest. 'Chasers' were needed to ensure debtors kept up their payments. The company knew most people would not want to do this sort of work for long and right from the start viewed most employees as birds of passage. Greengrass supplied two days' basic training and then turned chasers loose on 'clients.' Few applicants were ever turned down provided they were still breathing.

Barry was taken on immediately and proved an exception to the general rule. Quickly grasping every nuance of the job, he immersed himself in his new calling and blossomed as he began to explore its potential. Usually ignored and powerless over others, Barry now found his position gave him control over the financially vulnerable, many of whom, he was surprised to find, were much more exalted in their lives than he. Barry fed hungrily on the power Greengrass enabled him to wield, and relished every opportunity to flaunt his new-found domination. He could make unwelcome telephone calls at unpredictable times, send menacing letters threatening action unless …, or use emails and texts to surprise and alarm 'clients' at home or, even better, at work, to induce unease. In this manner, Barry was able to penetrate clients' lives in a most personal and, to them, unpleasant way.

The work tended to come in waves, relatively quiet periods being interspersed with more active stretches. Barry never figured out why this was, and did not much care. In the quieter moments he amused himself solving puzzles on the web: sudoku, crosswords, almost anything. He became quite adept at these, particularly crosswords, which were available on the web in much greater profusion than in newspapers, and were free. He could also use tools and resources on the internet to solve the puzzles by sorting out anagrams and finding synonyms and other information. Barry learned quite a lot by solving crosswords in this computer-assisted fashion, even though it did rather negate the point of doing the puzzles in the first place.

On joining the company, Greengrass told Barry the essence of his employment was to extract overdue monies owing to them whilst keeping clients in debt up to certain limits. His line manager had further explained that this was not best achieved by driving clients into the courts or bankruptcy. But Barry's secret enjoyment was precisely when that occurred, and he preferred the process to be relatively slow. He sipped it, savouring every taste as a connoisseur might enjoy a vintage Burgundy, and would feel equally as disappointed when the bottle was finally empty.

Gloating after work one day in a pub over one

such 'kill,' he could not resist sharing his thoughts with Dale Varney, a colleague in another office. Whilst consuming a few drinks less refined than Burgundy, Barry described to Dale his fantasy scenario of ultimate harassment. Pursuing a client to the point of bankruptcy, bragged Barry, conjured up for him an image of holding a frightened young woman close in a tight one-armed embrace while watching her eyes as he slowly, ever so slowly, pushed a knife deeper and deeper into her stomach. Barry then graphically described to Dale how he would twist the knife upwards bit-by-bit, and revel in the woman's screams and impotent blows whilst feeling her writhe and buck against his unyielding grip as she bled hotly over his knife-bearing fist, and died.

Fixing a quizzical eye on Barry over the rim of his half-empty glass, Dale asked:

"Are you some kind of perv, then?" before changing the subject so quickly Barry could not answer.

For several months afterwards, Barry heard nor saw nothing of Dale, but that did not bother him. Amusing himself in the evenings reading magazines, watching movies and making occasional calls to clients, during the days he progressed in his work and was promoted to supervise three other credit controllers. When news of his promotion was circulated, an email arrived unexpectedly from Dale. The subject line read:

"Improved collections with Rohana Stokes."

Barry read the email, which said:

"Hi Barry,

I reckon you'll like this. Rohana Stokes is in the collections game too and has certainly sorted me out.

Click the following link – it's quite an eye-opener."

There followed a link to Rohana Stokes's website and underneath was written:

"Regards, Dale."

Having read the short note from Dale, Barry hit the 'Reply' button.

"What did she do for you?" he typed, and clicked 'Send.'

But all he got in reply was:

"Dale Varney is out of the office. If your message is urgent, please call Greengrass Factors on 01587 763456."

Barry deleted the out-of-office message and clicked the link in Dale's email. Almost immediately he was rewarded with a browser-filling picture of a beautiful young woman with long bouncy black hair, wearing a skimpy white bikini, smiling and standing on a beach. Her legs were wide enough apart to form the outline of a capital A and she had one hand on her hip. Her other arm hung down by her side.

Surprised, Barry stared at the stunning beauty. He had been unsure what to expect on clicking the link, but he had not envisaged this unsolicited pleasure. The girl looked vaguely Asian, maybe Indian, but with paler skin than most Indian women; probably mixed race, Barry thought. He surmised that might also explain the rather exotic first name attached to the English surname.

Superimposed in white letters on the sand beneath Rohana's feet was a welcoming inscription, which read:

"Hi, Barry. I'm Rohana Stokes and I'm delighted to meet you. Dale said you might be along. To find out more about my business, please click here. By doing so, you accept my terms and conditions." The 'here' was underlined as a hyperlink.

Barry studied every detail of Rohana's ravishing body. Her picture was displayed to the highest resolution, making it possible to distinguish almost every hair on her head. Whatever Rohana's bikini was made of, it clung to her smooth, lithe body as tightly and accurately as paint, wafer-thin and revealing in shadowed relief every detail of the flesh beneath. Barry voraciously scrutinised every square inch of this gorgeous creature, his eyes travelling down over the swell of her half-obscured breasts, then over her flat stomach and navel and down yet further over her pale brown skin to those tantalising low white bikini pants, moulded ever so finely by her underlying contours.

Rohana was flawless; not a blemish anywhere, observed Barry. Dale had found a wicked wind-up, he thought, and had obviously gone to a lot of trouble, even arranging a personal introduction on the website. Barry felt chuffed. Discovering more about this beauty certainly appealed, so he happily clicked the 'here' link.

A pop-up message appeared across the screen. "Please confirm you accept my terms and conditions," it read, followed by an 'OK' button.

Again, the last three words formed an underlined hyperlink. It crossed Barry's mind that this was, after all, supposed to be a business site despite its initial appearance, so he clicked the link.

A long page of legal language appeared, beginning with the words:

"Rohana Stokes Collections (the Company), agrees with you (the Client) the following terms and conditions." Above the text were prominent 'Accept' and 'Decline' buttons. Barry scrolled down a few lines of the legalese and then gave up, impatient to make further discoveries about Rohana and her business. He hurriedly clicked 'Accept.' Another pop-up appeared.

"Are you sure?" it asked. There were two buttons, one labelled 'Yes' and the other 'No.'

Of course he was sure. Barry clicked 'Yes,' and saw a third pop-up.

"Thank you for accepting my terms and conditions," it read. "Please click 'Close' to proceed."

Barry clicked 'Close' and was instantly rewarded with another high-resolution picture of Rohana, standing with her legs apart as before. She had her back to Barry, but this time was topless, wearing only the clinging white bikini pants. To emphasise her toplessness, from the index finger of her left hand she dangled the white bikini top over her left shoulder whilst twisting round slightly, glancing coyly at Barry over her right. The bikini pants hugged her buttocks, low enough to show their upper slopes.

Barry studied the beguiling scene. Rohana was standing on the same beach as before. It was brightly sunlit, with the sea on the left-hand side. Sand ran to the far right-hand boundary of the view. Beyond the girl was a grass-covered headland projecting into the sea. Nothing else was visible except a vague pinkish patch in the far distance on the right, underneath the headland.

The patch looked odd, though at first glance Barry could not tell why. Then it struck him that, although everything else in the picture was displayed to a life-like resolution, the patch was not. Rather, it was blurred and indistinct. Wanting to get a better look at the patch, Barry wondered whether, if he saved the picture, he could enlarge it using various pieces of software at his disposal.

But his detective work got him nowhere. Whenever he tried saving or even printing the picture, he was greeted with a pop-up message saying:

"You cannot print or save pages from this website," alongside an 'OK' button.

Eventually, Barry gave up. Having only a relatively limited interest in the patch and slightly bored with seeing just the back view of the topless girl, he tried returning to the previous picture of Rohana, which had been more exciting.

But Barry found every attempt to do so was thwarted. He tried several times, but every time an irritating pop-up message would appear, stating:

"You cannot view pages you have already seen," always accompanied by an 'OK' button.

The message would stay onscreen about ten seconds, then disappear before the topless Rohana's rear view returned.

He was about to give up on seeing the earlier image, when he noticed a line of text at the bottom of the page. In white and superimposed on the sand underneath Rohana, the text invited him to click another link. Barry wondered why he had not noticed the link before. Maybe it just needed time to load properly into his browser, he thought.

Barry clicked the link. The picture of Rohana was immediately replaced by a blank white page stating in the middle:

"That's enough for now, you naughty boy. You will have to wait until tomorrow."

After about ten seconds, the message disappeared,

leaving behind only the blank white page. Nothing Barry could do succeeded in getting back to Rohana's website.

At this point, Barry's telephone rang and he was forced out of erotic cyberspace into the reality of everyday debt-collecting.

Arriving at work next day, Barry checked his email as usual. Some spam had got through Greengrass's filters, which he routinely deleted. He also found several messages from clients, almost all pleading for more time to pay and citing myriad reasons why. Barry always avidly read these pleading emails, partly because he needed to know the excuses put forward for non-payment, and partly because he found some of them creatively and imaginatively amusing. His habit was to read the emails whilst drinking coffee. But, having done so, he always ignored them all. Excuses were to Barry as popgun corks to a tank.

However, the subject line of the last email arrested his attention:

"Rohana wants to show you something."

The message was from Rohana Stokes Collections. Rohana's website must have recorded his email address when he clicked the link in Dale's message, thought Barry. Alternatively, Dale had given Rohana Stokes Collections his email address directly. Dale might have done that, particularly if the whole thing was a wind-up, as it seemed, rather like sending him a surprise strippergram.

Barry read the email, which merely contained a link to Rohana's website and another link which read:

'Click here to unsubscribe.'

He looked slyly round the office to check no-one could see what he was doing. Then he eagerly clicked the link to Rohana's site and was greeted by another screen-filling high-resolution picture of her standing on the beach. Rohana was still topless, but this time she faced him, star-shaped, with her legs wide apart and her arms flung high and equally wide, fingers splayed, her head back a little and slightly on one side, with eyes closed and her mouth slightly open, as though she were in ecstasy. Her long hair was blowing in a sea breeze.

For a while, Barry feasted his lascivious eyes on the topless beauty, devouring every glorious inch. He did not care the website was not, despite its earlier pretensions, a business site helping him with his work. Indeed, it was obviously no such thing. But that did not worry him. Why should it? He was enjoying himself.

Rohana's attributes were displayed in such fine detail it felt as though she was actually standing in front of him in the office. His eyes traced every curve and contour, every variation of shade and colour. After a while, however, he began to gain the impression there was something different about the remote object of his desire. He could not put his finger on anything specific, but an opinion gradually formed in his mind that Rohana might be a little older than she had been previously. Yet everything else about her seemed the same. She wore the same figure-hugging low white bikini pants and was on the same beach with the same headland; though he noticed that the odd-coloured patch on the right-hand side under the headland appeared different too. Surely it was slightly larger than before.

To get a better idea of what was going on, he wanted to compare the picture with earlier ones he had received. Wondering about his inability the previous day to view a past shot of Rohana, it now occurred to Barry that the website might have sent a cookie file to his computer preventing him from going back. But the coloured patch and his impression of Rohana's age left him curious. So he decided to write down the link from Dale's original email and load it into the browser of a spare computer on the other side of the room.

"You cannot view pages you have already seen," read the onscreen message. Barry was rather taken aback, and tutted to himself silently. How did the website know he was the viewer? He paused for a few seconds. Then, with a flash of insight, he guessed the site must have known someone had already used that particular link and was denying access the second time. Yes, that must be it. Couldn't be anything else. But … Barry thought again and studied the link he had written down:

'www.rohanastokescollections.com.'

That was all. Nothing else. There was no extension to the link address identifying it as having been sent only to him, just the website's core address. Barry was bemused. How did the website detect he was the person trying to gain access again?

Barry tried recalling exactly what he had seen the day before. He visualised the first picture, the one which came up immediately he clicked the link for the first time. He was sure the page had been specific to him: the inscription beneath Rohana's feet had mentioned both his name and Dale's. But now Barry began reasoning: why would Dale go to such lengths just for a bit of tomfoolery? There must be another explanation … Modern websites were very smart;

perhaps there was some other bit of geekery at work.

Barry gave up trying to figure it out. Instead, he went back to his own computer and tried saving the current picture, partly to compare Rohana's image with any others which might arrive, and partly hoping to examine the coloured patch again by enlarging it. But he remained out of luck.

"You cannot print or save pages from this website," was the uncompromising message he received on his computer.

He double-checked by trying to print the picture, but got the same result.

Barry returned to the screen, and lingered a little more over Rohana's female charms. Then he scrutinised the coloured patch as best he could. He could not understand why it was blurred, despite the sharp resolution of everything else. He was sure it was larger than before.

But that was as far as Barry could get. He could tell nothing further from the picture, and this time no link emerged to take him elsewhere. He ogled Rohana's outspread form for a few seconds longer, then left the site and went back to work.

After his lunch break, Barry tried returning to Rohana's website using the link sent to him that morning. Oddly, it was exactly the same top-level address he had found in Dale's original email. But, no dice. Another repeat of those annoying messages popped up:

"You cannot view pages you have already seen."

Barry gave up for the day, and consoled himself by making a series of aggressive telephone calls to overdue debtors.

Next morning, there was another email from

Rohana. The subject line announced:

"Rohana wants to show you more."

Irritating though her website was proving, its basic resource, large exposed areas of Rohana's very attractive body, remained a powerful inducement to Barry. He clicked the link in the email.

The result was another image of Rohana. She was on the same beach, but was now standing with her back to him, completely naked, with her legs together and her left arm straight down by her side. This time she was looking away from Barry towards the coloured patch on the right, under the headland. Her right hand was outstretched towards the patch, palm turned upwards with the index finger beckoning suggestively.

Barry took in the delights on offer. Rohana was certainly a beautiful woman. To Barry's mind, she was perfectly proportioned; he had always rather fancied Indian women. He wondered if Dale had known that. But, as his eyes travelled over her flesh, he again sensed she was older than she had been in previous pictures. Eyeing every detail of her image, he detected one or two signs of an aging process. There were, he observed, some wrinkles above Rohana's hips which had previously been absent. And maybe, just maybe, she had a slightly fuller figure. But Barry was not sure.

He was sure, however, that the coloured patch was larger. It was still the same pinkish hue, and had the same indistinctness, but this time Barry could discern a darker colour at its top. Also, whatever it was, it was taller than it was wide. He could distinguish nothing else.

Educated by his experiences of the day before and the day before that, Barry did not waste time trying to save or print the picture. However, his curiosity remained piqued, and he still wanted to retain a copy of the scene to compare it with others he might see in what was clearly emerging as an unfinished sequence. So he fished out his mobile phone to photograph the screen.

Looking on his mobile at the picture he was about to take, Barry made sure it displayed all of the naked Rohana as she stood on the beach with her back to him. But immediately after taking the photograph, all he could see on the mobile, superimposed over the original picture, was a just-decipherable message:

"You cannot print or save pages from this website."

Barry looked back to the computer screen. Sure enough, Rohana had been obscured there as well by the same annoying message, with its 'OK' button.

Barry thought back. Had he accidentally clicked a key or leant on the mouse whilst fiddling with his mobile? He was pretty certain he had not. Yet something must have occurred to produce this onscreen message just as he was taking the picture. Barry stared at the message, and felt a tiny knot of doubt begin to tighten in his stomach. Was he being watched? Was someone manipulating him, having a laugh? He looked round nervously, but could see no-one acting suspiciously. Could some so-and-so in the IT department be doing this?

Barry dismissed the thought. If the IT department was playing games, one of their anti-social number would have needed to see precisely when he took the photograph, and he could not think how that would be possible.

It must have been a coincidence.

Barry clicked the 'OK' button to remove the message and lingered a while longer admiring Rohana's attributes. But, as there was no link on the page, he could not progress to whatever was coming next, so he abandoned her for the day.

The following morning brought Barry another email.

"Rohana wants you to see all of her," announced its subject line. There was also another link just like the others, the ones which only worked the first time. Of course, thought Barry, as he clicked it. Simple! The website allowed access only once per day. Why had he not realised that before?

A new picture appeared on his screen. Completely naked, and facing him, Rohana was standing with arms akimbo, most of her weight on her left leg, with her right leg angled a little away from her body and her right foot slightly pointed. She was smiling coquettishly at Barry. Like the other pictures, it was startlingly well-defined. Indeed, every view of Rohana had been more life-like than anything Barry had ever witnessed before on his computer. However, right now he was not much interested in technical capabilities of computer screens. Rather, he was preoccupied with Rohana's female accoutrements, displayed in amazing reality before him. Every curve, every line, every nuance of shape and texture; Barry drank them all in, imagining what it would be like to actually touch and feel what he could only see electronically. It was not that Barry had never seen nor touched the unclothed female form before, but there was something overwhelmingly compelling about this particular woman.

And woman she was. In the first picture Barry

received, Rohana had been in her late teens, a girl just entering womanhood. But now he could see she was probably in her mid to late thirties; still strikingly attractive and well-kept, but with slight signs of maturing. A fuller figure without being in any way fat. One or two slight creases where before there had been smooth-toned flesh. Maybe not quite the tautness of skin, particularly around the tops of her thighs and around her breasts and midriff. The freshness and youth Barry had found so alluring was now replaced by an air of experience and depth. But Barry was not in critical mood. He savoured and enjoyed what he saw.

Eventually, Barry's attention wandered to the unusual coloured patch. Now more distinct, and closer and larger than before, it was forming into the shape of a person. The proportions were right, the flesh tones were right, and whoever it was had dark hair. And unless Barry was very mistaken, the newcomer was also naked, or wearing flesh-coloured clothes, though he could not be sure. Nor could he be sure of the person's gender: the image was still too vague.

The insistent ringing of his telephone reminded Barry he was supposed to be working and brought his solitary pleasure to an abrupt end. Having recently taken over the case from Dale Varney, he had written on several occasions to a young couple who had fallen badly behind with their mortgage repayments, each time instructing them to contact him urgently. They had borrowed far more than was wise, and now the man had lost his job and disappeared, leaving his partner, Louise Bartlett, with a ten-month-old baby. Anyway, that was what Louise claimed, but Barry did not care. All he knew was the loan had been sold on by the original lender to a third party, who had engaged Greengrass to harry the defaulting borrowers. Barry's job was to get the money out of them however he could. And in this regard, as usual, he was proving himself a pro-active employee.

The best way to get the money was normally to keep repayments coming. But Barry had tried that, and, reviewing the case with his boss, they agreed Louise was skint. Repossession had become the only approach. So when her call came, Barry knew exactly what he was going to say. Moreover, far from harbouring any qualms about what was going to happen to Louise, he extracted from the conversation exactly the kind of satisfaction he had described to Dale Varney. Laying down the law to her was almost as thrilling as examining Rohana. There was definitely something perversely exhilarating and infinitely satisfying about stifling the last vestige of hope in a squirming client.

Wrapped up in the Bartlett case, Barry was too busy during the rest of Friday to think much about Rohana. Besides, experience told him he could not view her site once he had left it until a new email arrived. He would just have to be patient and await whatever emails came after the weekend.

He was not disappointed. Sure enough, when he arrived back at work on Monday morning, there was an email displaying the interesting subject line:

"Rohana wants to dance."

Pruriently, Barry clicked the link it contained. Within seconds the same beach scene as before appeared. Rohana remained centre stage, though tantalisingly with her back to Barry again. But unlike the stills he had seen before, this time Barry was treated to a video. Rohana was dancing. Without a stitch of clothing, she danced smoothly, slowly and gracefully, her arms, legs and whole body moving as sinuously as a snake writhing and rippling its way across the sand.

Barry watched, fascinated. Rohana danced on and on, never apparently repeating a step or movement, though always keeping her back to him. Barry watched for some minutes before noticing that the previously indistinct coloured patch was now clearly resolving itself into human shape: a man, probably, and naked as far as Barry could tell. Despite the main picture's crystal clarity, the emerging figure on the right still lacked definition.

Returning his attention to Rohana, Barry could see she was again older. There was a dullness to her dark hair, he noted, which also had signs of grey roots in places, and the quality of her flesh and her gyrating behind spoke of a woman in her late forties. But she remained in quite remarkable condition.

He continued to look at the screen for a while, but Rohana did not turn round, nor was there any further development of the emerging person on the right. Guessing tomorrow would bring further delights, Barry closed his browser and resumed working.

His guesswork proved accurate. The following morning brought the latest in what was proving an extraordinary run of emails.

"Rohana: the works!" exclaimed the subject line. Barry rapidly opened the message and eagerly clicked the link as before. He had an idea of what he might see, and he was right. Still completely naked, but this time facing him, Rohana was dancing sensuously enough to make the one-armed Nelson leap off his column and cartwheel round Trafalgar Square. For ten minutes, at considerable risk of being observed, Barry could not take his eyes off her, as she pirouetted, bent, curled, swayed and sashayed across the sand, caressing and stroking herself as she went.

But Barry was not so engrossed in his drooling lust and overheated imaginings to fail to notice that the figure on the right was now clearly a man, also nude but looking downwards and still some distance away. He also observed that Rohana was in her fifties at least. She still had the illusion of an excellent, well-maintained figure. But there were flecks of white in her hair now, and creases in her flesh told of the loosening of its former firmness, yet she had that maturity of graceful movement younger women rarely achieve. The overall effect remained captivating.

Barry's appreciation of Rohana was interrupted by his boss coming into the room unexpectedly to discuss the Bartlett case. Barry had just enough time to close his browser and look busy. He felt deeply irritated with the wretched Louise Bartlett. Now he would be unable to watch Rohana again that day, given her website's usual response to second visits. When his boss eventually left, he nonetheless tried, but, as expected, had no success.

Instead, Barry proceeded to finalise action against Louise Bartlett, forcefully reiterating to her on the phone, with private relish, what was going to happen to her and her child.

The following day brought another email from Barry's sashaying acquaintance, the subject line this time rather disturbingly announcing:

"Rohana says it's your turn now."

Barry hesitated, wondering where this could lead. Somewhere in the back of his mind the thought arose that this might be an email he should not open. But the thought was stifled almost as soon as it arose. Barry's appetite for Rohana was too strong for irrational caution to intervene. He opened the email.

The message contained a link to proceed, and also an unsubscribe link. Ignoring the latter, Barry clicked the former.

When the image came onto the screen, it was not like the previous day's video, but another still. For a second only, Barry missed the critical feature it revealed. Initially, his eyes rested on the naked Rohana, who was standing slightly hunched, hands down by her sides, and facing him. But the view of her shocked him. Barry was beginning to think the image was out of sequence, not a further development reaching beyond the bounds of eroticism into pornography, when he looked at the other figure, now in clear focus next to Rohana. Standing with his arms by his sides was a man, staring blankly straight at him. His heart almost stopped. He was looking at himself.

Barry's mind reeled. He had not anticipated this. His eager expectation of more e-titillation died instantly. He studied the distasteful picture with growing alarm. Rohana was now well past her seventies, and looked it. Her hair was lank, thin and white, her breasts sagged and her expression was distressed, almost haggard. Her formerly unblemished skin was wrinkled and blotched by age. Veins prominently revealed their presence along those once smooth limbs. Rohana, gaunt and old, was the very opposite of an object of desire.

In contrast, the representation of Barry was youthful, still in his early twenties as, indeed, he was. Their standing naked together implied a strong carnal link. Yet the manifest differences in age and condition made the suggestion repellent and unnatural. It was a most disturbing image, and Barry shuddered.

Dale really had gone too far this time. Teasing him with the ravishing Rohana was one thing, but this was not playing the game. Then Barry began to consider whether Dale could actually have done this. How could Dale have faked that nude picture of him, even if he did possess the necessary skill and motivation? Barry was horrified to see that his own onscreen image photographically displayed every detail of his frontal physique, right down to various small moles and skin blemishes in positions neither Dale nor anyone else could possibly have known about. How on earth could that sort of information become available on the internet? Barry wondered whether his medical records had been hacked and published somewhere. But even if that were the case, there was no earthly reason why they should contain such intimate details, as he had never brought them to the attention of any doctor.

Barry decided it was time to speak to Dale. His last attempt, by email, only produced an out-of-office response, so this time Barry ferreted Dale's phone number out of the company directory and called it.

There was no answer. Irritated, Barry tried again. Still no answer. So Barry called the switchboard at Dale's office. A female receptionist picked up the call.

"Good morning, Greengrass Factors. How can I help?"

"It's Barry Allardyce, from the Bayswater office. Is

Dale Varney in today? I've tried calling him direct but there's no answer and no voicemail."

For a while there was silence. Barry was just about to ask if the woman had heard, when she spoke again.

"I am afraid Mr. Varney died three weeks ago."

It was Barry's turn to pause. The receptionist waited, until finally Barry said,

"Oh."

"Were you a friend?" she enquired.

"Not particularly," answered Barry. "Just workmates. We used to go for a drink together."

"I am sorry," the receptionist replied.

"What happened?" asked Barry.

"He committed suicide," said the receptionist. "He jumped in front of a Tube train at Golders Green. There wasn't anyone else near him on the platform, the driver said, so he couldn't have been pushed. I'm surprised you didn't hear about it on the news."

Even if Barry had heard about someone topping themselves on the Tube recently, it had not connected. Maybe the report did not name the victim. He had not heard anything on the company grapevine either. Though that was not particularly surprising; Barry did not socialise much.

"Oh, well," he said to the receptionist, and rang off with other concerns crowding his troubled mind.

Barry was now thoroughly alarmed. Dale had been dead two weeks before all the Rohana business started. So if he had been responsible for it, there must have been some kind of delay. Barry checked his inbox, which he only cleared from time to time. Sure enough, there was Dale's original email introducing him to Rohana.

Barry was glad he had not deleted the message,

because now he could see it was dated just over a week ago and had clearly been sent from Dale's email address.

Barry could not fathom what was going on, but whatever it was, he did not like it. He looked again at his computer screen. The picture of him and the ghastly aged Rohana was still there. Though this time, under Rohana's puffy, veined feet, Barry saw a message in white across the bottom:

"You must join in with Rohana now. Click here."

Had the message been there before? Barry was unsure. But he decided the one thing he was not going to do was click the link. He closed his browser and began to turn the whole affair over in his mind.

He concluded that everything about his recent online experience was odd and now, he realised, unnerving. He thought the emails had been started by Dale Varney. But now he had discovered Dale died two weeks before his first email introducing Rohana. Then, every picture of Rohana was of such high definition she practically jumped off the screen. He had never known computers display such detailed images as those of Rohana. Yet there had always been that strange indistinct area, which eventually emerged as the image of himself. This was the most astonishing thing of all, showing, as it did, details of him that only he could possibly know.

Barry had a peculiar sense of unease. He did not like it. He did not like it at all. There were just too many things he could not explain. Why had he been unable to print, revisit or even photograph any picture he had seen? And the girl, or woman's name. That was unusual, too, he thought. Rohana. He had never come across a Rohana before, let alone one with the far more prosaic surname of Stokes.

Barry's mind lingered on the name. Did it hold any clues? An idea occurred to him. He turned back to his computer, found an online anagram generator and typed in 'Rohana Stokes.'

A long list of computer-generated results came up, most of them useless. Why would anyone ever want 'roast hone ask' or 'snake root ash,' he thought? Even the more probable 'North Sea soak' could not claim to be a term in common currency. Barry wondered at the imbecility of computers.

And then, scrolling idly down the screen and on the point of deciding he was wasting his time, Barry jumped violently. Buried amongst hundreds of nonsensical irrelevancies, one result leapt at him.

"Satan's hooker," it said.

Barry felt his skin suddenly grow hot, with a prickling rush of sweat, then just as quickly grow cold again, leaving his goosebumped flesh feeling clammy. He looked furtively round the office and, only very slowly, what Barry took to be reason regained the upper hand. It must be coincidence. Nonsense, all of it. Some malevolent swine of a webmaster must be playing games with him.

Barry rapidly closed his browser and set his email spam filter to reject anything to do with Rohana Stokes or Dale Varney. Rather as a man with a serious hangover resolves never to drink again, Barry then resolved not to visit any more girlie websites. He undid the top button of his shirt collar, rubbing his index finger round his sweat-damp neck, and spent the remainder of the day mechanically doing what he was employed to do, though no longer with any relish. Even piling up the pressure on Louise Bartlett during a late afternoon phone call failed to cheer him. That night, he scarcely slept at all.

Tired and still a little shaken on arrival at his office the next day, the last thing Barry wanted to see was another email from Rohana. But one had evaded his spam filter and sat at the top of his inbox asking:

"Do you want to unsubscribe from Rohana's emails?"

Barry thought he had already set his filter to exclude every message that included the word 'Rohana' or any reference to her accursed website. But maybe the addition of the apostrophe 's' defeated the filter. Whatever the reason, Barry certainly did want to unsubscribe, so he opened the message.

The message merely said:

"Recommend me to three friends. Click here for my recommendation form."

Barry clicked the link. A form immediately appeared with enough fields to submit the names and contact details of three friends.

Barry examined what passed for his conscience, and did some logical deduction. If this was all nonsense, as his rational self believed, then passing on recommendations would do no-one any harm and would give three of his acquaintances an entertaining few days, even if there was a sting in the tail. But if it was not nonsense, which a more visceral part of Barry feared, then making recommendations offered him the chance of unsubscribing from Rohana's clutches and escaping whatever otherwise might await.

Barry did not think for long. He filled in three sets of details and clicked the proffered 'Submit' button.

A dialog box appeared on the screen, which read:

"Thanks for your recommendations. I am

delighted you enjoyed my nudity at your workplace over the past few days. But as you refused to join in as instructed, it is regrettably impossible to unsubscribe from my system. This decision is final. Your friend, Rohana. OK?"

"No, it bloomin' well isn't OK," said Barry out loud. Then he tried closing the dialog box without clicking the 'OK' button. Nothing happened. He tried again, with the same result. No matter what he did, the box obstinately refused to vanish. Neither could it be minimised. Then Barry found it also prevented him running any other program or rebooting.

Left with no other option, Barry eventually turned his computer off by removing the power cord. When he reconnected the cord and restarted his machine, to his dismay the dialog box was still there. He repeated the procedure several times. But the box stubbornly kept reappearing.

Barry was beside himself. He knew he could not leave the dialog box onscreen. But as he could neither close nor remove it, he was prevented from doing any work. Given the contents, he felt he could not let anyone else see the box, so asking the IT department to deal with the problem was out of the question.

There seemed only one way out of this hopeless paralysis. Yet something told Barry he should not take it. For a while, his unfathomed instinct wrestled with his wish to restore the computer to normality. However, in the end, Barry clicked the 'OK' button. The box immediately disappeared, and that was all. Nothing else happened. Barry breathed a sigh of relief. Problem solved.

At least, that was what he thought for a while. But, despite the spam filters, within half an hour another of Rohana's wretched emails arrived, the subject line stating:

"Rohana requires you to join her according to our agreement."

"What agreement?" wondered Barry. He thought back, then recalled he had clicked 'Accept' to some terms and conditions when the pictures first began appearing. So, despite his better judgment and all the trouble he had experienced with Rohana's communications, Barry opened the email, hoping for some release. This time, there was no link to click. Instead, he immediately saw another high-resolution video. It was a further development in the sequence of beach scenes, but this time it was nightmarishly gruesome. Still naked, Rohana looked ancient, probably in her nineties. Bent over with age, shrivelled, discoloured and wasted, she was kneeling over a prone Barry, who was still in his twenties, embracing him, caressing him, licking him and dribbling toothlessly. Nauseous, Barry closed and deleted the email as quickly as he could, with no wish whatsoever to investigate further.

Barry then deleted, unread, a continuous series of other bullying messages from Rohana. Her emails demanded attention with increasing stridency, and produced in the already severely rattled Barry an even more acute and rising sense of apprehension.

The subject line of the last email Barry saw that day, moments before he went home, menacingly proclaimed:

"Rohana will ensure you join in."

Sleep had been difficult for Barry for some nights, and this last message did nothing to induce slumber. Next morning, tired and fearful, Barry walked reluctantly to work.

His inbox contained only one email, stating it was from Louise Bartlett. Relieved there was nothing from Rohana Stokes, Barry opened it.

For a few seconds, he gaped wide-eyed in horror at the image confronting him. Then he started from his seat and rushed out of the office into the street for some fresh air.

As he blundered onto the pavement he nearly collided with a young woman walking towards him. He stopped just in time and looked at her. The woman wore a long blue overcoat, unfastened and loosely belted, with a gap down the front about nine inches wide. The gap revealed a white bikini underneath. Her left arm hung straight down by her side and her right arm rested across her stomach, disappearing under the coat. Frozen in fascination, Barry watched the woman withdraw her right hand from the coat's folds. In it glinted a long, broad, pointed kitchen knife.

Barry looked up from the shining knife into the woman's face. He recognised her from her file: Louise Bartlett. She had a flat expression, communicating no emotion whatsoever. Before Barry could move or speak, the woman's left arm encircled him with superhuman strength and squeezed the breath out of him. Barry struggled ineffectually to free himself, and saw the woman's eyes, now gloating with triumph. They gazed unwaveringly into his own and as he stared back, terrified, he suddenly felt the knife thrust upwards into his abdomen, whilst the woman jerked him even closer to herself to ensure maximum penetration. Just before he lost agonising consciousness, his assailant, twisting the knife, smiled and said evenly:

"Glad to meet you in the flesh. I'm Rohana Stokes."

The Detective Inspector finished scrutinising the pavement murder scene. He had ordered that nothing in Barry's working area be touched until he personally examined everything, which he now proceeded to do.

Barry's computer screen was blank, automatically turned off for energy-saving five minutes after the computer's mouse had last been used. The Inspector studied the desk round the screen, read a couple of nearby notes and then, almost idly, moved the mouse with the tip of his pen.

The screen flashed into life and the Inspector looked at it. A high-resolution video was playing and the Inspector's mouth dropped partly open. His stomach churned.

On a sandy beach, with a grass-covered headland in the background, a struggling Barry Allardyce was locked in a macabre dance with the decaying, discoloured and naked husk of what had probably been a woman, with long white tussocks of hair blowing in the sea breeze. Had the apparition been recumbent and still, the DI would have considered it a half-rotted corpse. But, grinning towards the observer most of the time, it was energetically waltzing on the blood-soaked sand without any assistance from its unwilling partner. A semi-skeletal left arm clamped the naked Barry inescapably hard against itself whilst its right hand gripped the handle of a knife, thrust upwards into Barry's stomach just above and to the left of his navel and running with blood.

To the right of the grotesque image, flung down upon the sand, were the two pieces of a white bikini and a blue overcoat. Underneath was written, in white lettering:

"The Company is exercising its rights under Clause 73 of their agreement with the Client, which is as follows: 'The Company reserves the right to retain the Client for ever.'"

THREE'S A CROWD

Montague Dewar's head shifted slightly on the pillow and a bleary half-opened eye scanned the bedside clock. Two-fifteen a.m. For a few seconds Monty was disoriented, groping his way out of the shifting fog separating sleep from wakefulness. His mind tried to fall back into the abyss. Then an unexpected noise from somewhere below blew the fog away, propelling him into the clear light of consciousness.

Monty listened, straining for further sounds. He was not quite sure what he had heard. Perhaps it was nothing at all. There was no rain or wind beating at his bedroom window. The night seemed still. Yet something was not right. What was it? Sitting bolt upright now, awake and alert, he caught the unmistakeable sound of his dining room door being opened. He knew the time had come. He reached under the bed.

In the hallway, a man said softly, "upstairs first for some fun. Then we do the rest."

Monty heard footsteps creak gently on the stairs.

With wildly pumping heart, he crouched in the dark behind his closed bedroom door, looking through the keyhole onto the illuminated landing, towards the top of the stairs. He had to get this right. Timing was crucial. He waited until he saw the top of a man's head rising from below. Then he stood up and threw open the bedroom door.

For a few seconds, Monty had the advantage of surprise. The nearest figure stared at him, immobile in astonishment. Monty raised both hands, targeted the man's head and squeezed the trigger. There was a sound like a heavy click and the intruder fell onto his companion, a few steps behind. Both tumbled backwards, fetching up against the wall at the bottom of the stairs.

Monty quickly crossed the landing, following his prey downwards. The lower man was partly trapped, face up, pushing his accomplice's bleeding body aside and trying to wriggle free. Monty fired again and the man instantly clutched his upper chest near the windpipe, writhing and screaming. Monty swore, and descended to stand directly over his target. This time there was no mistake. The silenced gun clicked once more and the man lay still, with a third and slightly off-centre eye about two inches above the original pair, weeping red tears.

Monty looked round rapidly for signs there might be more than two intruders. He saw no-one. He tried to listen, but his heart was pounding too loudly to hear. He sat down heavily on a Sheraton corner-chair, a recent addition to his collection of eighteenth century furniture. It emitted a disconsolate crack, but Monty ignored it. He no longer had the strength to get up, nor to hold the gun, which fell to the floor.

Monty's right hand fell limply after it, shaking like the rest of him. Jelly-like, he sat waiting for his composure to return in the terrible stillness of the icy cold hall.

Living alone, Monty always suspected he would be a prime target for intruders. And he had become nervously protective of his fine furniture collection, amassed over many years of happy visits to antique shops and auction houses. He was a practical sort of man, an accountant with a four-person practice of his own in Wetherford. He prided himself on the accuracy of his firm's work, and even named his boat 'No Comebacks' to reflect one of his key business objectives.

'No Comebacks' was a Hartley cabin cruiser, which Monty regularly hitched to his Land Rover for the twenty-mile journey to Seahaven Sailing Club. She was the largest vessel Monty could single-handedly launch and retrieve using a car-pulled trailer, and he was skilled at the manoeuvre. He had equipped the cruiser with the latest radar and navigation gear, and from time to time adventurously sailed along both coasts of the English Channel. 'No Comebacks' was Monty's treasure, and he relished every minute spent in her. Sometimes he invited a friend or two to accompany him on one of his excursions, and that was pleasant, too. Monty had a wide circle of acquaintances and, as well as sailing jaunts, he regularly enjoyed dinner parties with them. It was a conceit of his at dinners with these friends that finally led Monty into waters both turbid and turbulent.

Monty's friends were never quite certain what to expect when invited to dine. Possessed of a good voice himself, he might arrange sessions singing comic songs. Dinners might be themed – Hallowe'en was a regular – but poetry and story readings were fairly frequent features as well, with guests suddenly finding works by authors such as G K Chesterton thrown at them. Then, towards the end of an evening, Monty might produce samples from his wide range of drinks made with unusual ingredients, challenging guests to guess the contents. Intoxicating derivatives of prickly pear, artichokes and various Alpine herbs had all enlivened many a dinner party at Monty's old farmhouse in Featherden.

Friendly banter, and sometimes deeper conversations, would freely flow, especially when Monty used these dinners to fly verbal kites. A particular favourite had always sparked interesting comments. Ignoring debates about the European Union's common currency, Monty argued the EU would get nowhere without a common language. As no country would accept the native tongue of another, why not use Latin? It could be modernised to include words like 'computer,' 'nuclear bomb,' or anything else developed since the collapse of Ancient Rome. Though underpinning many EU languages, Latin was rarely spoken by anyone, with odd exceptions. The German Benedict XVI, for instance, the first Pope to resign in six hundred years, chose Latin to announce his departure. On other occasions, Monty advocated electing judges, on the American pattern, or argued that universal suffrage had coincided with the beginning of a long-term rise in inflation in Britain and may thus have caused it. He gleaned endless amusement from such arguments, though he intended nothing concrete to emerge.

Pleasantly provocative, though normally harmless, the nature of Monty's kite-flying forays would change when the greying accountant introduced the subject of burglars. Like many in his circle, he was greatly concerned about home owners he read of in the newspapers, who were being convicted of assault, grievous bodily harm, or worse, after confronting burglars who invaded their homes.

One conversation that particularly stuck in his memory occurred whilst Monty was holidaying in France. He had been staying near Épernay, as he often did, in a small champagne house which provided bed, breakfast, and occasional dinners.

On the evening in question, the diners had been Monty, the Flemish chatelaine, her hard-working French vigneron husband, and two other couples, one Welsh and one German. Conversation had been pleasant but bland, so, after dessert, Monty decided to enliven it with his most controversial topic. He began by mentioning there had been a series of burglaries in his part of rural Kent, mostly involving householders being beaten up and, in one case, stabbed to death. The problem, he said, had increased once the M20 motorway opened. Raiders were popularly supposed to come down the motorway from London before returning there, in 'boomerang raids.'

The police had proved useless. In country locations, they reportedly took at least an hour to arrive after alarms had been raised, giving offenders plenty of time to escape. For the benefit of the French and German couple, Monty explained that English law allowed householders to use force against intruders provided it was not 'grossly disproportionate,' although interpretation of the expression was left to the courts. He further explained that if a house owner harmed a burglar, the police would probably prosecute the householder to establish whether the force used was 'grossly disproportionate' or not. Monty thought this situation monstrously unfair.

"Why?" inquired Betje, the chatelaine. "Isn't it right to let courts decide?"

"No," replied Monty. "It means someone like me, faced with a burglar, has two equally unacceptable choices. Either I do nothing, allow my precious possessions to be stolen and face the risk of violence, or I act. If my actions don't work, I will be at the burglar's mercy. But if they do, I may well have harmed the burglar in some way. With the police and courts behaving in their usual stupid fashion, that will probably mean I will be the one prosecuted. If I lose, they will find me guilty at the very least of a criminal assault. Even if I win, I will have gone though the harrowing experiences of a burglary and a court action, through no fault of mine. Look what happened to that Norfolk farmer. He was jailed for murder after he shot two intruders who broke in. Even if his conviction was later reduced to manslaughter, is that fair?"

"Well," retorted Betje, "why don't you fit a burglar alarm?"

"I could, but as I mentioned, the police take ages to arrive. Serious thieves just brazen it out and simply ignore alarms. Besides, there are lots of other problems. What about people who rent and whose landlords won't install alarms? There'll be lots of people in that position. Good alarms are expensive, too. What about people who can't afford one? The law should protect them as well."

"Campaign to get the law changed, then. Write to your Member of Parliament," intoned David Tudor, a schoolteacher from Caerphilly. "Isn't that the way to do it?"

Monty laughed. "The law was changed. It was even worse before, but politicians bungled the chance to get it right. They are far too worried about criminals' human rights. And my MP's a certified moron."

"What's your solution?" asked Betje.

"It's not easy." replied Monty. "I would be grateful if anyone can prove my logic wrong. I'm nearly sixty, rather paunchy and unfit, and would have no chance against some young tough invading my property. If I do nothing, I'm a sitting duck. If I do something unsuccessful, I would probably get thumped or worse. But even if I survived the thug, the law would probably come down on me like a ton of bricks for attacking him. Furthermore, there would always be, lurking at the back of my mind, the fear that the thief might come after me later, probably with his mates. Unless …"

Monty paused for effect.

"Yes? Unless what?" David rose to the bait.

"Unless I kill the burglar and get rid of the body. Then no-one will know and there'll be no trouble."

The short silence following this dramatic suggestion was quickly broken by everyone trying to speak at once. Monty was amused. His dining companions were shaken out of their post-prandial lethargy. In the verbal kerfuffle, he heard "… it's murder …," "… exercise of gratuitous force …," "… good idea, if you ask me …," "… you'd never get away with it …," "… you've got to think it through …," "… grossly disproportionate, the law would say …," plus a good deal more besides. What he did not hear, was any challenge to his underlying logic. After the noise subsided, the German man spoke.

"How would you kill him and what would you do with the body?"

Monty considered. "Not sure. Could use a club or something, perhaps. Dumping the body might be a problem. Any suggestions?"

"Ja," said the German. "I would drop it off a bridge onto a busy autobahn at night. When the traffic had finished with it no-one could tell what happened before."

"Klaus!" Gretl Rindt was shocked by her husband's callousness, which, rather unnervingly, suggested he might have considered the subject before. Klaus ignored her. "Not if you shot him, though. Bullet holes might be awkward to explain."

"Guns are difficult to get in England," said Monty.

"And illegal," added David.

Jean-Luc Leclerc lacked the German's command of English, but he did have a contribution to make.

"I know a well. Very quiet and er … deep. No-one find 'eem zere."

"How would you kill him?" asked Klaus.

"I shoot 'eem. So I keep away from 'eem."

"What with?" asked Monty.

"A Luger. Mon grandpère … er … grandfather, got 'eet in 1944. 'Ee …" Jean-Luc checked himself, glanced at Klaus, then looked away. "I don't know 'ow," he lied, quietly.

Klaus smiled, but said nothing. Betje also said nothing, but did not smile.

David said, "I can't believe you're all talking calmly about murder."

"Not murder," retorted Monty. "You know if you do nothing to the intruder you're in for it. You also know by using non-lethal force you are possibly going to be jailed if the thief and his cronies don't get you first. I'd call my suggestions pre-emptive self-defence."

"Well, I wouldn't," said the Welshman. "And I don't like this conversation very much. I suggest we talk about something else."

Betje asked if anyone wanted some ratafia, and whether there would be any interest in a barbecue the following evening. Monty happily let the others drift into speculation about whether a fish or meat supper would be best. But he noted, with one exception, the group was broadly supportive or otherwise neutral towards his ideas. He had expected more opposition. Thereafter he began, semi-idly, to think through his logic.

The more Monty considered the Frenchman's remark, "keep away from 'eem," the more he thought it well-founded. A gun would be the obvious choice. Anyone without combat training would find it difficult to kill a strong, fit young man either by hand, or with any weapon requiring close proximity to the target. The outcome of such a struggle would probably be the reverse of what was intended. Besides, weapons such as golf clubs would be far too unwieldy inside a house. A gun would be better, he thought.

A shotgun, perhaps? No: indoors, that would be as cumbersome as a golf club. Sawn off, it would be more likely to maim than kill except at very close range, and it would have only two shots. Risky. A handgun would do the trick.

Monty also concluded that a silencer would be needed to minimise the chance of detection. Monty knew nothing about guns, but he did know how to use the internet, and during one session on a Saturday afternoon learned within three hours more about handguns than he had ever dreamed could be known. He learned about makes and types, sizes and calibres. In particular, he discovered silencers were more effective on semi-automatic pistols than on revolvers. The main problem was how to obtain such a combination as well as the necessary ammunition.

Monty considered the possibilities. All the items he wanted were illegal in England, but could they be obtained abroad? More internet research confirmed his suspicion that America would be the best place to buy. Guns were plentiful there, regulations relatively lax and the language familiar. Getting a gun home undetected would be tricky, though. To Monty, stuffing a gun into a suitcase, hoping no-one would find it, resembled Russian roulette with all the chambers loaded but one, rather than the other way round.

Many years before, Monty had exported a large Chevrolet from Baltimore to Southampton. Great fun to drive in England, and a powerful head-turner, it later sold for twice its value in the US. It occurred to Monty there were numerous places in a car where a gun and its accoutrements might be concealed. Perhaps he could hide a gun in a car, export it from the US and make money, too, on selling the vehicle afterwards. But that was not really his way of doing things and besides, it would still be exceedingly risky.

Maybe he could buy a gun illicitly in England, probably in London. But that thought did not last long, as he had no wish to become known to undesirables who might use the information for blackmail, or worse. Every time he considered the problem, Monty concluded there were no easy options.

Over the next few months, Monty held and attended several more dinner parties, and occasionally returned to his burglar theme. The subject gnawed away at him. He detested all the human rights laws that seemed to lead courts to protect the rights of criminals rather than those of people like him. It was not fair, and he never shied away from sharing these views. His comments always provoked interesting responses. On one occasion, they also produced something more.

Keith Foreman had spent a lifetime selling used cars which, in the early days, had been of dubious quality and often even more dubious provenance. As far as anyone could tell, he had gradually hauled himself out of the swamp and ended his business career some years before as the wealthy owner of a chain of car dealerships. He then retired to Featherden with his wife Angela. The Foremans seemed to spend much of their time travelling, but would occasionally join Featherden's dinner tables when not otherwise engaged. They came into Monty's orbit after attending the same dinner party, thrown by mutual acquaintances in a new development on the edge of the village. Despite suspecting he should not ask too many questions about their backgrounds, Monty rather liked their forthright approach and their apparent friendliness.

The day after most recently airing his solution for burglars, Monty received a telephone call from Foreman. Following initial pleasantries, Foreman said,

"I can help with your burglar problem."

"What do you mean?"

"You said a lot last night about burglars. I agree with you, and I can help."

"Oh yes? How?"

Monty heard a sniff at the other end of the line.

"You free for a drink tomorrow night – about six-thirty?"

Monty hesitated. Although he liked Foreman, this invitation, if accepted, might get him in too deep with the man. On the other hand, what harm could a chat over a drink do?

"Yes. Yes, that would be fine. Where?"

"My place. Angela will be out, so there'll just be the two of us."

"Fine. I'll look forward to it."

"'Great," said Foreman. And the line clicked off.

Something at the back of his mind warned Monty to be careful. Again he wondered if he was doing the right thing. True, he enjoyed the intellectual challenge of trying to shock people with semi-outrageous ideas. But acting on them ... ? Perhaps he should call Foreman back and say he'd forgotten a prior commitment. No; Foreman would think him either an idiot or a wimp, and Monty did have his pride. Besides, he need not commit himself to anything. Monty decided he would honour the engagement.

At exactly six-thirty next evening, Montague Dewar pulled the brass bell-chain outside Keith Foreman's iron-studded front door. Foreman appeared immediately, and Monty was ushered inside.

"Saw you on the camera, coming through the gate," said Foreman. "Wouldn't want to keep a mate waiting, would I?"

"Thanks." Monty entered and looked around. The building was a Kent hall house; very old, heavily brown-timbered, and, from his collector's viewpoint, furnished to a high standard, even if not exactly to his taste.

"I've always thought this was quite a place, Keith."

"Yeah, well, I've managed to put a bit away for my old age. There's no point slumming it, is there?" Foreman led Monty through a corridor into a large room, which he described as his 'observatory.' The observatory had a magnificent view over extensive and well-manicured lawns in one direction, and over a large swimming pool in the other. Beyond was woodland.

"What's your poison?" Foreman was standing by an enormous open cabinet, which contained enough alcoholic beverages to stock a pub.

"Dry sherry, thanks."

Foreman's left eyebrow twitched, but he said, "no problem," and poured a schooner of Tio Pepe. Then he filled a tumbler with Johnny Walker and a dash of water for himself. He joined Monty, who was observing the gardens through windows which managed to fill a large portion of one wall without detracting from the room's character. Monty took the drink and looked round. The domestic pub seemed to have disappeared. Then he realised the cabinet, when closed, looked like a seventeenth century linen press. Very clever - Foreman certainly must have money. The cabinet's doors reflected the glow of the fire which blazed invitingly in the observatory's inglenook.

For twenty minutes, Foreman gave Monty a verbal tour of the house. Then he said,

"Two nights ago, you stated burglars should be killed, and that, for someone like you, the best way would be to shoot them."

"Yes. I wanted to make a point. I am seriously worried about burglars. You know there have been many raids round here?"

"Yeah. But you don't have a gun, do you?"

"No."

"A bit futile, then, wasn't it? Or were you just playing games?"

"Well, I wouldn't say that. I wanted to make a point."

"Well, you made it. But were you serious?"

Foreman gazed quizzically at Monty. Monty shivered a little, and considered. If he answered in the negative, he would look a fool and Foreman might spread the word that Monty was all hot air. But answering "Yes" could lead into unknown territory. He dithered.

"Well?" Foreman pressed home his advantage.

Monty hesitated for a second or two more, then said, "of course."

Foreman studied him in silence for a few seconds, then opened an oak chest beside his chair. Bound in black iron straps, the chest resembled ancient coffers occasionally found in churches, but was smaller, and in better condition. Foreman extracted a large, stout-looking brown cardboard box, which he handed to Monty.

Monty studied the box. It was heavy.

"Open it."

Monty did so. Inside were five items, separately wrapped in chamois leather. Monty unwrapped one of them. A black pistol with a black grip. Monty stared at it.

"It's not loaded," said Foreman. "Interested?"

Myriad thoughts hit Monty simultaneously. He thought of his kite-flying, of all the friends he had wound up. He thought of the police, and of blood. He thought of Foreman, with that faint smile playing on his lips, almost mocking him. He thought of the raids on houses nearby, and of his own advancing years.

Monty asked, rather stupidly, "what sort is it?"

Foreman's mocking smile became briefly more obvious. Then it subsided, before he asked again, "do you want it?"

Monty hesitated. He shuddered inwardly at all the malevolent gun implied. Yet he had said dozens of times he was prepared to kill an intruder for 'pre-emptive self-defence.' He needed to prevent physical harm being done to himself. Using a gun increased his chances of success. That argument still held true. Monty crossed his Rubicon.

"Yes, yes," he stammered. "I never thought I would be able to get one. Yes, thank you, thank you very much indeed."

"To answer your question," said Foreman, "it's a Glock 17 semi-automatic, with a silencer. The other things are a spare seventeen-round magazine, a box of about two hundred nine millimetre cartridges and a gizmo to help load the magazines." Foreman paused.

"Ever used one before?" he asked.

Monty's inevitable "No" led to a short instruction

session in some dense woodland which formed part of Foreman's large garden. Monty handled, loaded and fired the gun, with its silencer, enough to become relatively confident in its use.

"Hold it this way," demonstrated Foreman. "Aim it like this; squeeze the trigger and the safety catch like that, don't pull; don't point at anything you don't want to kill or destroy. When you unload it, don't forget the one in the chamber. And use the loader to refill the magazines: it's easier on the thumb."

Afterwards, over a second Tio Pepe, Monty asked Foreman how much he wanted for the gun.

"Nothing."

"It looks expensive."

"Yeah," said Foreman.

"So, why are you giving it to me?"

"Let's just say I don't like being messed about by burglars either."

"Why don't you keep it for yourself, then?"

"Don't need to," said Foreman, grinning in a rather menacing way.

Monty realised asking where the gun came from would be pointless. Foreman clearly had connections he was unlikely to reveal.

Foreman said, "got a bag or something to carry it in?"

Monty tried to recall what was in his Land Rover. "I may have some carriers. Why?"

"Can't be too careful. We'd better get them." This they did, and returned to the observatory. On Foreman's instruction, Monty put the gun and its accessories into two carriers, one inside the other for strength. Foreman tipped the bullets out of their box into the bags, then threw both boxes and all the leather wrappers onto the fire.

"Why did you do that?"

"As I said, my friend. You can't be too careful."

Monty did not press for further enlightenment. He was no longer certain he liked Foreman. But he thanked him again and made his exit. As Monty approached the front door, Foreman said,

"If you have to use it, do it quickly and don't dither or the other guy'll get you. Don't use it at all in your own home until you've worked out what to do with the body – and I don't want to know what that is."

Monty had already worked out what to do with a potential body.

Through a window, Foreman watched Monty leave. As the gate closed, Foreman thought "what a berk," and picked up the telephone.

"Bernie," he said, when the phone was answered. "It's Keith. I've got a solution for those toe rags who think they managed to rip us off on that Gatwick job."

"Permanent?" asked Bernie.

"Reckon so. With no way of tracing it to us. I want them to turn over a place near here. Tell them to give the owner their special treatment. They'd enjoy that. But say they've got to clear the place out, trash it, get rid of the body and make it look like burglary was the motive. Got that? … Good. Here's the address …"

Two weeks later, Monty sat in his corner-chair in the hall at a quarter to three in the morning, with two corpses for company. His head was clearing and his nerve had steadied. Details of his plans, prepared for this contingency, were coming back to him. In the resolve he momentarily felt, Monty studied the bodies. The men were lithe-looking, and both about thirty, he thought. One wore black jeans and a tight black sweater, with dark-coloured trainers. He also wore a wedding ring. The other had a hooded mid-grey top labelled 'Oxford University,' and conventional blue denim jeans. He also sported a pair of dark trainers. Monty wondered who they were, whose sons they were, who loved them. Then he savagely banished such thoughts. By violating his home and clearly intending to commit theft and mayhem, these low-lifes had forfeited all right to normal human consideration. They had received the punishment they deserved, and Monty had no pity. They were rubbish, human rubbish, he told himself.

But this was dreadful, awful, worse than his worst nightmare. His beautiful home. Why had they come? He had not asked to be burgled. And just after getting the gun, too. Now there was blood on the stair carpet, the walls, the balustrade, his Afghan rug in the hallway. His pyjama trousers were splattered with it. A delicate Regency table had been smashed in the turmoil, as had a convex gilt butler's mirror high over the foot of the stairs. Monty looked at the mirror, still hanging in position, then walked over for a closer look.

Much of the mirror glass remained in place as curved shards, but where the glass had been dislodged Monty saw a bullet stuck in the wooden backing board. His brain accelerated. How many times had he fired? Three, he thought, but he was not sure. He searched the stairs and hallway floor and retrieved three spent casings. Then he picked up the gun and released the magazine. Yes, three shots gone. He knew he had shot one man twice, and two were dead. That accounted for three shots. So where had this bullet come from? Monty shuddered: it must have gone right through … It must have been the first man he saw, because he had shot the second one on the floor.

Something glinted at him in the shattered mirror, and Monty spun round. Nothing there. He looked back at the mirror. He had not noticed before, but small gobbets of bloody material were spattered over it. What were they anyway? Oh, God … Monty turned away, and threw up over the corpses.

It was not meant to be like this. He had not envisaged how messy things could be, nor his own revulsion. But there was no turning back now. He had to finish matters, and there was no time to linger. He became aware of a draught from somewhere. He went into the dining room and closed the French window through which the intruders had come, looking about outside as he did so. There was nothing there. Now, he must clean up.

Monty somehow managed to close his mind to the awfulness of his task. He became entangled in the filthy and furtive realities of 'grossly disproportionate force.' Thinking of the bullet in the mirror, he wondered if either of the shots he had fired into the second man had gone right through as well. He stripped the body and examined it for exit wounds. There were none, but an evil-looking flick-knife fell out of the man's trouser pocket during the procedure. Thank goodness he'd got the gun in time, rationalised Monty. For good measure, he checked the floor near and under the body for bullets and then, finding none, he stripped the first body.

In making his plans for removing dead intruders, Monty had obtained some rope, two thick white dust sheets, several lengths of rusty anchor chain and some motorcycle shackle locks. He fetched this equipment from his garage and went into the garden.

On top of the uncoiled rope, Monty laid out the dust sheets next to 'No Comebacks,' sitting on her trailer, then placed the chains across them. With strength he never thought he had, Monty dragged the cadavers out of his home one after the other on his bloodstained rug, and put both on top of the chains.

By now, Monty could scarcely bear to look at the Glock. He threw the repellent gun, its bullets, silencer, spare magazine and magazine loader, as well as the flick-knife, next to one of the bodies. Round these he tightly locked lengths of chain, with the dust sheets roped on top, completely enveloping their contents. The packages resembled two enormous white sausages, which Monty manhandled into the boat and crammed into its cabin. Every sound seemed to Monty capable of alerting half the neighbourhood, or reawakening the corpses. He prayed the dust sheets were good mufflers.

Then Monty got a Stanley knife from the garage and used it to rip out the stained stair carpet, which he piled in the middle of his large and, fortunately, secluded rear garden. Back and forth he went, as he placed his other ruined and tainted possessions on top of the carpet; the rug, mirror and table, plus the clothes he had stripped from the bodies. He covered the mound with some old sacking, weighted down with bricks. Then Monty concluded his labours by scrubbing and sweeping his home clean of all detectable traces of the event.

When he finished at six o'clock, Monty was filthy and shattered. He thrust his own soiled clothes into the washing machine, turned it on, showered, and went to bed, where he slept badly for the next six hours.

Monty knew the rest of the day had really planned itself. A quick slice of toast. Then, burn the carpet, clothing and other debris which might link the bodies to him and enable their identification should they ever be discovered. Book a glazier to fix the pane in his French window broken by the intruders. Finally, at dusk, launch 'No Comebacks' at Seahaven and deliver her cargo to Davy Jones.

On his way downstairs, Monty noticed tiny blood spots on the wall near where the mirror had been. "Must have missed them last night," he mused, as he wiped them off. He looked round: the hallway was clean. After a restorative cup of coffee and his toast, Monty went outside. The day was fine and still – perfect for his evening voyage. Monty set about making a bonfire of the stained carpet and other artefacts, using plenty of wood and paraffin to get the blaze going. Then he nervously checked 'No Comebacks.' Her chained passengers were still as he had left them.

The fire burned longer than Monty would have thought possible from its size, and smoked copiously. Even when, at last, the fire was nearly out, it still generated clouds of acrid smoke. Burning carpet, with rubbery underlay, was quite a business, reasoned Monty. Even so, the volume of smoke seemed out of all proportion. What was more, the smoke did not disperse, but spread slowly like a shroud over the surrounding neighbourhood. Its smell reminded

Monty of a cremation he once attended, when smoke drifted over the mourners.

Towards the end of the fire's life, Monty's doorbell rang. On opening the front door, he saw a figure standing outside enveloped in smoke, a vile-smelling cloud of which wafted into the house. The low sun had turned the smoke into a luminous aura round the figure, and for a few moments Monty could not tell who or what it was. Then his eyes adjusted, and Monty nearly fainted with shock to find himself face to face with a policeman.

"Montague Dewar?"

"Y-y-yes," stammered Monty. The figure stared him straight in the eye for what seemed an eternity, and Monty broke into a cold sweat of fear.

"I've come about your fire and the smoke, Sir. Not very considerate, having such a foul-smelling fire on a day like this."

"Er, er, no; I suppose it isn't," Monty answered, cautiously.

"Then please put it out, Sir," the policeman commanded.

"I think it is about out already," replied Monty.

"You won't mind if I take a look, then, Sir."

Monty did mind. He minded as though his life depended on minding. But he could not object. Hoarsely, he stuttered,

"N-no. I'll show you."

He led his unwanted guest into the back garden. As he had said, the fire was almost out, with only small fragments of material still unburned. The policeman asked,

"What was on it? Looks like bits of carpet."

"Yes, it was."

"You should dispose of rubbish properly, Sir, where it won't cause trouble."

Monty said, "yes. Yes, next time I'll do that."

"Good. Rubbish must be disposed of …" The policeman paused, then said, "… properly."

"I'll do that."

"You don't want …" Again the policeman paused, then added menacingly, "… trouble, do you?" He started back towards the road. Watching the man go, Monty thought there was something odd about him, but in his disturbed state almost everything seemed unusual.

His visitor's route took him close to 'No Comebacks,' which he paused to study. Monty stood stock-still, horrified. But the policeman only said, "nice boat," as he disappeared into the strangely pervasive smoke. It was all Monty could do to stagger into the house.

As he entered, he noticed more blood spots on the stairway wall. Monty was sure he had thoroughly purged the area earlier. Still, he had been highly emotional and may have overlooked them. They were very small. Monty cleaned them off before preparing to leave for Seahaven. He hitched 'No Comebacks' to his Land Rover, checking her contents were secure. Then he went to lock his house. Just as he was about to turn the key, the telephone rang. Monty cursed and went back inside.

"Yes? Dewar here."

At first, there was no reply, until a male voice said slowly,

"Liked the smoke, did you?"

Monty started a little.

"Who is this?"

There was no immediate response. Then, "you must have liked the smoke."

"Who are you?" demanded Monty. "Look, I'm sorry if the smoke bothered you, but the police have already been round. It won't happen again, I promise. Did you call the police?"

There was another long pause. Finally, the voice said,

"I'm sure you liked the smoke." And the line clicked off.

Monty stared at the 'phone, before replacing the handset nervously. He did not like the caller's tone at all. The smoke had obviously been much worse than he thought, but he had apologised, and had been admonished by the police to boot. Who on earth would be calling him like that? The voice was familiar. Monty had heard it recently, but tantalisingly could not place where. It must belong to a neighbour he did not know particularly well, who was now upset about the bonfire.

Dusk was fading into night as Monty finally left for Seahaven. Nervous about his unusual load, he drove slowly and carefully. He turned on the radio. Classic FM was his taste, and at that moment it was broadcasting Beethoven's Fifth Symphony. Monty turned the volume up, and tried to lose himself in the music.

On the dual carriageway just outside Seahaven, a siren jolted him out of his musical reverie. A police car was beside him, its blue lights flashing. The officer in the front passenger seat had wound down his window and was shouting at Monty. Over the racket of his engine and the radio, Monty could not make out the words, but the intent was unmistakeable.

Monty's strength left him. It was all he could do to apply enough pressure to the brake pedal to stop the Land Rover, which drifted to a halt under a streetlight. The patrol car pulled in behind.

A burly policeman in a luminous yellow jacket appeared at Monty's window.

"Would you mind turning your engine and radio off and getting out of the vehicle, Sir?" asked the policeman. "Leave your lights on, please."

Monty shakily complied.

"Come round to the back of your trailer, please," commanded the policeman.

A terrified Monty followed obediently. He noticed the second officer in the police car, watching them.

"What do you see here?" asked the first policeman, pointing to the back of the trailer.

Monty followed the officer's finger. At first, in his shock, he saw nothing wrong. Then he did. His offside tail-light was dead.

"Oh," he said.

"Yes," said the policeman. "A faulty rear light is an offence."

"It was working when I set out. I always check the trailer lights when I hitch up. The bulb must have blown since I started."

The policeman tapped the light with his knuckle. The bulb blinked on. Monty could not understand it. As usual, he had tapped the lights too, before setting off, and there had been nothing wrong.

"Going far?"

"No, just to Seahaven Sailing Club," blurted Monty, regretting his candour the instant the words left his lips.

"Well, get it fixed tomorrow, Sir."

"Yes, yes, of course. I will."

"Good," said the policeman. He moved back towards the patrol car, then turned and studied 'No Comebacks,' brightly lit in both the streetlight and the car's headlights, with her silent passengers. Monty felt a clammy vice of cold fear grip him. After what seemed like a week, the policeman said, "nice boat," adding "good night, Sir" as he got back into the patrol car. The car followed Monty for the rest of his journey.

Relieved to finally see the back of the car, Monty let himself through the Sailing Club gate using his pass key. The gate being locked was a good sign nobody was there, which was confirmed when Monty scouted past the buildings along the muddy track to the slipway. Perfect. With his now well-oiled technique, he launched 'No Comebacks' and sailed into the dark and welcoming English Channel.

In his planning, Monty had already considered depth, tides, currents, fishing and other activity and established where best to sink bodies. Now, in his time of need, he went straight there using his GPS navigation equipment.

The night was cold and moonless, with a slight swell running. When he arrived at his planned dumping ground, Monty checked there were no other boats nearby, then heaved the two chained corpses overboard. As the second went straight down with a gentle splash, Monty sighed, partly with the effort and partly from relief. He then washed down the interior of the boat, made himself a black coffee, and went back to Seahaven. There, he winched 'No Comebacks' onto her trailer and, for good measure, hosed her down. He also checked his lights again.

They were working perfectly.

Monty drove home in silence. His house was completely dark and, unlike the Channel, the very opposite of welcoming. To his surprise, wisps of smoke were still hanging around, and when he got out of the Land Rover, it seemed to cling to him. He rounded the building and inspected the bonfire. Though warm, the fire seemed out, but he soaked it with the garden hose anyway. Entering the house, his footsteps sounded hollow on the bare hallway floorboards. Inside, there was a strong smoky smell. It was both sickly and acrid at the same time.

Again, Monty had to clean tiny blood spots off the stairway wall. He was sure he had found them all before. But he was not himself. In the undiluted hell of the last twenty-four hours, he must have missed them.

Monty had a bowl of cornflakes, and went to bed.

After a few hours' troubled sleep, he was wakened by the telephone in the hallway. He stumbled half-asleep downstairs to answer it. A new, sunny day had broken. He picked up the handset.

"Dewar here."

There was no reply at first. Then, the same male voice which had called the day before said, "smoke and water. You like water too."

Monty jumped.

"Who the hell are you?" he shouted.

"You must like water, too."

"What do you mean, like water? If you 'phone again, I'll call … I'll call …" But Monty knew he would not call the police.

"Sure. I'm sure you like water." And the caller

ended the call. Monty sat down heavily on the chair next to the telephone, resting his hand on the table on which the instrument stood. He wiped his brow with the other hand.

What was going on? A neighbour could have complained about the smoke, and be playing a game with him, but this was going a bit far. Why would the neighbour have added water to the disturbing conversation. What water was he talking about? The water he sprayed on the bonfire? Or, and with this thought Monty felt a morbid horror creep over him, could he mean the English Channel and the water Monty used to wash the boat? No-one could have known about either of his uses of water unless … unless … unless he was being watched. Yes, that must be it. Someone was watching him, maybe following him. Must be. But who? Who? Maybe, yes, no, perhaps … yes, yes, there must have been someone else with the two intruders. Someone who stayed outside, but saw or heard the whole thing. Someone who was now watching him and trying to scare him. Well, Monty was not going to be scared. No, not Montague Dewar. Scared? No, no … but. This third man might try to do something else. He might return to do goodness-knows-what.

Monty was scared. Really scared. He stood up, and the hand he had rested on the telephone table felt strange. He looked at it. The palm was covered in dark, sticky, blood. Monty gasped, flung open the front door and ran into his garden.

Unable to recover from his fright, Monty spent the day away from his house. Home was no longer a cosy refuge from the world outside. It had been transformed into a place of dark and mutinous brooding, now associated indelibly in his mind with horror and fear. He would have to move, and passed much of the day in Wetherford investigating estate agents. He also went to a garage to deal with the elusive fault in his trailer lights. The garage could find nothing wrong, and Monty returned late in the afternoon.

From the front door, Monty looked nervously inside, not knowing quite what to expect. In particular, he listened for intruders and looked for blood spots, but he heard no-one and saw no more spots. Venturing further in, he made a cup of tea, and was settling down to drink it when the doorbell rang. Still carrying his tea, he answered the door.

Standing outside was another policeman. There was a patrol car in the road. Monty dropped his tea and stared in guilt, fear and amazement.

"Is there anything the matter, Sir?" asked the policeman.

Monty chuckled mirthlessly.

"No, no … someone just walked over my grave," he said, in the absence of anything better. Then, after shaking his head, he added,

"It's just that until yesterday I hadn't spoken to a policeman for years. You never see any here; that's the problem." He laughed nervously, thinking how different his situation would now be if policemen had been more prominent in the locality. "But within the space of twenty-four hours, I have had three separate conversations, with a different copper each time. It just struck me as very odd to see you there."

"I'm sorry to have startled you, Sir," said the policeman soothingly. "May I ask what the other two conversations were about?" Monty told him.

"That is strange," said the policeman. "My colleague and I were the only officers on duty in this area yesterday, and complaints about smoke or anything else would have come to us. If you can spare a minute or two, I'll check." Monty nodded, and the policeman used his personal radio to ask about complaints logged the day before. After a brief pause, Monty heard the operator confirming no complaint about smoking bonfires had been received, with the aside that it would not have been a high priority even if one had. Monty felt his barely-suppressed fear rising again, hammering at his sanity. The policeman had just clicked his radio off when, with a sudden flash of insight, Monty suddenly realised why yesterday's policeman had seemed odd.

"Trainers!" he almost shouted. He paused. "The constable who complained about smoke wore dark trainers, not policeman's beetle-crushers!"

The policeman stared at him silently for several seconds.

"Well, Sir, it sounds to me as though someone might be impersonating a police officer, which is a serious offence. Can you describe him in more detail?" Monty tried, but his recollection was sketchy.

"Hmm," said the policeman. "Leave it with us, Sir. Let us know if you see the man again. Now, the reason I called … There's nothing to worry about, but on driving past yesterday we noticed a white van parked in the gateway to a field round the corner. When we came back today, it hadn't moved and something told me I should check our database. The van came up as having been stolen in Islington last week. So I called to ask if you had seen anyone acting suspiciously. A possibly bogus policeman would certainly count, but has there been anyone else, or has anything else out of the ordinary happened?"

Monty stared at him, and experienced an almost insuperable urge to laugh at this grotesque question. But he managed to say, "nothing I haven't anticipated, really."

"Nothing? Someone you don't know wandering about – other than the strange policeman?"

"If I see anyone, I'll let you know."

"Thank you, Sir." The policeman turned to leave. Sitting on her trailer, shining in the sun, 'No Comebacks' caught his eye.

"Oh, yes," he said, appreciatively, "nice boat." Then he left.

I'm a fool, thought Monty, as he mopped up the dropped tea. They must have come in the van. They couldn't have walked, and couldn't have stolen much without a vehicle. Stupid, stupid, stupid. How had he forgotten something so obvious? And he began wondering about the third man, the watcher, the man on the 'phone, whoever it was. Why hadn't he driven away? Of course, one of the others must have had the keys.

"No wonder he's annoyed," thought Monty facetiously. "He had to walk home!"

But the relief of this shaft of whimsy did not last long, and Monty relapsed into a state of deep, deep apprehension and regret.

When he went to bed that night, Monty could not sleep. All kinds of terrible possibilities ebbed and flowed in his mind: the congealing blood on the table and walls upset him very badly. He was trying to determine what he should do about the anonymous telephone caller, when he heard a noise downstairs.

He looked at his bedside clock. Two-fifteen. He listened hard. He was certain he heard his French window being opened. Seconds passed. He heard more noises, in the hallway. And he remembered, petrified, that he no longer had the gun. He opened his mouth, to breathe more quietly so he could hear better. And what he heard was a now-familiar voice saying softly, no longer on any telephone,

"Upstairs first for some fun. Then we do the rest."

Monty's Land Rover and empty trailer at Seahaven Sailing Club did not arouse suspicion until they had been there for three weeks. Although good practice and club rules required members to leave a voyage plan behind when they set sail, Monty had often ignored this and vanished in 'No Comebacks' for two weeks at a time. Eventually, having failed to get any response from Monty either on his radio, his mobile, or his home phone, the club Secretary reported the vehicle's presence to the police. They had themselves been wondering about Monty's whereabouts, after one of his employees had reported him missing. They had inspected his home, but found little of interest except Monty's used and unmade bed and a peculiar smoky smell. The Land Rover advanced their investigations, though not very far. No traces of Monty could be found, nor of his boat. A general request was issued along the English and French Channel coasts for any news of 'No Comebacks' but nothing was heard. In their files, the police recorded their belief that 'No Comebacks' had come to grief at sea and Monty had perished with her.

Two years later, a group of scuba divers found 'No Comebacks' whilst looking for the wreck of a seventeenth century French warship off Dungeness. They inspected her, marked her position with GPS and nominated one of their number to report the findings to HM Coastguard, Seahaven.

It was definitely a case for the police, the diver said, because the wreck contained skeletons, tightly wrapped in chains secured with motorcycle shackle locks, and that wasn't normal with wrecks. Nor was their discovery of a gun with a silencer and a lot of bullets, and what may have been a flick-knife.

The Coastguard agreed. "How many skeletons?" he asked.

"Three," said the diver, who must have been a wit with a taste for sculpture, because he added, "all wrapped together in the same chains, having a group cuddle. Rather like the Three Graces."

The Coastguard knew the Seahaven police well, and made his report in person.

The policeman at the desk noted down the details, then remarked that he often watched the comings and goings down at the harbour.

"I remember 'No Comebacks,'" he said.

He paused, and added, rather wistfully, "nice boat."

THE LAMPLIGHTER

"Probability," said Mervyn with certainty, "is why I became convinced Barrington's was haunted. There was no other explanation." He picked up a wad of paper and waved it at his guests to emphasize the point.

Mervyn Drake would not have made this revelation to anyone other than close family or friends. He considered the modern world left little room for spiritual matters in most peoples' minds, except maybe as televisual entertainment. Such things were largely elbowed out by materialism, technology and science. Expressing belief in the ghostly, other than as a topic of idle drinking conversation, risked labels which would do no good whatsoever towards enhancing social or employment mobility. So Mervyn chose his sister and brother-in-law to witness his admission to supernatural conviction.

"Probability," mimicked his brother-in law, "suggests you are as nuts as your sister has always said you are."

"Sorry, Ben. Your amateur psychiatric assessment does not deter me. I intend to prove to you that something very strange indeed happened here which came to a conclusion this very morning."

"May we take notes?" asked his sister sarcastically. "We need to make the best possible case to have you carted away and get our mitts on your estate."

"Note away, Elsa, if it makes you feel better. Straight to the point as usual because, believe it or not, your comment is directly relevant to the story I am about to tell." Mervyn paused. "Anyone like a refill? No-one's driving tonight, and if necessary we'll sober you both up before breakfast with a refreshing dip in the briny."

Two heads eagerly nodded agreement to having their glasses replenished, and Bridget Drake circled the room, armed with a bottle of whisky and a jug of water.

"Right, then," said Mervyn, as whisky glasses were resampled and then put down. "Ready to rock?"

"Get on with it," said Elsa.

"According to Sherlock Holmes," started Mervyn, "when one has eliminated the impossible, whatever remains, however improbable, must be the truth. He should, of course, have said 'must contain the truth,' but I propose to apply his maxim to the conundrum of our bathroom light anyway."

"Your bathroom light?" guffawed Ben, who had expected to hear something less prosaic. "What's wrong with it?"

"It hasn't been a normal, contented, bathroom light." Mervyn glanced at his sceptical relatives, thought for a moment, then continued. "Before I go on, I suppose I had better give you some background

243

about our early involvement with Barrington's. I may not have mentioned this before, but I had serious reservations about buying this house."

"Mortgage beyond you?" asked Ben, competitively.

Mervyn ignored him. "I thought it might be haunted. I even delayed exchanging contracts because of it, though I was a little nervous about telling my solicitor why."

"Not surprised," retorted Ben.

"As it turned out, he was very sympathetic. He told me he had encountered similar problems with property transactions before. In his view, it was most important for buyers to be happy with their intended dwellings."

Mervyn paused as he recalled his solicitor's cramped little office, with its worn carpet and mismatched furniture.

"He even told me a story of his own, about a young man in his twenties who bought a flat in Eastbourne. You know, one of those Edwardian villa conversions. He developed doubts at the last minute, delayed purchase for a couple of weeks, and then bought it anyway, with disastrous results."

"What happened?" asked Elsa.

"Two days after he moved in, he went back to the solicitor and said he had to sell. He'd lasted just two nights in the flat, during both of which something cold, large, wet and invisible got into bed with him at about two in the morning. The first night he'd been out on the tiles and thought he must have dreamed it. The second night he was sober. It was impossible to stay. He shot out of the flat, found a hotel and never went back, even getting the solicitor to supervise the move." Mervyn paused again. "Which must have cost him a bit," he reflected, ruefully. There were knowing nods all round.

"Anyway, to get back to Barrington's. Before contracts were exchanged, I admit I did have a few sleepless nights of my own worrying about taking on such a large old building. And I suppose that may have been part of my reason for delaying. Maintenance costs certainly mattered as they can be very high with a property like this. You can see from the fireplaces and beams, parts of the house are early Tudor and the rest, apart from the abominable 1950s shop-front, dates from the mid-1700s."

Mervyn remarked how excited he and Bridget had been on first seeing Barrington's, with its mish-mash of rooms, including three with Georgian panelling, spread over four uneven floors. It had plenty of character and was only two hundred yards away from Hastings Old Town beach. What was more, it was surprisingly cheap considering its location and size.

Although they had not wanted to lose the chance of owning such an apparent gem, Mervyn related how, during the time it took to complete surveys and all the paraphernalia intrinsic to house-buying, other thoughts about the place had begun to creep into his mind. There had been something just a little odd about the first-floor landing and the bathroom leading off it, something he could not quite explain …

"I began to wonder," said Mervyn, "whether Barrington's was haunted. I therefore decided to test this theory by laying a verbal trap for the owners. We arranged another viewing. Whilst we were there, I suddenly asked them a question, without any warning. I said, "are there any ghosts?""

Elsa gurgled. "Clever, that, Mervyn. You always were a master of subtlety and guile. I bet they fell straight into that one." Ben smirked. Even Bridget smiled, slightly to one side, so Mervyn could not see.

"You may mock, you may mock," replied Mervyn, when the mirth subsided. "As a matter of fact, they did, although I did not realise it at the time. There was a very short pause after my question. Then the owner, Mrs. Vett, said rather wistfully, 'well, all these old places have their ghosts, don't they?'"

"It was very clever," explained Mervyn. "She knew we knew she had spent about thirty years of her life in the house and had raised three children there. She wanted to imply 'ghosts' meant 'memories,' and that was the message we took away. Beguiled by Barrington's quaintness and with house prices still rising, we went ahead with the purchase. It was only after we moved in that we realised Mrs. Vett probably intended both interpretations of her answer."

"It's obvious to me," said Elsa, "the last thing anyone selling a house would do is tell a buyer their home is haunted. Though I suppose an honest person would face a serious dilemma. 'No' would be a lie, but 'Yes' could lose the sale. So she would obfuscate, like your vendor. On second thoughts, I take back my comment about your question. It wasn't as stupid as it first seemed. But you were, for ignoring the implication of her answer."

"Yes, yes, we know that." Mervyn grimaced. "We didn't notice anything initially," he continued, "what with all the comings and goings of moving in, and with all the workmen around. But as soon as we had settled down a little, I began to observe the bathroom light on the first floor often glowed merrily, even when the room was empty. For safety, it's got a ceiling switch operated by a string, as many bathroom lights have. At first, I just kept turning the light off, but I found it on again and again even when there was no-one else around."

"Could it have been to do with your nightly barrel of Scotch?" Ben grinned.

Mervyn ignored him.

"Eventually, I asked Bridget, and she …"

"Yes," interrupted his wife, "I'd visited the local museum, as I wanted to find out more about the history of the area. It was fascinating, full of seafaring tales of derring-do. Smuggling was rampant in the town, right up to quite recent times. Everyone did it. Even the pub two or three doors down the road has an old smugglers' tunnel leading to the East Hill. The museum had lots of pictures, too," she said, adding excitedly, "Barrington's was clearly visible. You wouldn't believe it, but before all the Georgian developments this was one of the largest properties that nestled between the East and West Hills."

"After a time," butted in Mervyn, "Bridget convinced herself the house was haunted by a 'flashing' ghost signalling smugglers who had hauled contraband from the beach up onto the West Hill. But she didn't tell me at first."

"A 'flashing' ghost?" asked Ben. "You surely don't mean …"

"Not that kind of flasher!" exclaimed Bridget. "A light-flasher. The bathroom window, you see," she continued, "is visible even today from the top of the West Hill across the valley over scores of places where miscreants could lurk to watch for signals. What with getting up so early every day to get to

London, I wondered initially if I was leaving the light on myself. You know, darting around being careless. I soon realised, though, neither of us were to blame. But I desperately wanted to avoid Mervyn having his earlier suspicions about the house confirmed. To keep him quiet, I began making fun of my own suspicions about smuggling signals, saying I was probably being very silly and that I must be leaving the light on from time to time unwittingly."

"Well," continued Mervyn, "nothing else occurred, so I accepted Bridget's carelessness as the reason and left it at that. About a year later, the bathroom light switch jammed in the 'Off' position and had to be replaced. But even the new switch made no difference to Bridget. She still regularly left the light on. At least, that's what I thought, but then something else happened."

"Really?" asked Ben. "Did a merciful but invisible force try to hang you with the string?"

"No, you idiot. My foot went through a floorboard on the top floor, and I found something. Although the boards are very old up there, with large gaps between them and innumerable repairs, I hadn't realised any of them were rotten. But, one day, yours truly's right foot found a rotten spot and went through into a gap underneath, twisting my ankle in the process."

"What did you find?" Elsa sounded a little more curious than before. Despite her teasing, she knew her brother well enough to tell when he was serious.

"It was a book." said Mervyn. "A third edition of A.W. Eley's Morse Code Manual, 1941. I was too busy cursing about my ankle to pay much attention to the book at first. But there was something rather strange about where it was. It was sitting on top of a thick layer of what looked like dried, ground-up cow dung strewn between the joists. The mixture later turned out to contain sea-shells, chicken bones and hundreds of tiny pieces of paper torn from a Bible. When I came to fix the floorboard, I was all for getting rid of the stuff, but Bridget wouldn't let me and we left it there. Anyway, eventually I hobbled downstairs with the manual, and later, whilst absorbing a restorative Scotch, a thought struck me."

"What? You? A thought?" teased Ben, adding, "alright, go on, go on," when he, too, saw Mervyn was in earnest.

"Well, it was one of those odd connections one makes sometimes. Maybe the alcohol was instrumental, but I put together the flashing bathroom light, the date and nature of the book and the proximity of this house to the sea. Then I wondered whether Bridget had spoken truth in jest and whether the light really had been used for signalling, using Morse Code, maybe during the Second World War."

"Hmm," pondered Ben, "you mean for spying, or military purposes, rather than smuggling?"

"Possibly. But let me continue."

They all looked at him expectantly.

"I began to consider how the light could be used with Morse Code. The manual was full of detail about dits and dahs which enabled me to work out that transmitting letters of the alphabet by flashing a light, say, once a day would take over a week per letter. I reckoned if the bathroom light was being supernaturally flashed in code, I could tell after a couple of weeks, because some letters would have been formed. Also, I hadn't noticed whether the light ever came on more than once a day. If it did, I could decipher messages more quickly. The odd thing was, I didn't feel at all nervous that my pre-purchase suspicions about the house being haunted might have been justified after all. And when I mentioned my theory to her, neither did Bridget."

"No," said Bridget, "although I should have felt guilty about the light."

"Why?" asked Elsa.

"I don't really think I ever left it on by mistake. It is not something I would do. I had never done it before in any of the other houses we lived in. I just hadn't wanted Mervyn to worry about Barrington's being haunted when he was terribly preoccupied working so hard to pay for the place."

"That was very kind of you," said Mervyn. "But it should have been obvious something supernatural must have been turning the light on. There was no other explanation, Dr. Watson. And now I know it was a ghost."

"Why? I don't follow at all," said Ben, quizzically. "It could have been a fault, or anything."

"I don't think so. For a start, Bridget and I are the only occupants of this house. We have lived in seven houses before. They all had drawstring bathroom lights, and neither of us ever left them on. Why just in this house, and why so often? Even replacing the old switch made no difference. If the light came on due to a fault bypassing the switch somehow, why did it always turn off the moment we pulled the switch again? As I said, eliminate the impossible …"

"Hmm. I'm not convinced," said Ben. "And how can you say you now know it was a ghost? Was that communicated to you by Morse Code on your erratic light?"

"Yes."

Ben looked at his wife. "If I'd known about him before I married you," he said, "I would have had my doubts. This sort of thing often runs in families."

"Let him get on with it, Ben," said Elsa. "I want to hear the story."

"We decided to record the frequency of the light going on." Mervyn then displayed a well-thumbed green notepad. "It took eleven days before my weird idea began to look more likely." He opened the pad.

"This is what happened. On each of the first three days, the light came on once. Then it skipped a day, coming back on again on the fifth day. Nothing on the sixth day, then on again on the seventh. A three-day gap followed and then it came on again on the eleventh day. I was now fairly certain I was onto something. Ten days later I was sure, and then it was proved in a most dramatic way."

"Well, tell us, tell us," urged his sister, excitedly. "What did it mean?"

"In the second ten days, there was another sequence of ons and offs. Never more than one 'on' per day. From the manual I had so painfully discovered under the floorboards, the sequence in the first seven days was Morse for the letter 'D' followed by a space between letters and, on the eleventh day, the beginning of another letter. You can imagine how we felt, but it could have been a coincidence and we carried on. The sequence in the next ten days confirmed a second letter, 'R.'"

"DR? Was that it? Two letters in three weeks? Your flasher wasn't about to transmit the works of

Shakespeare, was he? Did you get any further than just DR? Drivel? Dry rot? Dracula?" Ben was having fun.

"I did get further, a lot further, but not by decoding the light. On the twenty-first day, I had a bath." Mervyn paused, and was rewarded by three smiling faces.

"Oh, I, well, of course, I do bathe more often," he grinned. "You …"

"Don't let us put you off," said Ben.

"I had a bath and, as I often do, I fell asleep. Only, as it turned out, I did so whilst pondering the question of the light, wishing I could find out more about what was turning the thing on. That point is crucial. What happened next is still incredible to me. I fell asleep, and started to dream about the light. But also," Mervyn paused again, "about the Lamplighter, whose name Bridget and I had imaginatively chosen mainly because of what he was doing. We also called him that because, in the twitten along the side of our house, there is an old Victorian gas streetlight, converted to electricity, and the name seemed appropriate."

"Twitten?" inquired Elsa.

"Sorry. It's a local word for a passageway," said Mervyn.

"I don't usually remember dreams." said Ben.

"Neither do I," replied Mervyn. "But in this case I certainly did and I recorded every part of it afterwards." He waved the wad of papers again. "Then I told Bridget." Bridget nodded, but said nothing. "Anyway, I'm going to use my script as a prompt." Mervyn then told them about his dream.

"Good evening," said the short, wiry man standing next to the toilet. "Nice bath? No, don't get up for me. Mind if I put the lid down and sit here?" He lowered the lid and sat down without waiting for a reply.

Mervyn stared at the intruder, open-mouthed. Oddly, he felt no alarm, only astonishment and annoyance at the interruption of his bath by an unknown man, wearing what looked like a naval uniform, sitting on his closed toilet.

"Who the hell are you?"

"Oh, don't say that! Ask who I am, by all means, but please! No references to … to that place."

"Well, who are you then?"

"I like the name you chose for me, the Lamplighter."

"You're … a ghost?"

"Ghost, spectre, apparition, messenger from another world, figment of your imagination, hallucination … what you will."

"You don't look like a ghost to me. Aren't you supposed to be able to see through ghosts? You're a solid as the Tower of London."

"Ah, simple word association: ghosts, Tower of London. Can't you do any better? Yes, I look solid now but I can also appear misty, transparent, swirling around in bits … anything I like. You wouldn't appreciate some of the disguises in my extensive repertoire, so I'm looking as I was the last time I breathed fresh air."

After all the months wondering whether there was or was not a ghost in Barrington's, Mervyn was not going to waste the opportunity to complain at the perpetrator.

"Perhaps you'd like to tell me what you are doing here. You've had me and my wife troubled for ages, fooling about with the lights like that. What's going on?"

"Hmm. Sorry, but it was the only way."

"The only way to what?"

"To engineer the conversation we're having now."

"I don't understand. If you wanted to talk, why didn't you come straight out and do it?"

The Lamplighter studied Mervyn for a few seconds. Then he said, "you clearly know nothing about the afterlife; I'd better give you a quick idea. Then I'll tell you what I want you to do."

"Do? Why should I do anything? I've never met you before and know nothing about you. Why should I do anything, other than have you exorcised?"

"If you don't help, you'll meet other … um, colleagues who are rather more persuasive. And you wouldn't want to meet them, I can tell you. Can I continue?" Without waiting for a reply, the Lamplighter resumed his thread.

"Firstly, you think you are awake, but in reality you are dreaming. 'Reality' is not quite the word, though. In this dream you can see me and talk to me. We are absolutely private. No-one will hear, as I am merely in your dream. Unlike normal dreams, though, in this one our conversation will be perfectly lucid. Also, when you wake up, you will remember every event and every word spoken, because I have a task for you and you will need to know the details.

"Your dream will only have lasted a few minutes in real time. Having heard you snoring, your wife is, in fact coming up the stairs right now to wake you up. Your dream will be over by the time she gets to the door, and she won't hear a thing, other than your snores. The bathwater won't even have gone cold."

"Very considerate of you," said Mervyn. "By the way," he added. "If it's not too much trouble, as you won't tell me who you are … er, were … could you tell me what you were? Navy, was it?"

"Merchant Navy, ignorant boy. I was a radio operator on a cruise liner. That is until, one fine day in 1970, when we were island-hopping around the Caribbean, someone you'll hear more of later cut my throat and heaved me overboard as shark food. It's not much fun watching yourself being eaten by sharks even if you are already dead. Would you like to see what I looked like when they had finished? No? Oh, well; never mind.

"Anyway, the first thing you've got to know is, ghosts have limited powers. When we first get here, by which I mean where I really am, not where you see me, we are awarded two powers, although they can be changed later. I've got lights and dreams now. No choice about the matter. You can see why. Imagine the chaos if we were all allowed the same powers we had on earth – there wouldn't be any difference between us, would there? Wouldn't be any point in being dead. Or alive, depending on your point of view.

"It's most unfair – I can type like lightning, and these new computer-thingies look dead easy to me, but I'm forbidden and there you are. Can't even speak to you, or appear, except in dreams."

Mervyn thought his visitor looked rather sad about this. "Why couldn't you have just appeared in a dream right from the start, instead of all this light nonsense?" he asked. "Seems odd to me."

"There are rules. Since the last re-organisation our system has been modelled on the Indian Civil Service. No idea why – something to do with fakirs, perhaps. It's a typical bureaucracy. Rules for everything. The over-riding one, for example, which shapes all others, insists no-one alive should ever be able to prove beyond doubt to others also not yet dead that ghosts exist. Proof would upset the relationships between the earthly world where you are, the one I inhabit, and the places we all eventually go to.

"Besides, if I could have started straight in on you with a dream, I might just as well have been given the power of appearance, you see. So, for a ghost to get in on a dream, the dreamer first has to go to sleep and voluntarily start dreaming about something relevant to the ghost. It's the rule. Then the ghost can muscle in and get his message across. The problem is, there's often no reason for sleepers to start dreaming about things relevant to the ghost, because they don't know the ghost exists. Chicken and egg. Thus I had to find a way to let you know I was here. Hence the lights."

"I see," said Mervyn, pondering. Then he asked, "what were you spelling out on the light? I only got to DR."

"I was going to say "dream about the light" but you did it anyway after two letters. Well done. Saved a bit of time, I can tell you. Now, what was I going to say? Oh, yes. You know all those ghost stories where the ghost can do just about anything? Mostly nonsense.

"As I said, you start with two powers. You might be awarded another if you do something beyond the call of duty or chalk up a singular success, but generally you get an extra power for every two hundred years' service. Which means very few of us ever get more than eleven different powers. Powers are the mark of respect here, you know. Like dans in karate, the more you have the more senior you are. You wouldn't fool with an eleven-power ghost."

"Two hundred years sounds a very long time," mused Mervyn. "Don't you ever get bored? And why the eleven-power limit?"

"Dead bored, sometimes - ha ha ha ha! Sorry. Anyway, our time here is limited. Have you noticed ghost stories rarely mention really old ghosts? I mean those of people who lived a very long time ago? That's because after two thousand years, give or take, we are normally moved somewhere else. Up or down, usually. It depends on performance. We could be moved before then, if the authorities want.

"Some of us are recycled; you know, reincarnation? It's for cockups and doubtful cases. There could have been a misunderstanding or mistake here and someone arrives too soon, with the problem not spotted before the body has been cremated or whatnot. Got to be careful there.

"Sometimes, our admissions department detects a premature arrival and sends him back without checking what happened to the body. The result is ghosts drifting about on Earth with nothing to do, or people waking up six feet under. Nasty, and it leads to more trouble, because they've got to be calmed down when they get back here again. Therapy is sometimes required.

"Anyway, those who get here too early are sent back. And then there are some not considered mature enough for existence here. They are usually sent back for another shot at it, too."

"You were talking about powers." Mervyn tried to get his dream back on course.

"Was I? Oh, yes. Well, the rules about powers are strict. Appearing and walking about are treated as two separate powers here, and they can be restricted even further. And you get quotas. You know, you've got to haunt a specified place for a minimum number of times in a set period. I always feel sorry for the ancient monk who was empowered to appear, and also to walk about his old monastery, but wasn't allowed to adjust his walk to avoid a wall built about fifty years after he died.

"The poor chap had to walk through two feet of limestone every time he appeared. Terribly uncomfortable. After he'd been doing it for about a hundred and fifty years, he got his third power, and some half-wit in Operations said it should be the power of speech. Can you imagine? The world's only swearing ghost monk."

Mervyn smiled, and the Lamplighter continued.

"I had a similar problem at first, you know. Often, you will initially haunt the place where you died, with whatever powers have been allocated to you. Having been murdered on a ship and thrown over the side, I was awarded powers to appear and walk on the ship. Made sense at the time, and I did have fun interrupting the nookie in some of the cabins, but the ship was scrapped after a few years, so I couldn't haunt it. I was left in Limbo while Operations thought of something else. Limbo really exists, you know."

"I thought being in Limbo was just an expression for being left stranded," said Mervyn.

"Well that's where the expression comes from. It's

got a children's division, for those who snuff it before anyone can instruct them about spiritual matters, but mainly it's a sort of supernatural labour exchange. There are all sorts there, mainly hanging about as temps until something permanent comes along. Want to scare the pants off a skinflint? See if Limbo can come up with a tax inspector.

"Sometimes, Limbo can't provide the right candidate, and some sinner who deserves a thorough and appropriate fright doesn't get it, or Operations has to be content with a mismatch or a second-rater. Limbo always wants to find unemployed spirits useful work, because otherwise they can get restive and rebellious. The pressure to have them doing something can lead to problems, though. You can get a Borley Rectory situation."

"Borley Rectory?"

"Yes. It used to be the most haunted building in England. Some Limbo go-getter said 'let's ease the unemployment problem by sending some redundant Limbans to practise haunting for a while. Let's see if Ops will let us try that Borley place.' Well, they stuffed it with demented nuns, dodgy vicars and other assorted misfits with different powers, and then one day one of them got carried away and the whole place went up in smoke.

"Thereafter, they strengthened the corps of training spirits – funny word, 'corps,' in the circumstances, isn't it? Training here is patchy, I have to say, and some of us don't get it until we've actually started haunting, but the Borley affair rubbed in the need for a professional approach. All the old wisdom was thrown out with the last re-organisation. These young Turks; they think they know it all. You wouldn't believe the difficulties we have here in the spirit world."

"What has this got to do with me?" asked Mervyn. "You're wandering."

"You forgive me and I'll forgive the pun. It's been a long time since I had anyone living I could talk to … Anyway, after my ship was scrapped, Operations decided my powers should be more focussed on getting retribution for the so-and-so who dumped me on them, so they sent me here with a different pair.

"Maybe it was a sort of initiative test as well: 'let's see if he can sort things out with only lights and dreams, har, har, har.' That's how I wound up in this house, and I have spent the last few decades frustratingly trying to convince its residents I was not flashing lights at the population of Hastings for idle amusement."

"How irritating for you," commented Mervyn drily.

The Lamplighter ignored him. "Luckily for me," he continued, "you and Sven came along. Firstly, you are bright enough to take a hint, and secondly, Sven is a first-class rotter. Now, don't get me wrong. I don't mean he's bad news. I mean rotting things is one of his powers. In your case it was a floorboard, so your foot could go through it. Sorry about the ankle.

"Didn't you think it odd the wood should be rotten only in one place? I showed Sven just the right spot. He owed me one for a favour I did for him just before Operations sent me here. By flashing a car's headlights in Stockholm, I was able to cause an accident which killed the man who had raped Sven's daughter. Sven was delighted.

"Anyway, years ago I lost a copy of Eley's Morse

Code Manual. When I got here I saw where it was, and got the idea of using Morse on the light to signal the owners about my demise and what I wanted them to do. Problem was, they didn't understand. At first each of them blamed the other for leaving the light on. Then they replaced the switch.

"Finally, although they came to realise the light was not entirely under earthly command, they just accepted it. Neither of them ever dreamed about the light, though. Unimaginative pair. How I wished for extra powers!

"But then you came along and after Sven had done his stuff, it wasn't long before your foot went right to where the book was. And, praise be, you connected it with the light, tested your theory and dozed off here in the bath dreaming about it. Hence this chin-wag."

"Why pick the bathroom?" asked Mervyn.

"Why not?"

Before Mervyn could think of an answer to this, the Lamplighter continued his story.

"I'm sure I had a good reason when I chose it. There may have been better rooms, but don't forget we ghosts are just as bright or stupid on our plane as you are on yours. Like they say about the House of Commons. Its composition reflects the nature of the public it represents: some are public-spirited, some are morons, while others are crooks or downright evil.

"Well, it's the same with us. We've got our ration of moronic spectres, I can tell you. Oh, yes. Mostly in positions of authority, if you ask me, but there are plenty on the ground as well. And in it.

"There's one dunderhead, with the powers of appearance and wailing, who haunts a sewer in

Bradford, the one he drowned in around 1960, and he's been there daily ever since. The trouble is, the sewer is only two feet in diameter – he was swept into it in a storm and they only found him because he blocked it two hundred yards in. So apart from a few passing rats, no-one ever sees or hears him. Pointless. A real head case. We call him Drain Man. He should have told Operations and applied for a transfer." The Lamplighter paused, grinning.

Mervyn thought for a moment. Puzzled, he asked, "the Morse manual. You didn't lose it when you were, well, like you are now, did you? You must have been here in the flesh, as it were. Did you live here?"

"Smart fellow. Now we're getting to the reason I'm here. I lost the book when I was re-wiring the top floor. Nice place, near the sea, full of character, worth doing the odd repair here and there … Anyway, yes, this was indeed my house until my untimely decease. The guilty party was my half-brother, a genial gentleman who by my death was able to inherit Barrington's plus a hundred thousand pounds of my cash. The murder was not witnessed and, as he fed me to the sharks, no-one ever knew what'd happened to me.

"The shipping company and police both concluded I had fallen over the side. There was a cursory investigation, but as my relative and I had different fathers, there were no names on the passenger list connecting me to the blighter, even if he hadn't used an alias.

"Had the authorities suspected murder, they might have unmasked him, but they never got that far. Although he is now approaching old age, I want the so-and-so to spend the rest of his earthly days in misery, and I want you to help."

"Oh, no. As Sam Goldwyn of the MGM film company once said, include me out. It's not my business." Mervyn did not like the sound of the Lamplighter's intentions one little bit. But the Lamplighter looked at him coldly and without sympathy.

"I've made it your business. Life happens, and so does death. You can't avoid the inconveniences of either."

"Nope. No way am I going to help you. I'm sorry for what happened to you. Most unpleasant and unfair. But I'm not going to try to catch your … what the … ?"

Mervyn had been looking hard at the Lamplighter. Suddenly, the solid, matey Merchant Navy officer disappeared. The bathroom disappeared too, and Mervyn found himself leaning over the taffrail of a ship, mesmerised by the phosphorescent wake under an intensely starry and moonlit sky.

The green churning water seemed to stretch to infinity behind the ship, and to Mervyn the scene had the breath-catching quality and beauty of a still winter's night at home in his native Sussex. Yet, inconsistently, the night was very warm. Mervyn fuzzily pondered this inconsistency, and also another, which he could not at first identify. Of course. He had not been born in Sussex, but in Liverpool. Why had he thought of Sussex?

Before he could resolve this puzzle, a hand was violently slapped across his mouth, wrenching his head backwards. Almost simultaneously, he felt a violent pain, moving rapidly across his throat from under his left ear to the same position under his right ear.

The pain seemed overpowering. Mervyn wildly raised his right hand to his throat and felt blood coursing out of it. For a few seconds, he thrashed as violently and uselessly as a fish on a trawler's deck, but his assailant held him fast and, just before consciousness left him, he became aware of falling, falling, falling towards the cleansing, bubbling sea ...

"Do you want to experience the rest?" As suddenly as he left, Mervyn was back in his bath, and the Lamplighter was studying him from his perch on the toilet lid. Mervyn gibbered incoherently.

"Not very nice, was it? Now, before you make up your mind about helping, I would like to say you're really very lucky, getting me. You might think you have just suffered a very nasty insight, and so you have, but it could have been a lot worse. In tough retribution cases, the authorities here sometimes use P&P, and you wouldn't want to meet them, not if you have any sense.

"P&P stands for Poltergeists and Possessions. They are the shock troops, with special powers. There is always some wrong to be righted with them. They're an aggressive lot, and they're only used when all else has failed.

"But you'll be OK, provided you do what I tell you. If you don't, well, there would be another reminder from me and then it would be P&P all the way until you did the right thing or died of heart failure.

"P&P are specialists in stepping up pressure until they get results. With most people, they start with something like banging doors and having objects turn up where they hadn't been left. Then they work up through smashing crockery, hanging the cat or writing lurid messages in blood on mirrors, et cetera, et cetera, until they get to pulling you out of bed at three a.m. and throwing you in the pond, or taking control of your steering wheel whilst you're speeding on the M6. A brutal lot, but usually fair.

"They've got a sense of humour too. Operations wanted one bloke to dig up his garden where an illicitly-buried body, murdered by someone else, would be discovered. He didn't respond to a quiet haunt by the body's former occupant, and Operations got P&P in.

"This fellow was cheating on his wife with a girl who didn't know he was married, so P&P got him in a sort of amnesiac trance for a few minutes and had him write an invitation to the girl to spend Christmas with him at the family home. Arrive 9.00 p.m. Christmas Eve, it said.

"Well, P&P thought this trick too good to keep to themselves and they let lots of us into the secret, resulting in about a hundred ghosts spending two hours watching the ensuing fun and laughing themselves hoarse. After the two women had finished mauling Mr. Cheat and each other they both left the house in complete indignation. The children went with Cheat's wife. It only took another short haunt by the murdered soul telling Cheat how his Christmas had been arranged, and how to avoid any further difficulties, to persuade him to get the shovel out there and then.

"As a bonus, Cheat's neighbours spotted him playing gravedigger. He had to spend Christmas week explaining to sceptical police officers in dingy interview rooms why he had been disinterring a body in his garden at midnight on Christmas Eve. Yes, we do get time off and some fun, sometimes – it's not just haunt, haunt, haunt, all day long."

The Lamplighter chuckled.

"P&P have always worked, shall we say, imaginatively. They have strict rules, though. For example, earthly retribution must always come with the involvement of souls still inhabiting earthly bodies. Otherwise, P&P could have dug the body up themselves, or transported it to Mr. Murderer's bed and left a message telling police where it was."

The Lamplighter paused, still studying his intended accomplice.

"Well?" he asked.

Still traumatised after experiencing the Lamplighter's death, Mervyn had no intention of tangling with P&P as well.

"What do you want me to do?" he croaked.

"You'll help, then?"

"Yes, yes, anything. That was awful, just dreadful. I don't want any more of it."

"Good lad," said the Lamplighter. "You want to go on?"

"I suppose so," whispered Mervyn.

"That's the spirit!" The Lamplighter grinned. "My half-brother, fortunately for my purposes, though not so fortunate for the person concerned, did not restrict himself to one murder. He was younger than I, and had a slightly younger full sister. Nice girl, she was. They were all the family I had. As with lots of people constantly at sea, I had made a will and divided my estate between the pair, the portion bequeathed to each passing to the other in case of prior decease.

"Unbeknown to me, my half-sister had already

been dispatched by the time I met my mortal end. Her body, like mine, has also never been found, but I know where it is. I also know my obnoxious relative interred her in a red leather overcoat. One of its pockets contains an electricity bill relating to the house she shared with her killer, and which he still owns."

The Lamplighter let Mervyn absorb the implications of this for a few seconds. He watched mischievously, as Mervyn's mouth dropped open with dawning realisation of what might come next.

"You don't … you don't … surely …," stammered Mervyn. "You don't want me to …"

"Dig her up?" interrupted the Lamplighter. "Not exactly. You see, she hasn't been buried."

"What!"

"My half-brother worked as a stonemason for a Hastings cemetery. More a necropolis, really, as it contains a large number of family mausoleums. Just before he murdered my half-sister, he was inspecting one of the more secluded ones, belonging to a now died-out family named Mulholland. When he found it had a loose iron grille which could be easily dislodged, and through which a man could get inside, he saw his chance.

"The contents of the mausoleum included a vast mahogany coffin on a plinth, enclosing the remains of one Peregrine Hereward Mulholland, who died in 1899. The lid, he discovered, though heavy, was not fixed to the coffin. It merely rested on top, positioned by a lip all the way round. The very same evening, he induced his sister to go for a walk with him on a route including the cemetery. My delightful relative then strangled her outside the mausoleum and deposited her body in the coffin. No-one has been inside the mausoleum since, and my half-brother inherited his sister's portion of my estate after she was declared dead seven years later."

Mervyn's horror had not left him, and he could not utter a word. The Lamplighter ploughed mercilessly on.

"So, lucky man, you are going to be her first visitor since my vile relative. I would like your visitation to occur at 8.00 a.m. on the morning of the day after tomorrow. But," he quickly added, before the dumbstruck Mervyn could respond, "you will not have to do what you fear. This is how it will work. You will enter the mausoleum through the still-loose grille, having first equipped yourself with that torch you bought about ten years ago, the one with a flashing orange light as well as an ordinary white one, loaded with the longest-lasting batteries you can get.

"You will also take a domestic duster and furniture polish, to enable you to polish the coffin lid to showroom condition, as far as possible. The lid only, mind. Your final prop will be an anonymous and fully detailed account of the deaths of me and my half-sister, which you will have written on your computer as though you had been an eye-witness. This will be enclosed in an envelope inscribed 'What is a strange woman, murdered by her brother, doing in this coffin on top of Peregrine?'

"You will place the envelope on top of the coffin weighted down by the torch, which you will switch on to flash orange. Then you will go home, but you will not replace the grille. On the way, you will use a public telephone box to inform the cemetery anonymously about a strange flashing orange light emanating from a displaced grille behind the Mulholland mausoleum. Within the next day or two the staff will investigate, and their curiosity about the polished lid and the envelope will persuade them to open the coffin.

"The police will call and find the squatter and, still not overly decayed in the relatively well-ventilated air of the mausoleum, her electricity bill. Modern forensic techniques, I am delighted to predict, will soon immerse my beloved half-brother in very hot water.

"You will not be seen, and no-one else will approach the mausoleum; Limbo has agreed to release some temps to deter the curious. Now, you will need some more details for your account, which will incriminate my half-brother beyond all reasonable doubt." Whereupon the Lamplighter supplied detailed information about both deaths.

"Are you asleep in there?" Bridget's voice suddenly penetrated Mervyn's consciousness, and he woke up in a warm bath in an empty bathroom. The dream was still vivid, but he decided not to repeat it to his wife until he had collected himself. He merely said, "no."

Next morning, Mervyn anxiously set about typing up his exceptional dream on his computer. At first he wondered why he had to skip a day before visiting the Mulholland mausoleum, but the Lamplighter's plan was correct. Not only did he need to locate the edifice, but it took him the whole afternoon to persuade his wife he had to go through with the Lamplighter's plan. Bridget was already convinced by the Morse test of the light's supernatural flashing, but agreeing to cooperate with Mervyn breaking into a mausoleum on the say-so of a ghost was a big jump. She assented only when she realised her husband was genuinely and completely terrified at what might happen if he did not fulfil his promise to the Lamplighter.

At the appointed time, Mervyn carried out the Lamplighter's instructions to the letter. Rather to his surprise, all went to plan. He had been exceedingly nervous about raiding the mausoleum, but he managed to get in and there had been no-one about to see him. Then he made the 'phone call to the cemetery administrator and went home. In the evening, Mervyn's sister and her husband arrived for dinner.

When Mervyn's relatives had finished listening to his story, they remained silent for several minutes. Bridget offered more whisky, which once more was universally accepted.

Then Ben asked, "didn't curiosity get the better of you, in the mausoleum?"

Mervyn said nothing.

"Curiosity about what in particular?" asked Elsa. Ben grinned. "About what was in the coffin," he said. They all looked at Mervyn, who flinched.

"Um," he said.

"Go on," pressed Ben. "It did, didn't it?" There was another pause. Then Mervyn said, "yes. It did."

"And?" asked his sister.

"I wondered several times whether I was being a complete fool," said Mervyn. "One never remembers dreams in anything more than vague outline, yet even now, two days later, this one is as clear as watching a film with soundtrack. Amazingly, I actually did what the Lamplighter asked. Then, while polishing the coffin lid, I realised lifting it would prove or disprove the dream. Admittedly, my curiosity struggled with revulsion but, deep inside, I knew I had to know for certain. It took a while before I could summon the will to go through with it. In the end, I did." He stopped, rather white at his very recent recollection.

"And?" repeated his sister. "What did you find?"

"I lifted the lid about a foot at one end and used the torch to investigate the contents. It took only a few seconds to see there were two, er … occupants, arranged head to foot. The top one was wearing a red leather coat. I lowered the lid, put the envelope and flashing torch on top, and got out quickly into the fresh air. Then I sat down for a long time on a bench outside the cemetery. Perhaps I should have mentioned opening the coffin before, but something told me not to."

"What state was the coat in?" asked Ben.

"Past its best."

After that, no-one spoke. Bridget silently refilled the whisky glasses, which were soon drained.

Eventually, Elsa said, "it's just too extraordinary for words. I'm going to bed, although whether I'll be able to sleep is quite another matter." Ben concurred, and they all retired for the night.

As Elsa lay next to her husband, she asked, "didn't the Lamplighter say there was a rule about living people not being allowed to prove the existence of ghosts to other living people? I wonder what happens when the rule is broken?"

"You're not saying he's proved the reality of ghosts to you?" asked Ben.

Elsa paused. "Well, I suppose not, but …"

"Go to sleep. I've always had my doubts about your brother, and I really don't know whether he's winding us up or whether he's suffered a series of hallucinations. I think the weight of this old house is getting to him."

But before Elsa had finished mulling this over, the whisky did its soporific work, and Ben received no reply.

Equally affected by the whisky, Mervyn too dozed off, thinking like the others about the Lamplighter. Suddenly, he became aware he was no longer in bed, but sitting downstairs again with the Lamplighter, who this time was standing in front of the inglenook.

"Mission accomplished," said the ghost. "My intelligence is that the cemetery staff investigated your call this afternoon, and my half-brother is now enjoying the hospitality of Hastings police station." He rubbed his hands together, adding gleefully, "I think I can look forward to a new posting, and possibly even a new power, after this."

"What about saying thank you?" asked Mervyn.

"Yes, yes, of course," said the Lamplighter. He paused. "But there is a difficulty."

"Difficulty?" repeated Mervyn.

"Well, I blame myself. I should have told you not to tell anyone about our earlier meeting. The Morse test you and your wife conducted merely proved the existence of ghosts to yourselves. Unfortunately, telling the others about the red coat will also prove it to them once the story gets into the newspapers, which breaks the rule I told you about."

"What do you mean?" asked Mervyn nervously.

"I mean I need help," said the Lamplighter. Whereupon he disappeared, and Mervyn's dream ceased as abruptly as it had started.

Next morning, at about ten-thirty, four souls gathered in the room where they had dined the night before.

"What a mess," said Bridget. "What were we doing last night? Look at all these glasses and papers lying about."

"I don't remember a thing," said Elsa. "I must have had too much to drink, or whatever …"

"I can't remember either," added Ben. "Weren't we talking about that old film 'Murder in the Fleet?'"

"Were we?" wondered Mervyn. "Or was that was when we visited you? Maybe these papers will give us a clue."

He picked up the papers, which included a well-thumbed green notepad, and studied every page.

"How odd," he said, after a long pause. "They're all blank."

NOT GONE

Oh, Rufus. I never imagined you would forget me. All those youthful years we spent together at school, then studying together the same science at university. Did they mean nothing to you? Those discussions we shared about the nature of existence: did they leave no lasting memory? Do you remember us reinforcing our increasing conviction that the universe and all things in it were sane and rational, totally explicable if we could but develop the necessary analytical techniques? Oh, dear! I can see by examining your mind now, that your memory is sadly hazy.

Young gods we were, with all things possible. I loved you then and love you still, after all this time of separation. Love is why, even now, in this state, I have sought you out to warn you we were so terribly, dreadfully and absolutely wrong. We were but gifted with the certainty of ignorance. I only hope you will remember and believe this message, in the morning, before it is too late for you as it is for me.

I married Flora three years after you moved to San Francisco. You never met her. No scientist or philosopher, she was nevertheless the catalyst which led to my changing convictions about the nature of things. An insomniac creature, she would leave our bedroom every evening, after kissing me goodnight before my descent into eight habitual hours of slumber. Then, as she gently closed the bedroom door, I would watch the light around it narrow to near-invisibility just inside its frame. As I watched the large heavy door close from the inside, and darkness enfolded me, I began to reflect. Here was a morbid parallel with my mortal end: one day someone would close the lid on my coffin, the light would narrow, but morning and new light would never flood around the lid again.

I would not witness that sight, or so I thought, at least at first. I would be physically there, of course, but dead, unaware and unseeing. And the thought was comforting. Death would be nothing, an end to all, as we believed, you and I. There would be no pain, no further concern for earthly cares, no intense sorrow at the appreciation of my own demise. Life would have been a single brief spark of self-centred strife, some joy and much worry in an eternity of oblivious darkness, and then forever gone.

But after a time I began to wonder, as I watched the narrowing light each night. Were there circumstances under which I could witness and experience that final narrowing? What if I were murdered: drugged perhaps, entombed whilst still aware of, yet unable to react to, events around me. Some medical error or condition might produce a similar fate. Those were, however, earthly and material events, and unlikely. I understood them and found the idea of them strangely undisturbing. They would also, in short though unpleasant ways, produce the ultimate extinction of life, memory and sensation: a consoling thought, perhaps, for one trapped in his own coffin. No, it was another possibility I found unnerving. A possibility of something eternal and not earthly or understandable to any degree by a living human being.

You may have guessed my meaning, Rufus: some part of me, or you, or anyone could survive body-death, intact with awareness and all that goes with it. Some part that, maybe, could not die.

I had not, until I began reflecting on the light disappearing round my bedroom door, given credence to spiritual existence. Darwin, Hawking, Dawkins and others of science appeared to have fatally damaged what you and I and many others saw as ancient superstitions. But in those transitional moments behind the closed door, briefly lucid before blurring into sleep, I came to perceive there might be more to understand, and maybe matters humankind could never understand. Perhaps, in searching for the tiniest sub-atomic particles, humanity was merely looking for the smallest cog in the single machine which is the universe. Perhaps humanity was merely bored with its old ideas, readily discounting the possibility of a designer or a purpose for the universe in its thirst for the new.

As you know, my lost friend, scientists talk of an expanding but finite universe. But if it were so, and if the vacuum of space were finite, what lies beyond? … Nothing? All human conception is of something detectable, or of a void with nothing in it. We cannot imagine anything which is neither of these things. Well, I could not.

There could, of course, be other things or

universes beyond the limit of our own, as Hawking theorises. But unless there were an infinite number of them, we would again encounter at their ultimate boundaries the incomprehensible nothingness of something which was neither matter nor a void.

Yet, just as I could not imagine what lies beyond a finite universe or a finite series of finite universes, neither could I truly visualise the infinite, either a single infinite universe or an infinite series of universes. The human mind, yours or mine, dear Rufus, is limited to conceiving things only in relation to other things. A chair may be conceived as a finite object inside a room. The room is conceived as a finite space within a building, the building as a finite object on the surface of the Earth and the Earth as a finite object within the universe. With none of these concepts do human minds have much difficulty: there is always a bigger space in which everything imaginable is contained and relative to which it is defined. But the universe, if infinite, is not contained within anything. It just exists, limitless in every direction, even if much of it is a void. At this point, as we so often discussed, Rufus, human understanding begins to break down.

Whether the universe is finite or not, human understanding fails completely when it asks "why does the universe exist and where did it come from?"

I know from your restlessness, Rufus, that I am making an impact upon you. I make no apology: it is my intention, and I will continue.

By and by, I came to believe humanity ultimately faces questions it cannot answer by science alone; certainly not by science as currently known. Man can only understand his environment as much as a rat born and living its whole life inside a box can understand his. The rat may live perfectly well inside the box and make observations and deductions about it and its contents. But the rat may only speculate about the box's purpose, what lies outside the box and how the box relates to the outside, even if the rat knows it is confined inside a box.

These conclusions could only limit my faith in human rationality. If I and others could not answer such questions, or perhaps not even frame the questions properly, confidence in human understanding must surely weaken. What else did I not know? Did I not know things I thought I did know? For example, could the ancient superstitions you and I derided have at least a grain of truth in them? Could they have arisen from realities beyond the limits of human rationality?

My mind was becoming prepared to admit that I might, terrifyingly, be able to witness the closing of my own coffin lid. I could be an entity not explicable by human rationality. I could be temporarily housed in a physical body, the death of which the entity could witness, experience and, chillingly, survive.

I can tell, Rufus, my thoughts are troubling you. Your sleep is disturbed, and you are subconsciously aware of my presence, and uneasy. But I have more to tell and will not yet let you awaken. Awake, your receptivity will be blocked by the surly experience of immediate reality.

Unfortunately, realizing death may not be the end came too late for me, although I had, as you now know, begun to wonder what to expect when death came. Nothing was still a possibility, of course. But so, too, was a scene from Hieronymus Bosch. Or angels, clouds and harps.

I did not have to wait long before I knew for certain, because shortly after reaching this stage of realization, I died of a heart attack.

You might have heard of my death, but death is the wrong word. I did not die at all. My physical body ceased to function but I, the entity living within, survived. And I wish most fervently I had not. How I wish you and I and all the others had been right about death being the end.

At first, I did not know what had happened. I felt nothing. I saw my own body lying lifeless in front of the television. I saw Flora kneeling over me, heard her shouting my name as she shook me and slapped my face. I saw and heard her calling the ambulance men, and watched them come. I watched them try to resuscitate me, and watched them give up.

"He's gone," one of them said.

I watched Flora crying. Irritated, I said to her, "why are you crying? I've not gone anywhere. I'm here. I'm not dead."

She could not see the real me in any way. She could only see my lifeless body. Again I said, "I am not dead. Here I am, look!" And I put my arm around her.

I could not feel her, and it made no difference to her. I screamed "I AM NOT DEAD! LOOK AT ME!"

She continued crying. She did not look at me and did not know I was there, cuddling her and yelling.

She left the room, but I did not follow. Instead, I looked around. Flora had turned the television off. I tried to turn it back on. My finger seemed to press the button, but I felt nothing and the TV stayed off.

Nothing I did made any difference. I realized I was unable to affect anything physical.

I found myself drifting around, always within sight of my own body. When, eventually, my body was placed in its coffin, I remembered the narrowing light around the bedroom door and my morbid thoughts about it. I imagined I was back inside my lifeless corpse to watch the coffin lid close, and suddenly found that I was! From the inside, I saw the final, total narrowing of the light as the lid closed. My earlier expectations of what it would look like were correct, but the sense of desolation and regret which immediately assailed me was so strong that I instantly wished myself outside the coffin.

To my amazement, my wish was granted! I found myself outside, looking down on my own sealed coffin whilst knowing my body lay inside. But the sense of absolute desolation and regret could not be wished away. I seemed to have turned it on by entering the coffin, and it still burns, like a white-hot sword constantly thrusting through me.

I have since experimented with the power of imagination. I now know I can go anywhere by imagining myself there. I have imagined myself in Tokyo, and been able to roam its streets. I have imagined myself inside a block of stone, and it has happened. I have imagined myself at the centre of the Pole Star, and there I went, instantly. I felt no heat.

I have not been able to imagine myself outside the physical universe, but lately I have become dimly aware it may be both possible and advantageous. It may be connected with communicating with you and others still physically alive.

So I have imagined myself inside your mind as you

lie in your beautiful home in California, and am in it now as you sleep.

But I must tell you, Rufus, although I can move myself at will, I have not been able to remove the corrosive loneliness, sense of loss or constantly gnawing remorse. So far, these dark miseries have only worsened.

After my funeral, the whole family gathered at home. My nephew asked his father if he could have a puppet, a goofy, floppy bird, with a squawker, which his aunt, my other sister, had given me to cheer me up during one of those fits of black depression to which I was more and more prone as I aged.

My brother-in-law asked my mother, who said, "Tony loved that bird. He used to tease me, making it squawk at unexpected times or in unexpected places. But I am sure he would have wanted someone to have fun with it now he's gone, so of course Jon can have it."

I shouted at her. "No! No! You can't give him away! He's mine, not yours!"

But, ignorant of my presence, she gave the bird to my nephew, who took him outside and promptly started throwing him around the lawn to see if he could fly. The bird squawked plaintively every time he hit the ground. Wanting to protect my poor, lovely bird, I screamed at Jon. "Stop! Stop it! He's mine, and he's delicate! You'll break him!"

Unaware of me, Jon continued his game, and, sure enough, the bird's head came off. He was in the waste bin before the day was out.

After that I left my home and did not return, but reflected, sobbing in the void, in isolation. I was tormented by being able to see and hear all the people and things I had loved and still love, whilst not myself being loved the same way. Nor was I even detectable to them, nor able to influence any of them one whit. My experience was too vivid, cogent and durable to be a dream. I was forced to accept I was indeed dead in earthly terms. I came to fear I was condemned to an eternity of solitary sorrow for irremediable error, loss and wasted chances. There was no hellfire, Rufus, but that could not be worse than lonely regret of infinite duration.

Gradually, though, a strange awareness began to impinge upon me. I began to experience a growing realization that I had a job to do.

I do not know where this command came from, nor exactly when it crystallized. All I am aware of is the material universe I can see and hear but not participate in. My sole alternative, when that becomes too much to bear, is an endless, cold, black and silent void. Perhaps I now know what nothingness is and what infinite means. Perhaps I also know what Hell is, or one form of it at least.

Although there must be billions of other entities suffering the same fate as mine, I have neither met nor been aware of even one. Maybe my command came, telepathically, from one or more of this discontented mass of mankind. I do not know. But I feel strongly urged to carry it out.

My task is to warn those I knew before I left the chrysalis I now know my earthly body to have been. I must convey to them the sense of futility I feel at the waste of a life and the sense of terror knowing I will remain sentient for eternity, with only biting remorse for company. For me this is for the friends lost, the children not had. The burden of wrongs committed and never corrected. The opportunities missed. But, most importantly, for the acquisition too late of knowledge that earthly existence is only a fraction of the whole.

I hope my visitation will convey to you the utter hopelessness, despair and sorrow I now permanently suffer as a result of former misjudgements. But that is not all. I can tell you, too, have your own reasons for sorrow, and fear.

I hope, Rufus, you are no longer as certain as we used to be that ghosts are merely echoes in time or hallucinations. I hope you will remember my visitation when I permit you to awaken, because your chance to avoid a fate like mine is now, whilst you still occupy your own chrysalis. Emergence from that can happen with no warning. One minute you are alive and well and the next ... bang! You cannot assume you have time to spare. To remove the remediable causes of your own regret, I implore you to change your life now.

When I first began to realise the true nature of the state I am now in, I wondered, "Is this the end? Is this all there is? Has all my experience gone to waste?"

I pray that the answer to all these questions is "No." If you act on what I have shown you, my efforts will not have been in vain. You may save yourself from my fate. And, as I end, a vague intimation has stolen into me that if I succeed in persuading you and others, I may eventually be freed from my anguish and exile.

Wake up, dear friend. Wake up and think, and help me, help me, help me.

ABOUT THE AUTHOR

Despite his Cambridge engineering degree, the author became convinced, after living in a 500-year-old house which proved to be haunted, as well as by experiencing some unnerving occurrences in other places, that twenty-first century sophistication and scientific knowledge afford no protection whatsoever against the supernatural.

He decided this realization deserved to be shared anew, following the example of the renowned M R James. The accounts in this book therefore attempt to remind modern readers that not everything can be explained rationally, and that some features of the unexplainable might be dangerous.